ℓ

—

THE
TRAITOR's WIFE

Also by Kathleen Kent

The Heretic's Daughter

THE
TRAITOR'S WIFE

KATHLEEN KENT

MACMILLAN

First published in the USA as *The Wolves of Andover* in 2010 by Little, Brown and Company,
Hachette Book Group USA

This edition published 2010 by Macmillan
an imprint of Pan Macmillan, a division of Macmillan Publishers Limited
Pan Macmillan, 20 New Wharf Road, London N1 9RR
Basingstoke and Oxford
Associated companies throughout the world
www.panmacmillan.com

ISBN 978-0-230-75057-9 TPB
ISBN 978-0-230-75504-8 HB

Visit **www.panmacmillan.com** to read more about all our books
and to buy them. You will also find features, author interviews and
news of author events, and you can sign up for e-newsletters
so that you're always first to hear about our new releases.

For Kevin and Kim

London, England, April 1649

THE WOMAN WORKED her way out of the crowd, grabbing Cromwell by the cloak, and pulled at it until he turned to face her. She was small with plain wheat-colored hair, but the blush in her cheeks was high, as with a fever, and her voice was surprisingly deep.

She said to him, "Sir, will you stay and speak with us?"

He had a mind to pull his cloak roughly from her grasp and move away into the darkened safety of the House of Commons, but he looked over the shifting, enclosing mass of the hundreds, perhaps thousands, who had come to petition him to release the imprisoned leaders of the Leveller movement and he tempered his voice to a fatherly tone. "It is not for women to petition, missus. You should be home at your plates and bowls."

"Sir," the woman said, "we scarce have any dishes left to tend, and those we have we are not sure to keep."

The minister of Parliament who had been close at Cromwell's heels, and who was eager to pass into the Great Hall, said with little patience, "I find it strange that women are now petitioning."

The woman cut her eyes to the man and said immodestly,

"That which is strange is not of necessity unlawful." When the minister brushed past her, she turned back to Cromwell and said bitterly, "It was strange that you cut off the king's head, yet I suppose you will justify it."

He stopped and this time he did pull his cloak roughly out of her hands. The supreme impudence of this little mouse, he thought, and turned the full import of his gaze on her. It was a gaze that had faced down generals in the field, brought court councilmen to anguished tears, and, some said, had looked without remorse or pity into the sightless eyes of the king as he lay in his lead-lined casket. There had been a time when he would have listened to the harpings of local women such as this, and their workaday husbands, when they still had the means to pay for armaments and food and fill the ranks with fighting bodies. But the Great War was over and he was nearly done with rubbing against the masses and would soon leave such rustic negotiations to the county councilmen.

He motioned impatiently for her to move away but she planted her foot in front of him and called out hoarsely, "If you take away the lives of our leaders, or the lives of any contrary to law, nothing shall satisfy us but the lives of them that do it."

To his dismay he could feel the crowd pushing against them towards the open entranceway of the House. At first he had seen only women in the surrounding faces, but he realized they were solely at the fore, being shored up from behind by common men as well as rebellious soldiers, some of whom had raised their cocked pistols into the air. He watched as twenty or so men rushed into the House, shouting, "Free them, free them, free them…"

Now half the day would be spent clearing the hallways of quarrelsome, menacing dissenters, his suit to raise the urgent funds needed to invade Ireland delayed for Christ knew how long.

The woman's sea green ribbon had slipped from her narrow chest, sliding down her arm, coming to rest like a wilted laurel around her waist. Two more women, likewise wearing the banner of the Leveller cause, emerged from the pack and entwined their arms with hers, forming a living chain to bar his movement forward. He had seen the same expressions on the faces of women fanatics of every degenerate caste and error-filled belief. Catholics, Anabaptists, Quakers, Diggers, Fifth Monarchists—they all carried the same look of unreasoning, unbending fervor. When he was a child he had seen a witch burn, and she had held that same unyielding, outraged mask until the flesh curled away from her skull like an Easter candle.

He took two steps towards the little mouse and, bringing his face close to hers, said firmly, "Will you to home, woman."

"This is England, sir. It is my home," she answered. Her eyes fluttered fearfully, but she tightened her grip on each flanking woman as though steeling for a blow, and pressed her lips together into a thin, implacable line.

And in that moment he recognized her. He had seen her many times from a distance: a screeching prophetess, standing on her box above the overanxious crowds, offering promises of impossible equalities. As though titled men of property would simply, upon hearing her words, yield up their ancient, hard-won inheritances to landless yeomen or their widows. He began to push his way around the women, using his staff to breach their clasped hands, demanding roughly, "What is your name?…By God, I'll have it, and you shall know the reasons why."

"Morgan, sir. My name is Mrs. Morgan." The fall of his staff had caught her sharply across the wrist and she pulled her stricken hand up to her breast, but she did not retreat from his path. She had spoken the word "Mor-gan" in two distinct parts, as someone in mourning would have said "death-knell" or "grave-stone" or even "mur-der," and for an instant he lost his footing. He turned his head to follow the tunings of his ears, and when he again met her eyes, he knew he had got it right. The image of fresh-laid straw fouled with the blood and brain matter of a headless corpse slid into his mind, like mercury poured into one ear.

"Jesu, woman, get you home…" He rushed past her into the darkened caverns of the House bristling with roaming bands of soldiers, clerks, councilmen, goodwives, and even a few doxies off the streets. Somewhere within the Speaker's chambers, there were shouts and a clash of arms, and bits of shredded parchment swirled around his head as though the very weather had begun dissent, bringing snow in April. He slipped into a privy, blindly closing the weighted door. He went hard to his knees and heard his thick cloak catch and tear on a nail. Two men scuffling, perhaps a guardsman and a dissenter, fell heavily against the door and then moved away down the hall, swearing and making oaths against each other.

Every undoing makes a sound, he thought, and these are the sounds of the unraveling of kingships and alliances and nations. For the hundredth, for the thousandth, time that day he prayed for guidance but felt his spirit blunted against the building noise and chaos outside. He heard his name being called from somewhere inside the chamber, faintly but desperately, sounding like a drowning man calling out for a line of hemp.

He stood and placed his hand against the door, dignifying his presence, setting his face to iron, and when he finally exited the privy into the tide of men-at-arms, he braced himself by saying, "Mrs. Morgan, Mrs. Morgan, if you can bear to carry that name, I can bear to remember it…"

*Lord, thou knowest how busy I must be this day; if I forget thee,
do not thou forget me.*

— SIR JACOB ASTLEY,
prayer before the Battle of Edgehill, English Civil War

*I had rather a plain russet-coated Captain, that knows
what he fights for, and loves what he knows, than that which
you call a Gentle-man and is nothing else.*

— OLIVER CROMWELL

*[The Celts] were chopped down with axes and swords but the blind
fury never left them while there was breath in their bodies.*

— PAUSANIAS,
Greek historian

THE
TRaitoR's
WifE

CHAPTER 1

Billerica, Massachusetts, March 1673

THE YOUNG WOMAN stepped from the wagon and turned to face the driver still holding the slackened reins. From Daniel's vantage point, looking through the shuttered windows of the common room, he could not read the woman's face but could see the rigid set of her back. The man in the wagon was small and as hard-set as a dried persimmon. The brim of his felt hat was slung so low and angled over his eyes that its very putting on must have been an act of vengeance. Daniel had met his wife's uncle only once at market, and the number of words exchanged between them could not have filled a walnut. But Daniel remembered well the look of triumph on Andrew Allen's face when the old man bested him at a calf auction. That he was now giving his daughter the last of his cautious, brusque advice was clear from the way he punctuated his words with a string of country sayings: "Hech, now listen to me," and "Hark you well to me now." The sorts of words that the old Scotsmen still used were like pepperweed in a mutton stew.

Daniel moved through the common room and stood at the

open door. He saluted the old man, saying, "Will you come in for a breakfast?"

To his relief Goodman Allen shook his head and with a few muttered words of good-bye pulled his wagon around, taking the road back towards Andover. The woman stood for a long while watching her father ride away, the hem of her dress slowly soaking up the wet, ice-filled mud of the yard. Daniel studied the unbending arch of her neck, thinking it was a sad thing that she be past twenty and not yet married, still sent out by her parents into service, her few things put into some bit of cotton sacking.

Taking the full measure of her forlorn appearance, Daniel shook his head in sympathy. Andrew Allen was prosperous enough; he could have at the very least provided his daughter with her own bed. But Daniel knew from his wife, Patience, that for all the old man's parsimonious airs, he swore, drank hard ale, and gambled at dice whenever, and wherever, the opportunity arose, and was tighter than a tick paying for anything he couldn't raise from the ground or fashion himself from driftwood.

It would be a blessing for his wife to have another woman at the settlement. He could hear Patience even now retching and puking into a bucket by the bed, as sick in her fifth month with their third child as any girl would be with her first. He was eager to see his wife's cousin settled into the house as quickly as possible. The roads were freeing themselves of ice, and though they be a rutted misery, Daniel had a certainty that if he didn't attend to his carting soon, others would beat him to Boston, getting the best of the off-loaded goods from England, Holland, and Spain.

He called her gently by name, "Martha," telling her to come in and settle herself by the fire. She slowly turned her head in profile to him as though still reluctant to give up her vigil on the road. A few dark strands of her hair, as coarse as a horse's mane, had blown free from her cap and whipped around her cheek in the damp wind. He braced himself for the onslaught of tears that surely must come in answer to being left, yet again, in the home of near strangers. But when she turned fully to face him, his breath caught in his chest, for there, in place of tears, was dry-eyed fury, and a mouth so pinched and implacably set that his first thought was to hide his tender belly from her approaching form. Good God, he thought, and cleared a wide space at the door for her to enter.

A HEAVY RAIN had started that morning, pouring in unbroken sheets, and though Patience had begged her husband to put off his leaving one more day, Daniel had thrown an oiled canvas over his head, mounted his carting wagon, and clucked his heavy gelding out of the yard and onto the road. But for the downpour, Martha thought, her cousin would still be standing at the door crying, holding her slightly protruding belly, seemingly unaware that Daniel had made all haste in leaving. Martha looked about the room, noting all of the tamped-down and dirt-ridden rushes scattered beneath the table, the scabs of food clinging to the previous evening's dishes, the soiled linen loosely draped over a chair—the entire unwholesome mess creating odors both fetid and close. Patience, finally closing the door against the rain, began showing Martha the places where the house goods were stored.

"Of the cellar," Patience said, motioning for Martha to lift the trap in the floor, "there are cranberries in a firkin of water, some wheat flour, cornmeal, two baskets left of apples, pumpkins, and squash."

Martha took a candle from the table and, lifting the hem of her skirt, stepped down the shallow ladder to the cellar. She held the candle high and saw at once that rats and mice had done their job during the winter months, chewing through the poorly tended baskets. Remembering her mother's stone-lined cellar, carefully cleared each day of blackening mold or encroaching pests, she wrinkled her nose at a braid of darkly speckled onions, rotted and evil-smelling from hanging too close to the sweating dirt walls. She could hear Patience shifting her weight restlessly in the space above her head. Finally Patience called down, "It's been a month or more that I cannot climb the ladder. I send the children down to fetch food for the table...and they...things may not be as they should..."

In the small arc of light, Martha quickly tallied the remainder of the cellar's holdings: one half-barrel of cider, thirty head of dried corn mixed with peas, two sealed pots of salted pork and salted cod each, one covered tin of autumn tallow, and fifteen candles in a box. The approaching scarcity of food would have to be addressed at once, as it would be days yet before any seed could be put to ground for the house garden. She had been told by Daniel that one of his two field men was a creditable hunter. They would need his skill, and soon, for they would all require fresh meat, whether it had swum or crawled, to have the strength to put the house to rights.

She prodded with her foot a bag of potatoes made unfit for eating by lying too long on the damp floor, but she reckoned with a hard boiling the spuds could be rendered to starch for the wash.

It would take a week at least to get clean all the dirty linens. Even now there were three or four baby's clouts hung close to the fire drying, looking as if they had not been scrubbed for weeks.

She held the candle up to light her way to the ladder and saw the pregnant woman's face appear at the hatchway, her eyes and lips still swollen from crying. Underlit by the soft yellow light, Patience looked like nothing so much as a petulant child, even though the woman was on the downhill path to twenty-five. As Martha climbed up out of the cellar, Patience was saying, "I think it fitting that Will and Joanna be made a porridge now." Two children, a boy of perhaps five and a much younger girl, came to stand behind their mother, yawning and rubbing at their faces. Martha bent to drop the cellar trap, hiding a look of disapproval, as it was long past the breakfast hour. When she raised herself upright again, she realized with a jolt that Patience had given her her first order. She'd been there only an hour and already she was being sorted like a common stone to the bottom in household prominence.

"When you are finished with the porridge you may—"

"Cousin." Martha's arms had crept together to cross in front of her apron, fingers gripping tightly at opposing arms. She saw Patience wince at the biting tone, and she quickly unclenched her hands, letting them fall to her sides. She cautioned herself from speaking so abruptly, a habit she had learned from her father, and one her mother had warned her would chase away flies, leaving only the vinegar.

She gentled her tone and began again. "Cousin, if I am to be both husband and wife to this house, there must be an order to things. Breakfast is past, and since there is no greater sauce to a meal than hunger, the children will eat at midday with the rest of us."

"Martha," Patience said testily, her mouth pinched and resolute. "The children are hungry. I cannot have them hanging about me, crying for their breakfast for two hours or more until their dinner. Cousin though you may be, you are here to aid me in my labors. So now, if you will be so kind, you may serve the porridge for my children."

Martha saw it all clear in that moment: this was the instant her place in the family would be decided. If she lost her footing at the outset, she would forever be dealt with as no more than a servant. She resisted the indignation that threatened to turn her voice shrill and said quietly, "Very well. But then Will *may* fetch the rain barrel, as he is such a great big lad, and if Joanna can stand on a stool, she *may* wash and wipe the bowls. You will need to call in the men straightaway and, *if* you can push a broom, you need to sweep free those rushes or we'll have rats crawling into the stew. I will soon need a book for the house accounts, a quill, and whatever ink you have for writing. The washing will be started as soon as we are free of rain, and I will want to strip today every bed and mattress and smoke them for lice."

There was silence in the room for a few breaths until Patience, grabbing the mantel for balance, retched violently into the hearth. After the spasms had passed, she took each child in hand and walked them back to the bedroom, firmly closing and latching the door behind her.

THE EVENING WAS late before Martha closed the door to her own narrow room. It was farthest from the hearth and cold; she could see her exhaled breath by the circle of candlelight. She sat carefully on the edge of the bed, feeling the ropes under the mattress give way, and began sorting through her meager belongings: two blankets and a pillow with ticking, a pair of summer stockings for the coming warmer weather, a good collar and cuff. Her father had given her a bowl to show Patience and her husband that his daughter would work to fill it with her own labors and not be a burden to them in this regard.

I have certainly been a burden in my own house, she thought bitterly—although not from what went into her mouth but rather from what came out of it. Earlier, Martha had tried to make amends for her harsh words to her cousin by kneading the pregnant woman's back with lard and mustard seeds. Patience had shown her gratitude with a kiss on the cheek, and Martha had felt a more amicable balance restored between them. But in her deepest heart, she knew that relations between them would always be more like servant and mistress. Patience as a child had been sullen and demanding, with an inborn grasping nature that had blossomed into a sense of entitlement after she had made a profitable marriage with Daniel.

Blowing out the candle, Martha pulled both of the blankets close under her chin and lay in the dark. Here I am, she thought, traded like a kettle to yet another family. She knew it was not just for the wages, though, wages that went to her parents; it was to find her a husband. Her father had said to her that morning as they rode in the wagon, "Ye've spent more time in the company of far relatives than in yer own house and ye still have yer maidenhead. Fer Christ's bloody sake, my hunting dog is more hospitable.

Yer twenty-three and I begin to despair of ye ever comin' to bed with a husband. Can ye not for once, just for once, guard yer tongue and mind yer place?"

It had been pointed out, and often, that Martha's own sister, Mary, had been married and settled in Billerica for ten years; she had a good home and a husband who provided for her, a son to share in their labors, and another babe on the way. Martha rolled over on her side, restless and overly tired, and spread her hands over her belly. She had at times wished it possible to be with child without having to be bothered with the needful attentions of men, their smells and their gropings, their intrusive probings. Even if she were to settle on a husband, and make children of her own, she doubted that her father would ever resolve his disappointments over her stubborn and contrary ways.

Sleep finally came, washing over the demands of her family, the calculations of laundry to be done, the setting to rights of the cellar, the sweeping of the floor, the scrubbing and sanding of pots. The imaginings of work yet to be done stayed with her through her dreams and left her exhausted and ill-tempered in the morning.

DESPITE A HIGH, buffeting wind and slanting rain, the entire household had embarked early on Sunday to attend the meeting-house in the town proper. The women and children rode in the horse cart, each one struggling to hold on to a corner of the oiled canvas draped over their heads, while the hired men followed behind on foot. Sodden dirt caked their boots to midcalf, and the younger of the two, a Scotsman named John with a ruddy childish face, mired himself again and again in the muck. The other, a Welshman named Thomas, walked between the ruts in easy strides. He was, without doubt, the tallest man Martha had ever seen, and though she was accustomed to having indentured laboring men about her father's house, he had a hard-bitten look about him that made her uneasy.

Past the one-mile mark, the cart tilted dangerously into a hole, one wheel sinking to its upper rim, and Thomas moved quickly to support its sagging weight. John took the horse's head and pulled at the trappings, but the cart would not be freed. They lifted Patience and the children onto a small hillock out of the ground water, but when Thomas offered his arm to help Martha down, she gave him a withering glance and waved him away.

She jumped from the wagon into the mud, and as she struggled to keep her balance, she saw John palm a grin. Her pride would cost a good hour cleaning clods from shoe leather, and her irritation grew as John passively eyed her wilting progress to join Patience and the children on the hump of ground, already crowded with furze and lichen.

Thomas bent his shoulder to the frame and, with little effort from the horse, pushed the cart rocking from the sump. There was no labored exhalation of air or grimacing of his face to prove to the women a superior show of strength. There was only a corded straining of tendons in the forearm and neck to mark the effort of freeing a baling wagon weighted with oak and a full morning's rain.

"As easy as plucking a plover's egg from a nest," John said with a grin and a whistle. He gave his hand to Martha to help her back into the wagon, but she refused it, barking her shins as she climbed over the spokes. He turned his head to stifle a laugh and she blushed with anger. The Scotsman may blow all he likes, she thought, but it did not give him a place to ridicule her. She would bide her time, waiting for the opportunity, and then he would learn who gave the marching orders in the Taylor household.

After the evening meal, Martha lingered at the table, watching John as his head drooped into the hollow of his chest. The meal she had prepared was sparse but savory, with heat and grease enough to loosen the day from the men's heads, and she knew John was thinking longingly of his bed in the new-built quarters behind the hearth. It was a room he shared with Thomas and was close and cramped. But the walls were boarded tight, the shake roof sealed properly with pitch, and, unlike the barn where the men had slept all last summer, it would not leak.

"I heard howling during the night," Martha said suddenly, turning to Patience. "The rustling of the hens has brought feral things from the brush."

John opened one eye drowsily and said, "Oh, it's only a fox come to pester the hens."

"No," Martha said, shaking her head. "It was a wolf I heard."

The rattling on the roof surged louder as the day's rain turned to ice. It would be an especially cold night, Martha knew, for anyone sleeping outside the walls of the house.

"Mark me," Martha said to Patience, her eyes resting heavily on John. "Someone should stay in the barn tonight or we'll wake tomorrow to find feathers with nothing besides but air."

John had been roused fully from his pleasant nodding and he lifted his head, cutting his eyes to Thomas, who sat close by with a whetstone, slowly sharpening a hoe. The stone made harsh scraping noises at odd intervals, and Martha sensed, although she was not certain, that the Welshman was marking every one of her pronouncements with purposefully long screeching sounds.

"But surely," Patience answered weakly, "it is too cold. And Daniel has never before insisted the men sleep in the barn before the first of April…"

It took another quarter hour for Martha to cow Patience into submission. She reminded her cousin that Daniel would be sorely disappointed to lose his prized hens to his wife's careless disregard, while bringing base and predatory beasts to their front door, endangering the very lives of their children, and on and on. Patience, complaining weakly, finally retreated to her bed, dragging the children along behind her. Martha, left alone with the men, turned triumphantly to John and pointed to the front door.

John, walking as though carrying a sack of stones on his back, took his time putting on his greatcoat and sighed at long intervals, hoping for some word of intervention on Thomas's part. But Thomas said nothing as he quietly put away the whetstone and walked to the warmth of his own bed. John soon followed him behind the hearth, harping at his bad luck. His voice carried back to the common room, muffled but angry. "She's a feckin' night-terror driven to ground, Thomas.…To be sent out to the barn like a dog.…Come morning she'll know what for…"

There was a dull creaking of ropes, as though Thomas had settled his tall form onto the rope bed, and he said in warning, "Lay it by, John, or she'll beggar you."

Martha walked to the linen chest and pulled from it the thinnest quilt. She waited for John to reemerge from his room and, handing the quilt to John, said pleasantly, "You'll need this. It's no doubt very cold in the barn." She opened the door and then, as John stepped into the chafing rain, said, "You'll next time think before laughing at me."

She firmly closed and latched the door behind him. Her mouth curled tightly upwards as she thought of John climbing, diminished and swearing, into the manger, the barn filling with the murmuring of hens and horses, a chorus blending with the sounds of wounded muttering.

BEFORE DAWN, MARTHA roused the entire house to help with the washing. She sent Thomas to fetch John from the barn and he appeared at the table sullen but silent, his hair and coat covered in straw. In the midst of the breakfast meal, the giving and taking of food and the talk of work to be done, Patience sat slumped in her chair, carelessly picking at bread soaked in milk. One lock of hair fell in a limp ribbon over her face and her skin held a greenish pallor.

Martha scratched with her nail a split seam in a stocking she had been mending and wondered if Patience would be well enough to at least mend some of the fraying collars and cuffs. A dark thought, playing beyond her work-filled mind, shifted and settled behind her eyes. It was common-enough knowledge among midwives that the unborn, to be born in good health, would by necessity make the mother sick, the mother's vital essences usurped by the quickening child.

But something unwholesome and yeastlike in the pregnant woman's sweat made Martha uneasy. She would try to remember later to save by her cousin's water. In this way she would sniff out the unbalancing elements. She had been present at numerous difficult, painful, and even violent births, but she had never yet lost a babe and had learned from older, more experienced women the collective wisdom of generations: the seeing, the smelling, the touching, the *knowing* of the sacrificial rites of birth. No, she had never lost a babe, but three women had been laid into the ground, two of them shrouded in cloth made to grace their infants' swaddling.

Walking out into the yard, she lifted her face towards the morning sun and, closing her eyes, felt the heat of it draw blood into her cheeks. The frigid sleet had ceased during the night, and the clouds, which had covered the skies for weeks, began to disperse into crisscrossed bands of gray. A crown of sweat soon prickled her skin under her cap and she opened the laces, pulling it from her head. An easterly wind, chilled and saltwater pungent, blew at her back, filling her apron like a sail and lifting the ropy strands of hair at her neck. She opened her eyes again, slowly, lids creased and fluttering from the sudden light and, with her fingers, smoothed away the sweat from the hollow of her throat. She tried banishing the dark thoughts about her cousin and filled her lungs with the briny air.

A lengthy shadow over the yard startled her and she turned to meet the unapologetic gaze of the Welshman. He had been studying her, she had no doubt, while her eyes were closed and had come upon her with soft-footed guile. Behind him stood John, who was also staring, but he dropped his eyes once she pierced him with a threatening look.

"Well?" she asked, jerking the cap back over her head, hiding the tangles of black hair. "The two of you won't work off servitude in the company of mischief."

"I need my man to come trapping with me," Thomas answered, his voice deeply resonant, as though he had swallowed pebbles with his mash.

Martha crossed her arms and considered him. She was a tall woman but next to Thomas she felt near to a child. She hated the way she had to tilt her chin up to see the whole of him. "My man," he had said. "My man," as though John Levistone were indentured not to the Taylors but to Thomas.

"You can tend to your traps when the other one has finished the clearing," she said, turning on her heel and walking away. There was a satisfactory silence that followed her to the house, and when at length she looked over her shoulder, Thomas had returned to the barn. John gathered up a hoe and a slotted rake and began pulling a winter's worth of dirt and leaves away from the damp foundation of the house.

She sat for an hour or more, sorting through the seeds that would go into the house garden. From time to time she looked up through the window or open door, following John's progress around the house. He sang snatches of a song, " 'For other manly practices she gain'd the love of all, for leaping and for running or wrestling for a fall,' " sometimes stopping to swear softly or moan to himself, "Christ, the woman is a tartar."

When she had finished counting the seeds, she glanced through the window and saw Thomas coming from the barn. He stood looking fixedly at the ground as though the firing pan had fallen off his flintlock. Something about the way he stared prickled the back of her neck.

Leaving her shawl in the house, Martha quickly crossed the yard to the barn, coming to stand behind Thomas, who had knelt down and was examining a late bank of snow worn down to gray, rounded lumps of slush and mud and pocked with deep channels and ridges. When her shadow crossed his path, Thomas stood upright again, suddenly alert, his gaze sweeping across the melting fields and into the surrounding woods. She followed his gaze but could see nothing beyond the bare trees.

He pointed to a marked depression in the mud. There, impressed like a mold into the wasting snow, were four distinct circlets over one larger circlet. Martha bent and spread her closed fist over the print and saw her own hand dwarfed by the size of it.

"Wolves," Thomas said, looking at her with frank appraisal. "Two of them. It seems John and I will both be in the barn tonight."

Martha hugged herself tightly with her own arms, shivering slightly in the cool, shaded air. There was no look of satisfaction on her face. Only a deepening crease between her brows, and lips that were open and moist, like a child's mouth caught at the moment of surprise.

LATE AFTER DARK, Martha kept vigil by the window, listening for the howling or yipping that was not from a fox or badger. She sighed, remembering her last worded exchange with her cousin. Patience, ill and fretful, wanting only to escape to her bed, had become overwrought and cried uncontrollably when Martha pressed her to take greater charge of the men, especially now that wolves had come prowling to feed at their door. Clapping her hands over her ears, Patience had cried, "Do what you will, only leave me be."

Rushing for the comfort of her bed, she had tripped over a stool, and when Martha rose to catch her, Patience waved her away and ran to her room, breathing bubbles of snot from her nose like an infant. Later, when Martha brought her a strained broth, Patience grabbed her hand and, holding it to her belly, wailed, "I am afraid of this birthing." She began to cry miserably and Martha stayed with her for a while, smoothing her hair and whispering reassurances that she herself did not feel, until her cousin had fallen into a heavy sleep.

In a year's time, Martha thought, shifting her weight to peer out the window again, Patience would be delivered of another child, with a husband and a home. Even Thomas and John Levistone would, next spring, have land on which to build. Earlier that evening Patience had corrected Martha's mistaken belief that the men were indentured for the accustomed term of seven years; Thomas and John had in fact been hired by Daniel to work for three years in trade for prime land owned by the Taylors on the Concord. They had one more year of laboring on another's land, and then they would have their own.

And what would she gain with her own sweat? Even the room in which she slept would have to be shared with Joanna and Will once the babe was born. And once Patience had recovered her strength and Daniel had returned, she would most likely be sent home. An unmarried woman too long in a strange household of men was a challenge to virtue, a carnal distraction not to be borne.

Well, then, she thought, spring would bring open roads, and if she had exhausted her chances for a husband in Andover, perhaps the market or meetinghouse in Billerica would bring more success. Tomorrow would be the first of April, a day of hopeful warming, and she would begin the cleaning in earnest. She would open all the doors and with sand and ashes and birch rods both dirt and despondency would be swept away with the old season as proof of renewal for the new. Perhaps, she thought, her mouth twisting into a grim smile, some journeyman, still damp from the crossing, would stumble upon their threshold and see some coveted quality beneath the gritty sweat over her lip, and the stains through her bodice, and say to himself, "Here is a woman to wife."

And thus would things be decided; for, Christ knew, the man who had a mind to marry her would not sit and talk to her about it. He would know that at her advanced years, if she had had a choice for husband, she would already have come to the marriage bed. It would be taken as a matter of course that the set of her back and the knitting together of her brows signaled the Work of Ages. It would be taken for granted that she did not have a thought or a wish for herself apart from carrying a man's seed in her belly.

"And if I hardly dare speak to myself of other hopes," she whispered, "how can I speak of them to another?"

She regarded for a minute more the ebbing light on the walls, and when the candle at last extinguished itself, she felt her way to her bed in the dark.

CHAPTER 2

London, England, March 1673

THE ANTEROOM OUTSIDE the king's chambers was cold and the braziers set out to take the chill from the air were ineffective, except to further smog the air with some musklike perfume meant to cover the evil smells pooling in the darkened corners. Henry Bennet, Earl of Arlington, rubbed at the black plaster covering the scar at the bridge of his nose and tried to keep his breathing from sounding ill-tempered. He knew for a fact that only a few nights before, the Duke of Buckingham had, in a drunken stupor, pissed in the corner. He knew it because he had seen it with his own eyes. The stain still marked the walls like a waterfall in miniature.

It had been close to an hour that he had waited on the king after being urgently summoned, and he resisted the temptation to sit in the one lone chair that had been placed there originally for Clarendon's use. Since the old man's banishment, no one had risked sitting in it for fear that the ex-chancellor's bad fortune would rub its way into the sitter's buttocks, clinging there like a painful boil.

He watched William Chiffinch standing patiently by the door like an old hound, and when the man looked in his direction, Bennet decorously gestured with one hand and smiled politely.

Yes, I'm still here, you old satyr, Bennet thought, setting his face to a courteous mask. Bennet had his own private entry from his quarters to the king's, but the sovereign of all England had been in a rare mood of genuine anger and had made it known that the only person he would be closeted with for the afternoon was his twenty-four-year-old French mistress, Louise de Keroualle. To be alone with one of his court favorites was Charles II's preferred manner of releasing tension, and the length of the assignation gave testament to his towering rage after leaving Parliament that morning.

Bennet took from his pocket a small jeweled case filled with snuff and allowed himself a modest pinch, bringing to his nose a lace handkerchief given to him by his own mistress, a Spanish lady who was not young but was very supple, and still very grateful to be kept. At fifty-five the earl knew that gratitude, combined with experience, brought a certain exquisite frisson to the bedroom, not yet the desperation of a matron in her declining middle years, but more the ardent willingness of a ripening woman to please. With the certain knowledge of decay comes true passion, he mused. It trumped the demands of youthful entitlement and inexperience in matters of sex every time.

The abrupt sounds of laughter, a woman's and a man's, drifted from the bedchamber, and Bennet breathed a sigh of relief. It would not be long now, as he knew the king liked to laugh with his women, but only after the serious business of bedding had been exhausted.

Chiffinch must have known from the muffled giggling that he would soon be escorting the Duchess of Portsmouth back to her quarters, because he straightened his drooping posture and wiped at his seeping eyes with one sleeve. The old man was over seventy and had been, as Keeper of the Privy Closet, one of the few men, apart from Bennet, who reported directly to the king. It always roused Bennet's suspicions when he personally could not bully, persuade, or buy a man into revealing court confidences. Unfortunately, thanks to the king's relentless licentiousness, William Chiffinch had already made a generous fortune taking bribes from every duchess, actress, or street moll who traipsed up the back stairs to the king's bed.

A gentle cough from inside the chamber alerted Chiffinch to the young woman's approach and he swiftly opened the doors, allowing Louise de Keroualle to exit the royal bedroom. She floated out in a cloud of pale blue silk, disarrayed artfully off both shoulders, her plump baby face pleased and self-assured. He made a deep courtier's bow, hiding a sudden amused smile. Nell Gwynn, another of the king's favorites, was sometimes mistaken for Louise. He had only recently overheard Nell sharply rebuke a confused gallant by shrilling, "Pray, good sir, be civil. I am the *Protestant* whore."

Nodding to Chiffinch, Bennet walked into the chamber and bowed. The king was already seated at the desk nearest his bed, papers and scrolls in an untidy pyramid, his shoes and his wig still in the chair opposite.

"Henry," he called, motioning to the earl to stand closer. "I trust I haven't kept you long?"

Bennet looked about the room, studying the dozens of clocks

all ticking in discordant rhythms as though seeing them for the first time, and said pleasantly, "Your Majesty knows my time is his own."

The king smiled, a cynical curling of the thick lips, and slumped back into his chair. "They've hurt us, Henry." Bennet took note of the "us" and was instantly wary.

"All our work," Charles continued, "is to be undone because Parliament will play the penurious husband to my wifely supplications. I tell you, I am quite undone."

Bennet waited for the king to speak again, but the smile was gone, and he knew the silence was for him to offer up some advice, some scheme that would circumvent the barrier that was Parliament. He had been with the king all through the Parliamentary sessions earlier that month, and had watched him try to cajole and charm both Houses not only into giving him the funds to continue the Dutch war but to continue the Acts of Toleration, allowing his close and powerful Catholic ministers to stay in power. The ancient fearful remembrances of Catholics overrunning the seat of government with the brand and the sword during the reign of Bloody Mary were even greater than the recent memories of the black plague and the great fire that had destroyed most of London.

But all of Charles's seduction and prevarication had come to nothing. Both Houses were clamoring for the king to nullify Toleration and pass into law the public swearing of sole fidelity and adherence to the Church of England. In exchange for the king's assurances, Parliament would release the purse strings. There was at present a very real and dangerous threat that Parliament would try to coerce, either through law or through blunt force, the monarch into compliance. It was the same impasse that had brought Charles's father to civil war and the executioner's ax.

"Sire," Bennet said cautiously. "Perhaps what is needed now is a gesture of, shall we say, grand and unifying proportions."

The king frowned more deeply, staring through heavy lids. "'Unifying' is to our liking. 'Grand' is not. In case you have been sleeping, Bennet, we are dry in the purse as of late." He stood up restlessly and turned to look through his window out into the gardens.

Bennet came to stand behind Charles and saw several of the queen's young women animatedly posing under the king's gaze. That the king had given him his back was a sign of the trust he put in the earl, but it was also a signal, and a threat, of the potential withdrawal of royal favor. Henry Bennet had been with Charles from the penniless, starving days of exile and had reached the highest of appointed offices by being made secretary of state. But his ambassadorial journey with the Duke of Buckingham to Holland the year before to force upon the Dutch the terms of peace had failed miserably, and the war continued. The fact that he, like the king, was a closeted Catholic, although he made a public show of taking sacraments under the Church of England, made him keenly aware of his precarious position at court.

Most of all, the earl knew he was despised by his Protestant colleagues and, worse, distrusted. His years in the Spanish court on behalf of the English monarchy had left about his person the aura of orientalist pursuits and popish ritual. Personally, he cared little what faith was à la mode, Protestant or Catholic; the important thing was what was expedient to further the king's, and his own, interests.

Bennet cleared his throat and offered, "Your Majesty knows that I have continued to have correspondences with the colonies of the Americas, and that despite two expeditions to the new England some years past we have had no luck in capturing the murderers of your father."

Charles grunted his assent but continued staring out the window. "I am painfully aware that the colonists have hidden and will continue to hide Cromwell's covey. It hardly matters now. Natural death will soon do what the hangman has not been able to."

Bennet moved slightly nearer. "I have recently received a packet from an agent of mine in the governor's office in Massachusetts. It's true that Edward Whalley is reputedly in poor health and is likely to die soon. Of William Goffe and John Dixwell, the other two regicides in hiding, we have had little word of their exact place of concealment. However"—and here Bennet paused, knowing the silence would pull the king's attention away from the spectacle of youthful exuberance and back to the matter at hand—"we have placed the whereabouts of the chief of Your Majesty's ills in this regard in the person of one Thomas Morgan."

Charles did not turn around, but Bennet knew he had his full attention now. He leaned in closer, enough to smell the orange-water cologne of the French girl, and said, "I am fully prepared, Sire, to use my own resources to fund this expedition. What I propose is to send a few, perhaps four or five, expertly trained men on a merchant ship." The last expedition, nine years earlier, had been composed of four ships and four hundred and fifty men; the rattling of sabers must have been heard a hundred miles out to sea. Not one arrest in the colonies had been made. "In this way, Your Majesty, we can take by stealth what has eluded us by force."

Charles tapped sharply on the window, drawing the attention of the young women, who giggled and turned away in practiced, coquettish flurries.

Bennet took a deep breath to make his words more forceful and said, "Sire, I will speak plainly. There is ill feeling in both Houses. The Dutch, the French, and the Spanish are all waiting to cut our throats, or worse, cut off our trade routes. Now is the time to bring to justice, in a very public way, a man who has been hidden in plain sight by a gang of ill-bred rustics. By doing so you will make it clear to the world that, though it take years, the seat of English government will not be deterred in its will. An exhibition of the hanging, drawing, and quartering of this criminal who held the ax will make a powerful statement, Your Majesty, to the people, and to Parliament."

"Arlington, do you know why I depend on you?" Charles turned and smiled perfunctorily, though his eyes remained thoughtful and hooded. "Because you are ruthlessly dependable." In a distracted motion, he rubbed one hand over his closely shaven head. "Do you know what I wish for more than anything in this world?" He had spoken quietly, almost to a whisper, and there was a brief pause before Bennet realized the king had asked him a question.

"I wish to dream of nothing," Charles said, tracing with his eyes the opulent fittings of the room: the lavish tapestries, the intricate gilt-laden furniture, the mammoth canopied bed. "Giving me the body of the man who murdered my father will give me a quiet sleep." He smiled lazily again, saying, "And, Henry, it will give *you* a duchy."

Bennet recognized the subtle signs that he had been dismissed: the look of restlessness on the king's face, the turning away again to stare out the window at the beauty of St. James's Park, the language of the Royal Body which stated, "You are no longer in my presence."

"Thank you, Your Majesty," Bennet said as he bowed and left the chamber. He passed Chiffinch, returned to his post by the door, and thought, The next time you see me, you old goat, you'll address me as "Your Grace."

CHAPTER 3

MARTHA STOPPED HACKING at the weeds in the house garden and dropped the hoe to give her aching arms a rest. She cupped her hands over her eyes and looked across the adjoining fields, four acres in all, black and undulating from the rigors of the plow. The sowing had been well begun and would be finished before the next sabbath. She heard the strangled yerping of the old cock again for the hundredth time that day, made nervous and full of fight because of a coming change in the weather. She had learned to place such readings into the noises of an old rooster from her mother, who had recited to her many times, "A rooster crows at the sun and the moon, but peckish and quarrelsome, rain will come soon." Rain would be a welcome beginning to the sprouting, even though the sky overhead was clear except for a few high wisps of mottled clouds far to the west.

She heard the sharp squeal of the sow coming from the barn and knew John was feeding her extra mash to make her fatter. She had been held back from slaughter in the fall for breeding, and by the way her belly hung low to the ground, Martha knew they would have piglets soon. Perhaps, she hoped, as many as eight. She sensed Patience was already regretting having promised to give her any piglets over the number six. If the sow had eight, then Martha would get two, enough to buy four yards of good cloth for a new dress. And perhaps a new dress would make her more attractive to a suitor than her present worn and spotted skirt.

She had seen her reflection in a bucket of water often enough to know she had a kind of beauty, mirthless though it was; her skin was clear and unspotted, her forehead high and sloping. Her black hair, thick and ropy as a horse's mane, was no doubt her glory, but she knew her brows knitted together too often to be pleasing, causing a deep well to form between them. But beyond all of that, she feared, she had too much force, too much animal vitality, to be winning; at least to any civil, unprotesting sort of man.

Picking up the hoe once more, Martha called to her cousin, idling just inside the door, to come spread topsoil in the garden. Patience pushed herself from the door frame and slowly made her way into the garden. The smell of dried fish and manure, coming in waves from the bucket at Martha's side, made her gag and she clenched her teeth.

As she dragged the heavy bucket behind her, Patience ladled the sticky mess over the loosened soil. As soon as she had covered a small area, she picked up the short hoe and tamped it into the dirt. She continued in this way until a spasm, just below her breast, made her catch her breath and drop the bucket. A look of fear eclipsed the frown on her face, the fear of slipping too soon, in a wave of blood and viscous matter, the nesting bit of life in her womb. Martha quickly caught up her cousin's arm, her eyes questioning, but Patience shook her head and motioned Martha away.

Martha upended a bucket and settled Patience down on it, tucking her skirt over her lap and out of the dirt. She kneaded the pregnant woman's shoulders and clucked vaguely to soothe her. Martha knew her cousin mistrusted midwives who used slippery elm to ease the passage of the babe through the birth canal; "a squaw's poultice," Patience had called it, a custom of native savagery. But Martha decided that she would go soon and harvest enough for the birthing. Patience would be glad enough of a liberal application between her legs, she thought, when her labors came.

Thankfully, Patience let herself be led into the house. Martha steeped mint leaves in water to quell the griping, assuring her cousin she would soon enough want to eat again. But Patience bleakly eyed the suet pudding made for their supper, and she managed to whisper through gritted teeth that she doubted with her whole being she would ever again eat anything but bread.

ON A SATURDAY morning a harried-looking yeoman appeared at the door soon after breakfast, holding an ancient matchlock. He stood to the fore of two younger men, both carrying hay forks, and all looking as nervous as cats on a sinking ship. He nodded to Patience when she came to the door and asked, respectfully, for Thomas. When she asked their business, he told her that a pair of wolves, perhaps a male and his mate, had felled two lambs on his farm in Andover.

"They have seemed to bound up, fur, teeth, and claws, from the very ground of that place," he said, his tongue working carefully through broken teeth. "So clever were the beasts, they et through the high leather latches on the lambfold. The Town Fathers has charged us to kill the wolves what killed my sheep." At Patience's blank face, the farmer continued. "There be a bounty of fifty shillings apiece for the pelts. And twenty shillings more if the pair be skinned doubly so...at the same time, is what I mean to say...that is, together..." His voice trailed away and he stood, looking baffled by the ensuing silence.

Martha, coming to stand at the door, huffed air through her nose and said, in a loud aside to Patience, "Your boy, Will, would have better luck with my garden trowel against the beasts than these men here with their forks." Patience covered her mouth against a sudden smile.

"Now, missus, you'll not laugh when these great monsters climb through your shutters. They've come to Billerica now to do some mischief. As your man Thomas is a creditable shot, and as he has his own weapon, we are here to ask him to lend aid in rooting out and killin' these here wolves. We'll pay him a part of the boun—"

The sight of Thomas's towering form approaching the house cut off his speech as cleanly as a hand around the throat. They watched him set by the door a hundredweight sack, his head grazing against the beams at the ceiling, and Martha realized for the first time that he must duck or bump every time he came inside.

"You'll not catch them by day," Thomas said, wiping his hands over his shirt. "They'll be hidin' in a thorny lair. And if you did find them, you'd need to climb in face-first to kill 'em. No, a gun's not the way to catch a wolf." He looked significantly at the rusted barrel of the cradled matchlock, and the farmer bristled.

"Well, then," the man said hotly, "if you're too afraid to come, you only need say so." Thomas shrugged and, wishing the men a good day, walked back into the fields. The lead farmer motioned for his men to follow away, and they walked in single file down the path like geese tied bill to tail feather.

Soon after, though, Martha saw Thomas returning to the house and, with a flash of irritation, thought he wanted his dinner before the appointed hour. But he gave her no notice and instead addressed himself to Patience.

"Missus, if you'd be willing to give over a hen, I can kill those wolves. I'll buy you back a hen from the skinning bounty."

Patience looked at him in surprise and said, "But you told Goodman Shed he could not kill the wolves." Will, who had spoken of nothing else since the farmers took their leave, clapped his hands and tugged at his mother's skirts, shouting, "Mamma, Mamma, Mamma, let me go. Let me go hunt the wolves with Thomas. I can help, I tell you I can!"

Thomas laughed and answered, "No, Goodman Shed could not kill a cow with that rusted pipe of his, little less a wolf. But I can."

Patience pulled Will from her skirts and shushed him, but a calculating look had settled into her face. Martha looked from Patience to the Welshman and realized a deal was being struck; Thomas had sent the other men away so he could collect the bounty for himself. She looked with new eyes at his raw-boned figure; his face, cut by hard living, was well beyond comfortable middle years. But as he inclined his head to Patience, she saw ambition flare in his eyes, like a sudden sharp flame.

Martha, thinking a knotted cord the best way to plumb deep

water, clanged the spoon loud and long against the cook pot. "Well, then," she countered. "You're going to spend the night thrashing about after the wolves yourself, are you?"

His eyes shifted to Martha's, and for the briefest moment, she felt the short hairs on her head bristle. He turned his attention back to Patience.

"I'll build a pen, missus. They'll come for the hen. Once they're inside, I'll spring the gate behind them, and shoot 'em dead."

After some pointed haggling, it was agreed upon that the bounty would be split three ways, John getting the third equal share for helping build the pen. She felt hostile eyes on her and turned to see Will regarding her with a jutting lower lip. He was a sweet child, she knew, but a handful at times and rebellious.

"What is it?" she asked crossly.

"You shouldn't look so at Thomas. He's been a soldier in England," he said defensively. "Haven't ya, Thomas?"

Thomas nodded briefly, but there was a sudden guardedness about his posture, a wariness that made Martha think there was a good deal more to the story. The angling scar dividing one brow neatly into two halves took on a more interesting history than a careless fall onto a harvesting blade, or a village brawl. Her father used to say that eight parts of speech came into the world at Creation and that women made off with seven of them. The eighth part held by men was the language of war, conquest, and bragging. The Welshman, like most men, had a tongue for boasting; and she was sure, with the right abuse to his pride, those secrets could be tipped into revelation.

"And what kind of aimless fables have you been throwing the boy?" she asked dismissively. "You're too long in the tooth to have served the king as soldier. More like stable boy or muck-about..." Her voice trailed off as she watched his jaws working together, knotting the skin at his cheeks. There was a slight lowering of the chin, but nothing was said, no gestures made nor distracted shuffling of feet. He merely stood, hatless and calm, and in that moment all other action in the room ceased. And settling over every motionless figure, like gilt over wood, was a lingering, brittle tension.

CHAPTER 4

TIERNAN BLOOD STOOD quietly in a small alley off Pudding Lane and watched the night-soil men carting their refuse noisily over the stones. It was only just past midnight, but from the bawdy laughter and the unsteady stopping and starting of the handcart, Blood knew the refuse men were well on their way to being insensible with drink. It was dark, with no moon, and he could hear more than see the watchman in the alley opposite him stir with the noise. He had been waiting for three hours for the watchman to fall asleep, and he cursed, resolving himself to waiting another quarter hour for the man to nod off again.

He heard what sounded like a woman's shriek, in anger or in pain, he didn't know, but it was brief and soon the street emptied into relative quiet again. He thought about where he had dined earlier that evening, a fine tavern in Covent Garden, and smiled thinly to think that he should now be waiting on the main pathway populated with the night-soil men; the midden men, taking the worst of London's droppings to the barges moored on the Thames. A solid river of shite, he thought, the overarching smell giving proof that even the leavings of privilege stank as highly as any laboring 'prentice's.

Blood's dinner companion that night, among some ladies of rank, minor nobility, rakes, and assorted whores, was Wilmot, 2nd Earl of Rochester, who had recited to them all a new poem he had composed specially in the Irishman's honor. "Since loyalty does no man good, let's steal King and outdo Blood." The fact that Rochester had already pulled down his breeches in preparation for mounting his dinner companion, a fair-haired whore improbably named Honour, when he was overcome with his muse gave the recitation boundless hilarity. From the time of Blood's release two years earlier for trying to steal the royal jewels from the Tower of London, and his subsequent pardon from King Charles II, he was the most sought-after rogue in court society. The fact that he had blackmailed the king into a full pardon by threatening to reveal state secrets was known to no one else, except perhaps for Henry Bennet, the Earl of Arlington. If nothing else, Tiernan Blood, the son of an Irish blacksmith, with his nose in every backroom dealing, knew how to keep secrets, if it benefited his person. And he knew many secrets, from chambermaids' to the highest offices' in England.

He felt under his cloak for the cudgel and the hooked latch lift he kept tucked into his waistband and peered cautiously into the street. Gentle snoring sounds came from the watchman, and Blood quickly crossed over to the house opposite in the middle of the lane. It was an old house, one wall leaning against the neighboring house, and the door was made of heavy oak, although the portal was split and spongy from rot. Built in the time of the Great Queen, the house walls, half-timbered with wattle and daub, were dark and spotted from a hundred years of fire, rebellion, and neglect. The great fire of 1666 had begun on Pudding Lane, but somehow this row of houses had escaped the worst of the flames. Pulling the hooked lift from his waistband, he passed the thin piece of metal through the gap between the crumbling wall and the door and deftly raised the latch.

Blood passed into the house at the moment he heard another cart rumbling down the lane, but it didn't concern him; he was inside and the watchman had seen nothing. He paused for a moment, listening for any sounds coming from the common room.

From his stance at the threshold, he imagined the stairs roughly ten or twelve paces from the door. He walked carefully forward until he felt with the toe of his shoe the first riser to the stairs. Placing his feet as close to the wall as he could to prevent the boards from creaking, he lifted his weight from stair to stair. He took his time, allowing his eyes to better focus in the dark, and when his head passed above the second-floor landing, he saw a faint glimmer of candlelight leaking through the gap beneath the large, iron-banded door of the bedchamber. A segment of the lime-washed wall under his fingers crumbled and showered the steps in a brittle cascade. He froze and listened for steps approaching from the other side of the door, but there were no footfalls, and he climbed the last few stairs to the landing.

He reached for his cudgel and pulled it from his waistband and, with a few gliding steps, positioned himself in front of the chamber door. He lowered his head, placing his ear next to the splits in the wood. He heard nothing; no movement, yet no sounds of deep sleep either. If he hadn't known better, he would have thought the room completely empty.

Raising his cudgel, he pulled down on the rope latch and threw his weight against the door, which swung freely open on its hinges. Blood counted on the sudden violence of his forced entry to surprise the man he knew to be in the room, and it was the total astonishment on his target's face that gave him the greatest satisfaction.

The man, of course, had no pistol; he never carried a pistol, relying rather on the weapons of those who guarded him. He had been reading by candlelight, and he dropped his book to the floor as he clutched the arms of the chair, awkwardly rising to his feet, his mouth open in alarm. The small sea-coal fire had burned down close to ashes, too weak to illuminate the intruder's face.

Blood could have laughed out loud with delight, but instead he said to the man, "I'm here for my ruffian's pay."

A spark of recognition passed over the man's face, and he fell back into the chair, his terror quickly replaced with anger; and just as rapidly, in a series of winking spasms and tics, a forced calm settled over his face as he bent to pick up his book and place it carefully on the table next to the chair. He said tightly, "These games of yours, Blood, are most tiring."

Blood dropped his upraised arm still holding the cudgel, curling his lips unpleasantly. "Did I scare you, Sir Joseph? My apologies. It's only to drive home the point that I can breach any hindrance you put in my way, find any place you care to hide, should I be played falsely or go unpaid. But more than this, Sir Joseph, I do it for my own amusement."

Sir Joseph grunted impatiently. "You realize, of course, that if you've murdered the guard, it will come out of your wages."

Dragging a small wooden stool closer to the coals, Blood said coarsely, mimicking the lilting accent of London streets, "Sir Joseph, ya know I'd never hurt yer man. I left him sleepin' th' sleep of the innocent." He straddled the stool and, placing the cudgel in his lap, rubbed his hands with exaggerated briskness over the small hearth. It gave him no small pleasure to give Sir Joseph Williamson his backside, and though he could feel the other man's eyes on his neck, he took his time before speaking again.

"Your letter intrigued me," Blood said, finally breaking the silence, all traces of street cant gone. "You intimated you had an offer for me, an offer that would pay quite well. And that it was a venture—how'd you put it?—that would bring to bear all of my multitudinous talents." He smiled broadly at the older man and then shifted his attention back to the hearth.

"No," Sir Joseph said, "I wrote you that it would bring to bear the talents of those you have in your employ. I'm not paying you to do the work. I'm paying you to find the men to do the work. And just so we're very much of like mind, I'm *not* paying you to play the shuttlecock."

Blood stood and stretched and then dragged the stool closer to Sir Joseph's chair. He placed the cudgel on the table, setting it carefully over the book, and leaned in close, as though preparing to relate a confidence.

"I *am* a shuttlecock, Sir Joseph. A vainglorious shuttlecock of monstrous proportions. But it's you who've made me so. I am, after all, only the creature of your designs." He sighed and, reaching into one of the pockets in his greatcoat, pulled out a handful of singed chestnuts, which he placed on the table. They rattled and rolled together sharply to the lip of the slanted tabletop.

Picking up one of the nuts, Blood began to peel back the charred skin and said, "What is it you'd have me do?"

With his eyes on the cudgel, Sir Joseph distractedly brushed one hand up the length of his yellow silk vest as though searching for something. His fingers found a pocket and he extracted a small scrap of paper and handed it to Blood to read. He watched carefully as Blood first squinted against the darkness to decipher the amount of money written on the paper and then whistled softly. Sir Joseph took back the paper and folded it once more into his vest. "This, as you must have guessed by now from the size of the bounty, comes directly from our Catholic friend the Earl of Arlington."

"Ah, yes," said Blood, rubbing at the bridge of his nose, "our friend with the sinister yet obvious reminder of his service to the Crown. I've heard that black plaster bandage hides nothing but warts. It is a goodly amount. But considering the scope and size of the venture, Sir Joseph, . . . I'm afraid it won't be enough."

The startled look from the older man gave Blood another surge of satisfaction. "How could you possibly know what it is that you are to do?" Sir Joseph asked, a small bubble of spit forming at the corner of his mouth. He quickly wiped it away with the back of his hand, but Blood had seen him do it, and a look of distaste crossed the Irishman's face.

Smiling thinly, Blood said, "I know everything, Sir Joseph. It's what you pay me for. I can tell you how much and from whom you've bought this safe house, as well as the name of your tailor. I can even tell you" — and here he paused, resting one hand on the cudgel, fingering the long handle — "how many spies you have on your payroll. I can tell you the names of all of your enemies in the ministry and the names of all of your friends, among whom I'd like to count myself. But, as you well know, you're not the only one with a pair of ears…and a purse."

Even through the dim light, Blood could see the renewed flush of anger on Sir Joseph's face, and the tic which began fluttering beneath one eye. "You may be a Protestant dog," Sir Joseph said, spittle forming again on his lips, "but you're an Irish dog as well, and had I less need for the fleas off your back, I'd have you drowned in the Thames, if only for the pleasure of seeing you float downstream, all the way back to the Irish Sea, where you came from."

Blood's fingers closed tightly around the grip of the cudgel and he brought it quickly up over his head and then down again, crushing the remaining chestnuts and precariously rocking the lone candle on the table. The swift action caused Sir Joseph to flinch, but before he could move to stand, Blood's hand rested firmly over his arm, pinning him to the chair.

"Aye, Sir Joseph. I am a dog, but a dog must eat. A dog must have a place to sleep. And a clever dog never puts his muzzle into a fight unless he can feel the breeze of the open back alley at his arse. I know what you want me to do and I know you've already failed twice at it. I need the funds to hire the men to do it, as well as the funds to pay for passages, bribes, and, for myself, a retirement from having to pursue the vagaries of a restless marketplace. I know your little schemes. You take more bribes in one year running parcels and packets through your royal postal offices than most lords do off their lands. I'll find your man. But for that you have to pay." He pulled out of the same pocket from which he had extracted the chestnuts a piece of parchment and showed it briefly to Sir Joseph, until he was sure the old man understood what Blood expected in payment for his services.

Blood then stood up and, throwing his scrap of paper into the darkening coals, walked from the room, leaving the cudgel and the withering shells of the chestnuts behind him.

He stepped rapidly down the stairs and back into the street, hurling a chestnut hard at the sleeping guard's head as he passed. The guard snorted himself awake and looked upwards, as though the stinging missile had fallen from the sky.

As he strode down Pudding Lane towards the docks, he mused on the work that was yet to be done. He would need men and armaments, although the men he had in mind for the job could make do with a knife or length of rope to get the business done. He would hire Brudloe and Baker for certain; they were cunning. There were killers enough in London to populate a large town, but most of them were unreliable in their loyalties and, worse, stupid.

He'd need a big man, as well, with great strength, for the man they were to bring back was rumored to be quite large; although it was so often that the size of a man, like the size of a battle, grew in the retelling. Also, he would require a man who knew the colonies; that was essential, for the colonists were a prickly lot, small-minded and close-fisted when it came to protecting one of their own. The king had attempted the grand folly of sending bustling troops to the Americas twice before, and his prey, the regicides, had gone to ground, hidden by men who wouldn't be bribed. Perhaps he would bring in Samuel Crouch, a man who had lived for a time in Boston before returning to England.

It would prove to be a simple thing, he thought, bringing back to England one man; but there was much to do before the ship upon which he would book passage for the bounty men set sail. Five men should be able to overcome one colonial lout. His pace quickened, and he figured, based on the call of the street watchman, that if he could strike a deal with the gun merchant within the hour, he would have time to pay a visit to Fanny Mortland's whorehouse before she closed her doors at dawn.

CHAPTER 5

THE WOLVES RETURNED to Billerica, killing three more of the neighbors' lambs and savaging a milk cow so that she had to be taken for the butcher. Hard by the barn, Thomas made his wolf pen from woven willow and birch rods staked to the ground, and he scattered cow offal about as a trail to lead the wolves to the hen tied within the cage. If the beasts entered to devour the hen, the men, hiding up in the hayloft, would then pull the trip rope, trapping the beasts inside.

At dawn, Martha dressed quickly and slipped from the house to inspect the cage. There were no large, hulking forms within, only the hen, which sat ruffled and shivering in the morning cold. She could hear the sound of lax-lipped snoring coming from the open hayloft above, and she shook her head at the thought that the men would catch anything other than a wet lung from sleeping in the open air. The trip rope, snaking its way up the side of the barn, was still taut, and she thought to give it a good pull and startle the men into waking.

A movement at the far edge of the yard caught her eye. Thomas stood alone, raking the ground over with the heel of his boot. A knot of flies rose and fell with the movement, finally settling back onto a clot of what looked to be blackened entrails. She could smell the rotting bait mixing thickly in the morning breeze and knew that if Patience caught a whiff of it, she would have her face in the bucket all morning.

Thomas scratched his chin thoughtfully as she approached, and she fought the impulse to cross her arms in front of her chest. She regarded the swarming mess with a disapproving sweep of her hand. "Well, I see we have caught something, and plenty of those. It's a pity, though, there's no bounty on *flies*." She ejected the last word as though she had said, "Satan, the father of *lies*."

He ducked his head, the brim of his hat hiding his face, and said nothing. But she sensed it was not an attitude of submission, rather more a desire to hide his expression.

"The wolves did not come," she said with certainty. "So you must wake John and clean this mess from the yard before Patience can wake to find it…"

"You're wrong," he said suddenly. "They did come in the night." He motioned for her to look past the bait and she saw the depressions in the mud. At that moment the breeze lifted, carrying with it the odor of stinging musk; a wild, uneasy odor like the pungent smell of a dog in heat.

There were two sets of tracks, side by side, one smaller than the other. The larger of the tracks was bigger than any dog or fox could have made. The paired wolves had been standing, perhaps for a long while, regarding what lay in the clearing beyond the forest. The sharp imprint of their nails pointed, like an arrow's mark, back towards the house. Then the tracks wheeled sharply about, disappearing into the bracken. She saw a soft bit of gray undercoat still clinging to a thorn briar, insubstantial and filmy like the downy top of a puff-away weed. She plucked it from the branch and brought it to her nose. The heavy, musky smell was stronger there, reminding her of her own body at the bleeding time.

Once, when she was fourteen and living in Andover, her father had trapped and killed a young wolf. The wolf was small enough for her father to carry the carcass home over one shoulder. "Hardly worth the skinnin'," he had said. But he had skinned it nonetheless, making a fur frill for her cape. The fur, more white than gray, had a warm lair scent about it, as though the pup still carried within his very skin his mother's milk. It had been a rare kindness from her father, and he was wounded deeply when she gave the fur over to her sister, Mary. It was the smell of it she couldn't abide — the overwhelming smell of brutalized innocence.

"These are smart ones," Thomas said. He had come to stand next to her and she startled at his voice. "I've never seen the cunning like. They never even touched the bait."

She took a few steps back from him, hiding the bit of fur under her apron. "Well, what are you going to do about it?" she asked impatiently, coloring darkly at her own thoughts.

"We'll need a sweeter come-hither," he answered.

The tone of his voice was hard to place. Not mocking, but flat and dry in a way that made her think he was masking something not quite proper. Narrowing her eyes, she said, "I suppose you'll be wanting to risk freezing two chickens now instead of one?"

She snapped the hem of her apron, clearing away some unseen clod of dirt, and fought the impulse to move back another step.

"No," he said, drawing out the *o* as if singing the final amen to a solemn hymn. "I'll be thinking something larger, and more tempting." He said the words slowly and carefully, as if speaking to someone cleft in the head.

A bead of sweat vibrated at the curve of his jaw, like oil on heated metal, and the heavy scent of musk and burned wood pulsed from his clothes and skin. She paused and waited for him to speak. She was not certain he had been sparking her with his talk of tempting, sweet come-hithers, for men rarely spoke true their intentions, but she would be wary for a reach and a grab nonetheless. Yet Thomas only stood, his arms tightly crossed, the vertical lines of his face impressed deeper into the hollows of his cheeks.

When it was clear he wasn't going to offer anything more, she returned to the house and began cleaning in earnest. The boards on the floor were swept, scrubbed, and sanded. The table was polished with butter and ashes, the great pot scoured and greased. The pewter was rubbed, and the blankets were shaken, the ticking boiled, the mattresses taken out to be emptied and refilled with new husks. The great cloud of winter's detritus was lifted and settled back down over her head, and with it came a growing irritation.

She set a narrow-backed chair under the eaves to stand on and began sweeping out the gutters with violent thrusts of the broom, practicing in her mind what she could have, what she should have, said to Thomas. The leaves, erupting with spiders and mice, first exploded in rustling showers, falling to the ground brittle and sharp, like shards of thin glass. Will soon began to scatter the leaves over the newly swept yard, throwing and kicking them into the wind. Martha had only just resolved to chase him away when Will asked, "Who're ya talkin' to?" He had come to stand next to the chair and craned his neck to see what lay on the roof. From the look on his face she knew she had been revealing her thoughts aloud.

"I'm talkin' to the mice," she said, her irritation firing to red, and with the next jab of the broom she felt the handle break in two. "Now see what you've made me do," she muttered, stepping off the chair. Will retreated quickly backwards, his arms shoved behind him, wide-eyed and frightened, as though he had broken the shaft himself.

Seeing his stricken face, she softened her tone. "I don't suppose you can mend it, then." He shook his head, and fearing he would begin to cry, she asked, "Have you ever seen the down of a wolf?" She pulled the tuft of fur out from under her apron and showed it to him. He looked at her wonderingly as he stroked it gently with one finger.

"Will Thomas kill it, then?" he asked. His childish wriggling and shifting about had given way to a sudden, doubtful silence.

"He will try," she answered, nodding what she hoped would be taken for a certainty.

"And what if he cannot?" he whispered. His face had begun to crumple into fear, his brows crouching low over his eyes.

"Then," she said solemnly, smoothing her hand once across the runnels of his hair, "we shall have to run very fast indeed." Her lips, which had been downturned, arched up into a teasing smile, and the boy whooped away, loosening his fear into the cascading piles of leaves.

Watching his exuberant dash across the yard, she was suddenly very tired, the last of her anger extinguished, smothered within the press of punishing labor. She sat on the chair and brought the bit of wolf down to her nose. She breathed in the wolf's scent, a scent brought from ceaseless roaming over darkened fields and haunted fens, through gates of slanting twilight. The odor, both sharp and intimate, offered up the violent submission of the kill, and a no less forceful submission into coupling. Thoughts of an obdurate Thomas slipped unwanted into her mind, and she opened her fingers, letting the wind blow the clump of fur across the yard, where it mixed with the leaves and was gone.

THE BOUNTY FOR the wolves was raised to seventy shillings apiece and Patience agreed to sell to Thomas the smallest of her four lambs for the pen. Martha took the hen, still ruffled and peevish from spending the night in the open, and put her back into her roost. Thus was it ever with men considering women, she mused, watching the bird settling herself deeper into the straw; plain and pecking creatures, such as herself, were passed over for those more meek and tempting.

A heavy rain had fallen the night before, bringing with it a chill wind that blew and cracked at the roof with empty branches. With morning, the wind had stopped, leaving pollen-green ponds in each rut in the yard. Early buds, torn loose by the storm, floated like rafts on miniature oceans, making intricate swirls and arcs in their wake.

From the open common room window Martha watched Thomas as he stood in the yard, looking for rain to fall from the clouds dispersing darkly over the rooftop. She knew he was ruminating over his plans to bait the pen with the lamb. From a reeking pail he spread new entrails in a line to the pen, wiping the trap door with the oozing guts to hide his own scent.

He led the lamb struggling and bawling against the tether, wild-eyed at the coppery smell of blood, and tied her to a stake inside the pen. The creature was still piebald from having the wool eaten off her back by her brothers, hungry and near to freezing from the desperate winter. Still, she was clamorous and lively and would bring the wolves to trap, if they hadn't already tracked onto another's field.

Patience came to stand in the yard as well, watching Thomas carefully, her every gesture a testament to her worries over the possible loss of a valuable lamb. She called tersely to Will, who had followed Thomas inside the pen, laughing and excited to a fever by the thought of wolves coming to their very door. Jabbing at the lamb with a stick, the boy cried desperately, "Can't I help kill th' wolves too, Thomas?"

Thomas shook his head and, leading the disappointed boy out of the pen, set the trip rope to the swing door carefully. When he was satisfied, he started for the house, to gather up his gun and some quilts for the long night in the barn, Martha thought. She could hear John rustling about in the hayloft, excited over the prospect of the kill, singing a fragment of some bawdy tavern song, the lyrics sly and unseemly.

Thomas whistled a warning to John to lower his voice, and glanced at the open house window. He startled to see Martha's face peering out at him, motionless and staring. She quickly closed the casing, but she continued her vigil through the small leaded panes. Outside, beyond the window, she could see the dark, rippling shape of a crow settling itself on the last small island of snow in the yard, picking at the still-red spatters of blood from the bait.

A rushing, half-formed thought of silent beasts with snapping jaws made her head jerk up and she grasped suddenly at the casing. Thomas, sensing her alarm, even through the barrier of glass, wheeled about to find only the wet and glimmering yard, reflecting the last of the day's curdling light.

Martha could feel Thomas watching her during the supper hour as she ladled soup mindlessly into bowls. Her usual precise movements, economical and sure, became, as the hour passed, disjointed and awkward. Even as Joanna knocked over her bowl, a thing that would normally have set her to scolding, it only served to further dispirit her, and she sopped up the mess without a word.

They had no sooner finished scraping the last of the soup from their bowls when Martha stood abruptly from her chair and walked to the shuttered windows, opening them to peer out into the blackened spaces of the yard. The lamb had ceased its crying and there was no sound beyond the caustic settling of the hearth.

Patience, anxious and fretful, took Will and Joanna by the hand and retired to bed, the men leaving soon after for the barn. Martha quickly cleared the table and, pinching out the candles, placed herself at the open window to keep watch.

She followed the scattered rays of candlelight from the tin lantern in the hayloft, and then, as the men settled themselves, that light, too, was extinguished. Martha raised herself up on her toes, elbows braced against the windowsill, and arched her neck to follow the clouds lifting ever higher into the ceiling of the sky. Through the scrim of vapors the light from a slivered moon glowed dully, like a flame through smoky glass. The evening breeze blew in chilling gusts from the west, where the forest bracken grew, and she knew the wolves, when they came, would not be able to smell her scent from the open casing. She heard a rustling behind her and turned to see William creeping along the wall towards the door, his fingers outstretched as though he would open it. Her glance startled him and he pulled back his hand, but he stood his ground for a moment, looking defiantly at her. Shaking her head, she gave him a cautious eye and pointed him back to bed.

For hours, a fragment of song she had learned long ago worked ceaselessly through her head. She had heard it from an ancient virgin aunt who had come to be nursed through her decrepit ravings, finally to die in her father's house. In truth, the old woman was her mother's great-aunt, and was hardly a corporeal being as she lay shivering beneath piles of quilts, her bones loose and untethered beneath her skin, like sticks inside a bleached linen bag. She had been laid on a cot close to the hearth, and through every meal, through every task done within the house, the Allens listened to the old woman mumbling in fear or to her shallow, whispery singing:

> *What comes at night, with scalding breath,*
> *With teeth that bite and claws that tear,*

With cunning eyes and fur doth wear;
It is not wolf, but man, and brings a maiden's death.

And as the old woman died, she had caught hold of Martha's wrist and, motioning her closer, said through laboring, gaping lips, "Young woman...be ye 'ware of untrue prophets that come in the cloth of the lamb...for they be wolves...and wolves be footmen to the Beast...." When Martha raised her head again, the aunt had passed beyond, her eyes still open and fixed on the lintel above the door.

A swift movement of shadows at the outermost rim of the forest, like water over rocks, caught her attention and she poised, motionless, gripping the sill with cramping fingers. She could see no definable figures in the yard, only bands of greater and lesser darkness. She listened for something beyond the gentle rustling of branches above the roof but could hear nothing moving across the damp earth.

A sudden, bleating scream was cut off by a ripping noise, like cloth being torn from a loom. Then, the dull snapping sound of the trap coming down brought an enveloping silence. The scream had come from the lamb, she was certain, and yet an unreasoning, terror-filled image assaulted her that William, restless and curious, had crept out undetected from the house. With a hammering fear she ran to the door and, flinging it open, realized she had left it unbolted. She stumbled off the steps into the yard, not thinking if the trap had been sprung too soon, or too late, leaving the wolves free and blood-lusting, thinking only of what might be trapped inside the pen.

Nearing the barn, she heard a low, throaty growl. The sound

was close, but she could see nothing between herself and the woven structure, which in that moment appeared as insubstantial as tatting lace. There were noises of a weakening struggle, a high-pitched whistling squeal which could as easily have come from a small child as from an injured lamb, and then more tearing sounds. The dark was absolute, as though black curtains had been hung within, and she took another two steps forward, straining to see through the slats. She could hear breathing then on the other side of the slender barrier, the cautious, overlengthy intake and exhalation of air, like muffled twin bellows, accompanying the wet and urgent sounds of feeding.

"Move away," Thomas said tensely, appearing out of the darkness. She heard him curse and call to John for more fire for the firing pan; the fuse on the flint had gone out.

The illumination from John's open lantern now flooded and filled a good two-thirds of the pen, but she could no longer hear or see the wolves in the shifting wall of shadows that clung to the back of the enclosure. She cautiously pressed herself against one side of the cage, her fingers encircling the coarsely woven slats. As she pressed one eye to an opening, she felt, rather than saw, the rush of heavy form and energy.

In an instant, Martha was eye to eye with the great wolf as it stood on its hind legs, its scabrous, working jaws on a level with her chin, its pelt yellow from the wavering light. The wolf's hackles were raised in a great bristling collar about its ears, and as the steam from its mouth spackled her face, she could feel the other, smaller wolf catching hold of her skirt, jerking her body hard and holding her against the shattering wall of the pen. She heard sharp, cracking sounds and felt the wood weakening beneath her fingers. The wood cut sharply into one side of her face, drawing blood, but for every effort to free herself, the frenzied surge of teeth at her hands gave her no purchase to push herself away. Her captive eye, pressed against a widening gap in the slats, could not close itself for terror, and she wildly tracked the wolf's eye within a hand's breadth of her face, reddish gold and unblinking like a rust-stained moon; and she saw there was no vengeful, manlike designs in its gaze, only the singular will to free itself.

The world narrowed to the closing span between them, and she inhaled sharply, breathing in a fleck of bloody foam from its laboring tongue, and tasted the salt from a still-warm body. Her jaws, unhinged by fear and anger, became an open cavern and she screamed. A sulfurous explosion behind her deadened her hearing to all but her own voice. She felt a forceful ripping away of her hem as the smaller wolf was flung backwards from the bite of the lead shot. Still she screamed into the roaring mouth of the standing wolf, as though she would offer up every part of her frothing innards, liver, spleen, and heart, feeding them to the beast one by one like boiled sweetmeats. The second shot exploded, shattering the wolf's throat, laying open the tender gray neck. And with a great geyser of blood, it crashed heavily to ground.

As the wolf fell away, she felt hands grabbing her shoulders, encircling her, dragging her away from the pen. She was spun about and shaken, her neck bobbing loosely over her shoulders, spineless and weak with terror. She could see John, ashen and spent, as he stared at her with bulging eyes; and her cousin as well, standing barefoot in the yard, open-mouthed and sobbing over the children, who were safe at her side, hiding their faces within the folds of their mother's thin night shift.

Thomas bent over her and wiped the blood away from the scratches around one side of her face where the wood had gouged the flesh, looking for and finding an open bite mark at her lip where a wolf's poisonous spittle could hide, turning her from woman to changeling, to be chained to a post, ranting and howling away the rest of her days. He carried her to the house, where Patience bathed her face and hands and spread a quilt over her quivering form.

Later, she would come to stand in the rim of torchlight, silently watching the men winching up the wolves, one male and one female, side by side in death as in life. With immense skinning knives, the men opened up the carcasses like wings and sluiced buckets of rainwater over the fur, carving out the organs until both were clean of blood. It was only when they began to strip the fur away from the muscles and sinew, revealing the pink and defenseless flesh beneath, did she slip away again.

CHAPTER 6

THE FIGHTING BITCH was short in stature, her forelegs deeply bowed, but with a massive head. They called her Whistler, not for any sound she herself made, but for the sound the opposing dogs often made through their throats after she had buried her teeth deep into their windpipes. This was to be her fifteenth fight, and her owner, Samuel Crouch, had bet heavily on her. She was the odds-on favorite to win, even though the brute in the ring with her was larger and younger as well.

Their two respective handlers held tight to the straining leads, the dogs already lathered in great, glistening mantles of sweat and spittle, their snapping jaws tearing at the air. The crowd standing around the circular walls of the pit pushed aggressively forward, each man eager to see the match. A roaring had begun that was greater than the usual gaming noise. Bettors called encouragement to their fellows standing close by or threw insults, friendly or not, to men on the other side of the ring.

Sam Crouch caught the eye of a gaunt, dour-faced man standing on the far side of the pit and, with the barest possible movement, raised his chin in recognition. The dour-faced man spat and shouted last-minute instructions to his handler to hold more tightly to the brute's lead.

Crouch laughed and turned to his companion standing nearby. "He'll look even sourer when my bitch chews his dog's balls clean off."

"God, what a stink," the man said. He smiled approvingly, taking in another deep breath.

Crouch tugged at his sleeve, leading him away from the ring, and signaled for more drink. "Come, Brudloe," he said loudly over the din. "We have a few moments yet before they let slip the dogs."

A serving man brought two heated ales and they drank deeply, their eyes like twin beacons searching the room for newcomers. Crouch noted the hulking shape of Brudloe's bodyguard, Cornwall, at the far side of the room, leaning against the wall as though propping it up. Brudloe himself was a demon in a fight, fast with a knife and tireless. But one look at Cornwall's bulk gave even the most obstinate aggressor pause for thought. Cornwall's first loyalty, however, was to the master spy Tiernan Blood, and he would most likely report everyone's actions directly to him. It was through Blood's directives that Crouch had called for a meeting with Brudloe and his associates after the match.

Crouch leaned closer to Brudloe's ear, saying, "I have all that we require: maps, our contact in Salem, the captain for transport."

"Guns?" Brudloe asked.

"Aye, that, too. Blood has seen to that." Crouch tipped the mug up to his mouth again, draining the last of the froth. He'd never actually seen Tiernan Blood eye to eye, always dealing through an intermediary. And he doubted whether Brudloe would know the man by sight either. The Irishman could well be in the room at that moment, in one of his many disguises. The only one who would know him for certain would be Cornwall, who'd been with Blood from the early days.

Crouch saw a group of men and women tumble into the smoky room, dressed in heavy velvets and brocades. They were all masked as though, he mused, every ripe son of a whore in the room wouldn't know it was the Duke of Buckingham with his cronies and their mistresses. He saw one of the duke's men pay out the wager, a sizable stack of coins, and Crouch grinned. Tonight's wagers would make him a handsome profit. This, along with Blood's pay and his bounty for passing English secrets on to Spain, would see him comfortably through the next few years.

The crowd's sudden deafening cries signaled the release of the dogs, and he pushed his way forward to the circular pit wall. He could hear the frenzied snarling, and when he had elbowed away the last man blocking his view, he saw the dogs locked muzzle to muzzle, the vicious twisting of their heads spraying blood and saliva over the walls in oozing ribbons. A fine mist spattered the face of one finely dressed woman, her satin bodice stained red, and she screamed in outrage over her ruined dress.

The brute had latched onto Whistler's ear, ripping it away from her pelt, and she locked her teeth into the back of his neck, worrying it like a rat. He staggered under the attack but managed to twist out from under her, clamping his jaws crushingly onto one of her forelegs. A sound like the breaking of ice was followed by a screaming howl as the bitch tore her leg away, pieces of her hide shredding like braided rope. She staggered, and the brute rammed her onto her back, leaving her belly exposed. He began to flay open the hollow beneath her ribs, her legs scrabbling at the air frantically, but he had left his neck exposed, and Whistler's fangs found the killing spot at his throat, and until he bled out, she would never let go.

When the brute had finally collapsed, Whistler clinging fast to him like a monstrous tick at his neck, she staggered to her feet, holding her shattered foreleg aloft, her belly bleeding heavily onto the sand and sawdust of the ring. The riotous shouting and whistling swelled, filling the space like a tidal rush, and Crouch acknowledged the approbations and cheers from Buckingham's corner.

Whistler's handler cautiously slipped the lead around her head and quickly examined her wounds. Looking up, he shook his head, and Crouch exhaled resignedly.

He heard Brudloe's voice at his ear. "You can buy a dozen prized bitches now with your winnings."

Crouch gave the signal to the handler to dispatch her, thinking, were he to have a hundred more dogs, none would be as sporting as Whistler; and, truth be known, he had grown to love the dog and would have retired her soon to breed. To him, it did not bode well that she should die before his taking on a dangerous new venture.

He gathered his earnings into a pouch at his belt and left the ring with Brudloe, Cornwall lumbering after them like a baker's kiln with legs. They walked out of the gaming house, behind the Royal Exchange, and the three of them stood taking in the damp, cold air, the street a well of silence after the din of the baiting pit.

Crouch had a mind to go to a private room at an inn at Aldgate within a few minutes' walking of Cornhill Road, but Brudloe beckoned him in another direction, saying, "We need quiet; too many eyes and ears. I know a house that will serve."

He led Crouch south on St. Botolph's towards the wharves next to London Bridge, his scarred and closely shaven head turning this way and that for signs of alley cutthroats, Cornwall close behind them with his hand on the hilt of a large dagger. At the head of Lyon's Key, a form slipped out of the shadows, wrapped in a heavy cloak, and approached them on the pier. Crouch tensed, looking for Cornwall to move defensively, but Brudloe placed a hand on his arm, saying, "Be at ease, Samuel. This here is our new partner."

The hooded figure nodded and Crouch took his hand away from the pistol hidden under his greatcoat. In a loud whisper Brudloe said to Crouch, "He's *titled*, is young Master Thornton." Brudloe snorted unpleasantly and Thornton responded with a tight exhalation of air that could have been laughter.

They followed Brudloe into a shoddily built house perched on the docks, newly built since the fire. The door was opened by an old bawd who signaled them in, and at a large table set with food and drink sat Baker, a placid, cadaver-faced man known widely as an artist in the application of torture. It was said he could make the pope give up the names of his own bastards. For a moment, Crouch paused at the door. He found Baker at all times abhorrent, but of late, it seemed, where there was Brudloe, there, too, was Baker.

Shoving aside a large trencher of meat, Crouch pulled from his coat pockets maps and documents that he spread on the table.

The others moved to the opposite side of the table to be seated, and Crouch regarded them silently. Like the Four Horsemen of the Apocalypse, he thought, each with his own talent for destruction. His eyes returned to the youngest man's face, studying the refined features, certain he had seen him before. He was dressed expensively, much too richly to be a deserter from the army or a common street bravo.

Crouch pulled off his wig, scratching at the thinning halo of rust-colored hair, and pointed to the pile of papers. "Here are the Letters of Transport, signed by the office of Sir Williamson himself. The voyage to New England will take at least three weeks, maybe four. The ship is *The Swallow.* Captain's name is Koogin. Our passage is already paid, supplies on board. Do not," Crouch said, holding up a finger for emphasis, "do not underestimate the discomfort of the passing. March storms are fierce."

Brudloe sniggered. "The only discomfort for us will be the lack of women. Except for Baker, here, who may make time with the cabin boy."

Baker smiled benignly, scratching casually at his brow.

Crouch picked up a map out of the pile and turned it around for the four men to better see. He jabbed at the point of entry. "This is Boston Harbor. The captain will see us to a reliable boardinghouse. We will gather food and water and, as soon as we are able, leave Boston for Salem." His finger traced inland on the map. "We can walk it in a day. In Salem we'll contact a man named Rogers. Goodman Rogers."

"Oh, Christ. A Puritan," Brudloe muttered.

"They're all Puritans," Baker said under his breath, fingering through the documents.

Thornton sighed impatiently, saying, "Tell us about this man Morgan."

Crouch reached for a tankard and filled it with ale from a pitcher. He had it now; he had seen Thornton not once, but several times in the inn at Aldgate. The young rake had watched him more closely than was usual for a fellow reveler. On those occasions Crouch had thought Thornton, with his mincing gestures and embroidered coat, merely a wastrel with unnatural appetites. But now he couldn't be sure he hadn't been scrutinized for other reasons. His eyes met Thornton's, and the man's lips curled in a knowing way. Crouch's flesh at the hairline glazed with sweat.

"He was a soldier," Crouch began.

"Twenty years ago." Thornton sneered. "He's an old man now."

Brudloe poured himself more ale, adding, "And bleeds through the navel like any other man."

Baker smiled and offered, "One can only hope."

"He's a giant." Cornwall's voice suddenly erupted into the room. It made a cavernous, almost mournful rumbling, and there was silence afterwards as the four men looked at him in surprise, but nothing more was said. He only hoisted from the platter the largest joint of meat and began to eat.

Crouch placed his hands flat against the table and leaned closer to Brudloe. "Our job is to bring Morgan back alive. That's what the king wants. Not dead. Alive. He wants the pleasure of killing him himself, and to do it legal, which means publicly sanctioned, he needs a statement given in front of a bonded witness." He nodded to Baker, who inclined his head graciously in turn, as though at a compliment.

"We'll do our best," Brudloe said and held out his hand. "And now, about the pay."

Crouch reached into another pocket and pulled out a leather sack heavy with coins. "There's fifty pounds here. Another fifty upon completion...if Morgan is transported alive. That's twenty pounds total each for the five of us when he is brought back to London."

Brudloe exhaled through his teeth and reached for the coins, but another, larger hand was quicker. Cornwall had pushed up from the table, his fist closing over the sack. He tucked it away inside the tentlike folds of his greatcoat and moved slowly to the other side of the table, coming to stand behind Crouch.

"Any last words, Sam?" Brudloe asked, all emotion evaporated from his face. He raised his chin and stared at Crouch in stony silence.

Crouch stiffened, suddenly wary, and looked at each man in turn. He could feel Cornwall behind him, his breath at the back of his head. It came to him then that he was the only one in the room whose first name had been freely used. He knew the others solely by their surnames: Brudloe, Baker, Cornwall, and now Thornton.

His hand crept towards the pistol at his waist and he said, "Only that you'll not get far without me. I'm telling you, so help me God, the wilderness there will make these alleys look like a maiden's romp."

"*Traidor*," Thornton said, the Spanish word for "traitor."

A crushing blow at the back of his head knocked Crouch off the chair, blinding him momentarily. He could feel Cornwall grabbing at the top of his breeches, pulling away the pistol.

Crouch lay on the floor, a searing pain at his temple, under-standing fully the unyielding conditions of the new England; the unbearable harshness of the seasons, the strange, brutal obstinacy and unnatural pride of its inhabitants, the daily overarching fear of being ambushed by natives. He looked at Thornton's fine clothes and snorted bitterly through his nose.

Brudloe's voice came to him in blanketed waves. "You may well laugh now, Sam, but it's never wise to be buggered by Spaniards."

Crouch could see the wavering shapes of Baker's shoes coming to stand at eye level, and a large leather bag being dropped next to his head.

"But worse," Brudloe concluded, "is taking Blood's money while you're doin' it. I wonder what all you've passed along?"

Baker knelt down next to Crouch and began removing from the bag the instruments of his trade: gleaming prongs, probes, and small boxes studded with nails. He cocked his head at him and asked, almost sympathetically, "Shall we begin?"

CHAPTER 7

MARTHA SAT AND stared at the scarlet leather-bound book in her hands. The last words she had written with an unsteady quill blurred and dissolved into meaningless swirls that threatened to slide off the page. Patience had given her the book days ago to keep the house accounts, thinking to distract her from the terrible palsy that had fallen on her after the wolf attack.

Upon presenting the book, Patience had said in an overly cheerful manner, "Daniel traded an entire load of cod for this book. See how it's red, red as a cardinal's cap. It's rare fine, don't you think? And look how fast the color holds. It never bleeds, even into a sweated palm." When Martha had not reached for it, or even acknowledged her cousin's words, sitting listlessly and staring into the fire, Patience had placed it gently on her lap and tiptoed away.

Martha looked again at the pages and was able to read:

Received today, a letter from Daniel, written by a parson in Malden. He does profitable carting along the coast roads from Boston to Cape Ann. He returns for a visit in May bringing: 3 parcels of English broadcloth, cotton wicks, 1 new ax, leather hides for harnesses, and a young rooster, as the cock now in the barn is getting too old to bother the hens…

Suddenly the effort to pen even a simple account of the house was overwhelming. The last few words she had written, "bother the hens," rolled repeatedly through her mind like the last of an echo. A remembrance from childhood of swirling feathers discharged by frantic chickens in a small laying shed brought with it another, darker memory of the man whose lurching, desperate actions had created the panic. The man with whom she had once lived, and with whom she had come to believe that God, in his infinite scope, could never be found in a space as small as that inhabited by a terrified child. She watched as splatters of ink dropped from the quill poised over the page. Shaking away the old thoughts, she dipped the quill into the pot again and continued to write: "The talk with the meetinghouse men in Billerica makes much to do with Thomas and his wolves. The gossip with the women is much to do with my town dress."

The brittle sounds of coins being counted and recounted on the common room table, still strewn with the leavings of supper, cast an edge to the otherwise silent room. Martha could sense them—her cousin, Thomas, John, and even the children— eyeing her in a doubtful, speculative way. It was out of concern for her, she knew, for she'd lain in her bed senseless and feverish for a day following the butchering of the wolves. She had woken at night, thrashing the air with her arms and legs, moaning and shrieking defensively, until Patience took up sleeping in the room with her, bathing her head and neck with cold cloths.

But the scrutiny of the Taylor household was also of a fearful sort, as though her screaming at night signaled some sort of separation from reason or, more darkly, the beginnings of ravings brought on by the infection from the wolf's fang. She fingered the cut on her lip, which had already begun to heal cleanly without redness or swelling, but she knew it would leave a scar.

She had no fever left, but her hearing, diminished from the blast of the gun, had not fully recovered; and, all through the day, a high ringing inside her head set her nerves to fire and made her restless and curt. She bent her head closer to the page, hiding the next passage with her free hand, and penned quickly, "My dreams are all of dying, shredded joint from socket, and of the One who comes for me in the dark. I thought this remembrance to be tamed."

She read the words again and frowned. She had not meant to give form to her most intimate thoughts and, for a moment, was poised to scratch the words over with concealing lines. Instead, she quietly placed the book on the table, thinking to later blot out the last passage; or, better still, tear out the page entirely. She looked about to see if her cousin had been watching, but the rattling on the table continued as Patience restacked her piles of ragged shillings. Martha, suddenly irritated by her cousin's deliberate show of coin, muttered impatiently, "You'll burnish those coppers to gold before you're finished."

Even John, as he sat idly staring into the fire, fingered the coins inside his money pouch possessively, as though he'd wear through the seams to touch the metal. His share of the one hundred and sixty shillings could buy a goat and, if he was shrewd in his bargaining, a new doublet, breeches, and worsted stockings still smelling of salt from the crossing.

Thinking of her own ragged skirt that could not yet be replaced, she picked up a piece of linen she had been mending and gave the cloth an exasperated shake. With a sharp exhalation of breath, she leaned closer to the hearth to capture more of the failing light from the embers. When all eyes turned to her, she realized she had startled every one of them. She put her head down and put her mind to the needle.

Thomas had taken the prime spot on the long bench, nearest the fire, and was rubbing an oil rag over a trap. Through her lashes she studied his sharp profile as he bent over his task, his brows furrowing with concentration, and felt a sudden flare of resentment at his quiet, solemn pridefulness. He never once boasted or swaggered with any of the other men about besting the wolves, turning over to John the pleasure of describing the capture and the kill. But there was a look of satisfaction in his bearing and she envied him his bounty.

He had given no special notice of her presence after carrying her to the house, and yet that morning she had found a new broom propped against her chair, a solid, tightly woven broom to replace the broom she had broken. She had no doubt that Thomas had made it, but he had said not a word to her.

Keeping her eyes on her piecework, she said quietly, "I thank you for the broom."

She could sense his eyes on her for a moment and then he answered only, "Aye."

John had begun a teasing play with Will, making growling and snapping noises with his mouth, pawing the air like a beast, until Will squealed loudly in terrified delight. Martha felt panic, like a taut, vibrating rope, in her chest, and at every shrill, piercing scream from Will, she felt her hold on any moderate reserve slipping away.

"For pity's sake," she snapped. "Can't you leave us in peace?" Boy and man, startled from their play, looked at her in reproachful silence, so equally matched in hurt that had she not felt so weary, she would have laughed.

Following the sudden silence, images of the hens began to plague her again and, to dull her own thoughts, she asked tersely, "And what is it you plan with your share of the bounty?"

Thomas, finally realizing the question was to him, answered solemnly, "It goes, missus, to my house that is to be."

Martha had asked the question lightly and had expected his answer to be more homely: acquiring a brace of pigs or a breed cow and a gallon of hard cider to be drunk in spartan sips through the long winter's night. A new, deeper sense of jealousy pricked at her as she remembered his plot of land to be granted by Daniel after one more year of work.

Patience, relieved to see her cousin out of bed and anxious to make peace of the night, offered eagerly, "Martha, now that Daniel is bringing us cloth, I'll make you a new skirt myself. Then, if there be enough piglets, you can trade them for the making of a cloak as well." She continued chatting in an idle way about Daniel's return and the goods he would bring them, all the while petting and rocking Joanna, who had fallen asleep on her diminished lap.

Will, restless and weary of uninteresting talk, began to pull at

John's shirtsleeve and begged, "Tell us a story now. Tell us about when Thomas was t' soldiering."

The childish pitch of his voice carried through the roaring in Martha's ears and she instinctively looked to Thomas, whose gaze was still bent to the now-glistening workings of the box trap he had been oiling. Without looking up, and with no great emphasis on the movement of his head, he turned his chin slowly, first to the left and then to the right, moving in a ponderous and stately manner; an arc so subtle that its meaning, an irrefutable no, would be discovered only after the motion had stopped.

She could sense John shifting nervously about in his chair, shushing Will, trying to placate him with a cat's cradle made from an errant piece of string. John's deft hands quickly made a Jacob's ladder, and as Will's two fingers climbed the rungs from bottom to top like pale, naked feet climbing a set of stairs, the image of fluttering hens and an unformed, but terrifying image at the periphery of her memory threatened to unseat her and set her to screaming once more.

"There is a tale of Gelert," Thomas said abruptly, his few words rumbling through the common room, which had grown almost entirely dark from the lack of new wood to the fire. The one candle, set next to Patience, guttered and smoked, exaggerating the shading beneath every slanting surface and under every angled feature of noses, brows, and lips, so that even Will's childish face was painted to a savage mask with the ink of shadows.

"I have the tale from my own country," he began. "Gelert were a hound. Given to Llywelyn, a prince of Wales, by King John of England, Gelert were the best of hounds. He could hunt game and bring down a wolf, so large and fearless was he, and Llywelyn loved him beyond anything else but his own son." He stopped for a moment to set down his trap and picked up another, larger one.

"One day, that prince goes hunting with his hounds and his men and his hawks. A deer were killed, but Gelert is not to be found, and the heart of the deer, by rights to be fed to Gelert, grows cold within the corpse. But no one can find him. So the prince goes himself to home with his hounds and his men and his hawks and is greeted at the door by Gelert, his muzzle blooded up to his eyes."

He stopped for a moment and his long arms reached for the water urn and he upturned it, taking deep, unhurried drinks. Martha jumped to feel a soft hand creeping under her arm, and she turned to see Will trying to climb his way into her lap. She pursed her lips at him but pulled him onto her thighs and was grateful for his weight and warmth. She hugged him to her breast, her arms encircling him tightly.

"Seeing the gore, a terrible fear overcomes the prince and he runs to his son's bed to find it o'erturned, bedclothes scattered and bloody, the boy nowhere to be found. A terrible rage builds within the prince and he takes from his belt his sword and pierces Gelert through the heart. Upon the dying howls of the hound, the prince hears a babe's mewling, and throwing off the bedclothes, he finds his son, whole and unblemished. And next to his son is the body of the wolf Gelert has killed, keeping safe the boy. From that day, Llywelyn never smiles or laughs again and it's said in Beddgelert, the place where the hound was laid, that you can of an evening hear his dyin' howls."

Martha turned her face from the remaining light of the hearth, carefully brushing away with her fingertips the water pooling at the corners of her eyes. She could hear Patience sniffling and sighing, giving full import to the sadness of the story, and she bit the inside of her cheek in aggravation that she would be so close to tearfulness over such a rustic, overworked tale, the kind of tale that would have sent her father into a spasm of ridicule.

She gently dislodged Will from her lap and directed his nodding form towards his mother. Patience stood awkwardly holding the sleeping Joanna and, gesturing for Will to come, carried the sole candle to her room. John stretched elaborately and, muttering and grimacing, followed his own feet to bed.

Slumped deeply into her chair, Martha let her chin fall sharply against the hollow of her chest and watched Thomas gathering up his traps, stringing them together as he would trout on a length of heavy string, his fingers finding the open hooks that his eyes could not see in the dark. The remnants of embers, briefly pulsating in orange and vermilion, lit only the most prominent features of his face and hands, leaving them to float, disembodied and massive like a statue buried to the neck and wrists in black tar.

The knot in her throat had finally dissolved, and though she granted dignity to the grave telling of the story, she resented her own response to it, as though he had deliberately sought to draw her out of her protecting reserve. An irrational play of thought rose up behind her eyes along with a sudden, embittered anger, and she remembered the brown hen passed over, not even worthy of sacrifice to beasts.

"D'ye think of yourself as the wolf?" she hissed, the words overdrawn and sibilant. "Or is it the wrongly accused dog that lives to serve and is trampled underfoot for it?"

He stood carefully to his full height, mindful of the beams above his head, and at that moment the last of the embers were extinguished. She listened for heavy footfalls as he fumbled his way to his room behind the hearth; but she heard nothing, as though he had disappeared along with the light.

A panicked nervousness began beneath her ribcage and she blurted out harshly, "Or do you imagine yourself a prince from Wales?" Her hands gripped the loosely jointed armrests, causing them to creak loudly. "Well…?" The room was an endless cave, the dark subsuming every familiar object, vanishing the floor beneath her until the chair in which she sat balanced solely on the points of its four slender legs. "Tell me, which are you?"

Against the river of noise in her head, she thought she could hear the cadence of his breathing, a slow and steady inhalation and exhalation, as though he had begun to slumber on his feet, and she strained to hear his advance or retreat.

"It's not about me, missus." His voice floated somewhere over her head, a bass counterpoint to the brittle rustling of the traps. "It's about yourself."

He moved expertly past her, not touching the chair, or any other thing in the room, causing only the boards on the floor to creak rhythmically, stirring the air briefly with the scent from his body.

CHAPTER 8

ANNE CARTER STOOD at the groaning board, surveying with satisfaction the thirty or so men who sat in the tavern eating, but mostly drinking, their Thursday-night suppers. They were almost to a man dockworkers, off-loading bales and crates and barrels from wherries and barges bringing their loads direct from the large merchant vessels anchored farther down the Thames. They were, as dock laborers went, a quiet lot, there to drink their ale, eat their bread, and stagger off to their crannied bunks to sleep for a few hours before starting again in the morning, hours before dawn.

She had been keeping a careful watch on the man leaning comfortably against the far wall near the fire, and when he raised his chin to look about the room, she shook her head at him. He had been nursing the one cup of ale for more than an hour and she teasingly rubbed her fingers together to show him he should order another cupful and spend some coin or leave the premises. He grinned at her, tucking his neck further into his coat, but made no move to comply.

There was a feeble pounding at the door and she sighed, leaving her station at the table to go and open it. The men were quiet but not above stealing a pie or a few oysters when she wasn't guarding the food. The main tavern door was heavy with iron cladding and, in moderate weather, left open during hours of business. But a cold and brutal wind, a Normandy blow, had raked its way from east to west, and Anne had closed and latched it earlier against the rain. She opened it to a boy straining to hold with both hands a bucket of eels, thrashing and boiling in dark coils.

"Oh, Georgie," she said. "Sweetheart, come in." She laughed as the buffeting wind blew them both back into the room, and as she struggled to shut the door again, she felt the man at the fire come up behind her. He pushed his hands against the door to help her, but his thighs pressed against the back of her legs. Giving him a warning glance, she expertly danced away and put her arm around the boy.

"Georgie," she chattered, "did ya swim here with the eels? Look at ya. With a towelin' ya'd still be drownin'." He laughed with her and shook himself like a dog. He snuck a peek at her bare arm wound tight around his neck, and blushed to purple. She smiled at his discomfort and teasingly brought her wrist to his mouth, wetting his lips with the rain off her skin.

Anne looked into the bucket and clucked approvingly at the muscular slapping of the eels. "Ooh, sweetheart. Go now into the kitchen and tell Min to give ya some oysters and bread. And tell her I said ya'r to have ale and not the small beer, mind ya, but a proper cup with both legs and a head."

She gave his ear a playful tug and he colored again up to the roots of his hair. He went into the kitchen, carrying the bucket, and she walked through the room, table to table, checking each man's portion to see if all had been paid for. In the corner farthest from the hearth she passed a makeshift table with a dead rabbit, head and feet intact, lying starkly on the naked boards, a small pinprick of red staining the wood beneath its neck. She was pleased to see every man in the place had taken note of the warning and had steered well clear of that corner of the room. The dead rabbit was Tiernan Blood's mark, and his little joke to the world. His trade name on the streets and alleyways of London was the Gaelic word *raibead*, pronounced like the English word "rabbit." Translated, it meant a man greatly to be feared. But to those outsiders who did not know his reputation for violence, it often meant fatal misjudgments in their dealings with Tiernan Blood.

A wind at her back caused her to turn, and she saw a cluster of men come into the tavern, unwrapping themselves from layers of cloaks and hats, carelessly spraying the laborers around them with drops of frigid rainwater. They walked without hesitation towards the table where she stood, and she hurried to the kitchen to bring them cups of ale, warmed earlier with a heated poker. They settled themselves onto chairs and stools and once seated began to look about the room, studying every downturned face, noting the sudden quiet. The man at the fire had turned away, but his head was tilted in an attitude of cautious readiness, as though listening for sudden footsteps from behind.

When Anne returned with the cups, she startled to see the fifth seat empty and whispered to the man at her elbow, "Here now, Brudloe, who's missin'?"

He snaked his arm around her hips, pulling her closer, and said, "Poor Sam Crouch. He's lost his last argument."

"What d'ya mean?" she hissed. Brudloe had begun to pull her onto his lap, but she grabbed his thumb and, pulling it back painfully in its socket, said carefully, "This won't play. Ya know Blood asked for five men, five *ready* men, and unless ya can increase yar number as quick as a whore's plague, ya'll have to answer for it."

Brudloe freed his hand and shook it with elaborate hurt, laughing. "Annie, d'ye reckon there's not bullies and bravos enough in London to replace Sam Crouch? Or d'ye think we can't take care ourselves to advance Blood's scheme?" His smile was suddenly gone and she regarded his small frame and balding head, crosshatched with scars from a knife fight that had separated his scalp down to the skull. He had, after finishing the fight, pulled the shredded skin back over his head, paying a seamstress to sew the wounds together with silken thread. She knew that his greatest asset was his surprising strength and agility, far beyond most men twice his size. His weapon was a short-bladed knife because he preferred plying his trade up close, but his true pleasure lay in tying intricate knots; some for immobilizing his victims and some for garroting. She looked at his forearms and knew he could strangle a cow if he needed to.

Anne turned to the others in quick succession and had to admit the four men together could be formidable against all but a heavily armed group of mercenaries. Baker, seated next to Brudloe, was unremarkable in either size or appearance, although he was rather tall, and he sat alternately studying his nails and observing the room in affable silence. He was a professional torturer, sometimes taking his victims north to Scotland, where the rack and the wheel were still tolerated, if not readily accepted. She also knew he had a wife and five children in a house on St. Mary-at-Hill, only a few streets from the tavern which stood on Lower Thames Street, within the shadow of the Tower of London, where he sometimes worked late of an evening.

Next to him was seated Hammett Cornwall, named after his place of birth, though past infancy he'd never traveled beyond the walls of London, and so massive that his coat was made from two cloaks stitched together. He never asked questions, never lost in a throw-down, and had been in with Tiernan Blood when he planned and executed the robbery of the Crown jewels from the Tower. He was the only one of the men who had seen Blood's true face, and he had been known to break an opponent's neck without beading a sweat.

When Hammett felt Anne's eyes studying him, he said suddenly, "Enough talk, yeh? Sausage."

The fourth man, the youngest, dressed in the elaborate sword and scabbard of wealth, said, "And bring something other than this piss. Rhenish or, better yet, Canary." He had the weak good looks of any young titled man she had lifted her skirts to because they paid in ready coin, although of late she had had to do her business in light enough to see that the coins weren't Dutch stivers or a French sou picked up in some foreign war.

"Who's this?" Anne asked Brudloe, jerking her thumb over her shoulder towards the young rake, ignoring his demand for costly drink.

"Edward Thornton, late of the Dutch wars," Brudloe answered, leaning in closer to Anne. "Though, to my mind, the most action he'd seen in the Low Countries was in turning over his shaving razor." He smiled at Thornton, who stiffened but said nothing. "All in all, though, Annie, he is a man for us." When she still looked doubtful, he whispered loudly. "Edward here turned out Sam."

"Samuel Crouch was a trimmer," Thornton said, frowning distastefully into his cup of cooling ale.

When Anne looked in surprise at Brudloe, he nodded his head. "It's true. Sam'd been takin' money from Blood as well as from some tangle of pope's whores out of Spain. Thornton caught him out and Baker trimmed his buttons." He snorted gleefully at his own joke. When she looked at Baker for affirmation, he nodded pleasantly and made snipping motions with his fingers, as though holding a pair of shears.

"Sausage," Hammett said again, more forcefully, and as Anne turned to go to the kitchen, Thornton thrust his cup into her hand and said, "Canary wine, sweet bird." He slid his tongue between his first two fingers, silently casting for a quick lay, but she decided she would turn him down. Something about his eyes made her stomach clench; he would probably ask for something unnatural.

She walked quickly towards the kitchen, passing the tables emptying as the men finished their dinners and ducked back out into the rain. The man at the fire had not moved and seemed to have fallen asleep in his chair. In the kitchen she gestured for Min to prepare more food and turned to see Georgie sitting by the hearth, stuffing the last of an oyster pie into his mouth. He smiled at her broadly and she regarded him thoughtfully for a minute.

"Georgie," she said. "How old are ya now?"

"Fourteen, if an' it please you, Annie," he said with pride.

She nodded and stood closer to him, waving her apron at the cook fire, stirring up the scent of her body like fresh-steamed bread. "A great big boy, now, ain't ya? How's yar traps workin' at catchin' eels?"

He wiped at his face with his sleeve, cleaning off the dirt around his forehead and chin, saying, "The traps is mostly broke, and that's the truth."

She pulled up a low stool and sat close to him. "Ya know how th' French catch eels, Georgie? A sailor told me. They takes a horse's head and ties it up good to a line. They throws it in the river for a day, mebbe two, and when they pulls it out, it's filled with eels. Coveys of 'em. It sometimes takes three men t' pull the head out, so heavy is it. The eels, ya see, they've sneaked inside th' brain, t' eat." She had absently picked up his hand and was toying with his fingers as she talked. He shivered slightly, though she didn't know whether it was from the thought of the eels burrowing deep into the horse's flesh or from her touch.

"Would ya like me to find ya a horse's head, Georgie? I could ask my ol' man. He's a carter with more dead nags in a week than there'r martyrs in Heaven."

He smiled at her gratefully and she sent him away, promising to meet him at the tavern before daylight with a handcart bringing a fresh-severed head.

She brought food to the table and the sweet wine for Thornton, ignoring his disapproval over the crusted, half-emptied bottle. She seated herself in the fifth open chair and turned to Brudloe, who was speaking softly of the ship that had been chartered.

"The captain's name is Koogin," he said, spearing a sausage

with his knife. "He was born a Dutchman, but only insofar as his mother's cunny was filled up with some Low-Country yeoman. He's of no country now. His only 'vestment, and loyalty, is to his own pockets and he's been proven more than once. He's run powder and flint to the colonies for ten years or more and he'll ask no questions. His ship is a three-masted hull with a crew of only a dozen or so men."

Baker roused himself, saying, "Blood's paid for five men and he'll know if we board only the four of us. How do we propose to fill our fifth?" It was the first time he'd spoken and Anne marveled at the gentleness of his voice. She tried to imagine how many times he had softly, and reasonably, questioned prone men screaming out their last agonies into his face.

Brudloe said, "There's only a few left alive, or out of prison, who'll serve for our purposes. There's Pillater, for one." He looked around the table and seeing no affirmation or dissent continued, "What about Knox?" He looked to Cornwall, who shrugged and rolled his head. "Christ on a cross. Well, then, there's Markham."

"Ah." Baker smiled musingly and shook his head.

"Frig me, then," Brudloe muttered. "We're in for four, and Blood will take his own back."

Thornton snorted. "Four of us and one colonial dirt farmer…"

An enormous hand wielding a knife plunged onto Thornton's plate. The knife slowly removed the remaining sausage, dripping grease over the younger man's velvet breeches, and Thornton's startled, angry gaze turned to Cornwall, who shoved the sausage whole into his mouth. He chewed thoughtfully for a moment and then rumbled, "Big man. Big, *big* man." He pointed the knife blade at Thornton and uttered carefully, "Little man."

Brudloe guffawed and clapped Cornwall on the back, saying quickly to forestall Thornton's reach for the butt of his sword, "Calm yerself, Edward. Do you know what it means when there are three nuns together with a horse? It means the horse is in for a rough ride." His smile vanished and he gave the rake a serious look. "You're the young blade here, laddie. Keep quiet, listen good, and you'll live to collect yer pay."

"I reckon a ship's passage to be a danger," Annie said suddenly, as though thinking aloud. Her voice cut through the fog of tension and she looked cautiously around the room, seeing only the sleeping man left at the fire. She lowered her voice to a forced whisper. "Who's to say what will happen on the water with a hard blow and a rollin' deck so bad as to pitch a man o'er the side?"

Brudloe smiled and reached for her arm. "What are you sayin', Annie, dear?"

"I'm sayin' five men board a ship and four men get off." She looked to each man but when her eyes fell on Thornton, he smirked and said, "Look out, boys, she'll snap your wick right off with her cunny."

"At least any of *their* dicks'd be stiff enough t' hit the mark," she snapped.

Thornton scowled but buried his face in his cup.

Brudloe tapped her arm and said, "Go on."

"What if I can find someone t' fill the gap? No need to pay the impress men. I'll find th' mark and we'll split the fifth man's pay." She turned to Thornton and said, pointedly, "Equal shares."

"Blood won't like it," Brudloe said.

"Blood won't know," Anne answered, looking around the table, each man giving his nod of complicity.

"He always knows," Cornwall mumbled sadly, eating the last of the damp morsels off the table with his fingers.

As Brudloe signaled for the men to go, she saw that the sleeping man had left his place at the fire, the door just closing on his retreating form. As Baker stood from his stool, he pointed to the rabbit and asked politely, "May I take the rabbit for my wife?" She nodded and he saluted her, his fine hands gently folding the rabbit's corpse into his cloak.

She locked the door behind them and smiled at her own cleverness. As long as the work at hand was attended to, Blood would never begrudge her initiative. He had sparked to her abilities, and though he could have his pick of any woman, he had chosen her for his special attentions. It wasn't merely the sweaty business in bed that she was partial to; his parts worked like any man's. It was the talking he did when they were about it. He would whisper wetly into her ear, "My oyster, my briny-dewed oyster…my careless pearl…my wine-dark abyss," and other such nonsense. The words stretched out into the long groan of rutting, words which uttered at any other time would have brought laughter from her mouth, but which, at the frantic moment of release, brought violent and thrilling images of falling from a vast height, with nothing but rocks below to catch her.

One brief moment of doubt crossed her thoughts, that he would settle on her harshly for dealing him false; but it was only flickering, soon gone with the rapid pulse of her breath. Blood would be in her room close by, still warm from the long wait by the fire, perhaps yet good-humored that his hired assassins had been so close and yet unaware that he had been seated in the tavern all along. She would trust, due to their greed and their fear in equal parts, that none of the men would reveal their little plan for the fifth man, and though she had grown fond of Georgie, it would be a very small thing to replace one eel boy with another.

CHAPTER 9

THE STRENGTHENING SUN had passed the noonday hour, and already Martha had hung clean shirts and breeches along low-lying bushes, dividing her time between watching the level of the boiling water in the great iron wash pot and spying on Will as he marched up and down the yard, a stick balanced over his shoulder the way he had seen Thomas balancing the long barrel of his flintlock.

The quiet, solitary preparations of the wash had come as a soothing ritual after a frantic morning preparing the house against the plague. They had learned of the outbreak from the Taylors' nearest neighbor, who shouted out the news from the road, not wanting to come even so close as the yard to prevent contagion. Martha had painted the lintels with vinegar, smoked the rooms with sage, and regardless of the warmer breezes bringing the scent of early iris throughout the house, she had closed all the windows tight to keep any errant winds from bringing ill humors into the house.

She had not spoken more than a dozen words to Thomas since

the evening he told of the hound, Gelert, and the meaning of the tale, or lack of it, had rankled her as though she had swallowed a smelt whole, one whose bones had stuck in her belly long after the flesh had melted away. The hot and piercing rage she had felt after the wolf attack had passed away, taking with it the savage dreams; but now, in place of anger she had a restless, almost hostile, curiosity about the Welshman.

She pulled a tiny fragment of cone sugar out of her apron and called to the boy. She smiled at his eagerness to grab at the sweetie and she toyed with him a bit, holding it just out of his grasp before placing it with her own fingers on his tongue.

She pulled him down to sit with her on a patch of drying grasses, the sun hot at their backs, and asked, "What, then, do you know of Thomas?"

He answered, smacking his lips, "Thomas has been all t' way to London."

"You mean New London, don't you, Will?" she asked, giving him a doubtful look.

He boldly reached into her apron, looking for more sugar until she pushed his hands away, shaking her head.

"More," he demanded, his mouth opening like a baby bird's.

"Tell me, then," she said with mock seriousness.

"He was t' London, *old* London, and he fought the king, with Cromwell. John told me an' he hasn't told you." He began to squirm, and she knew he would tolerate only a few more questions before he dashed away.

"Want more?" she asked, taking his hands in hers, tethering his restless form a moment longer. "Tell me and you'll get another pinch of sugar."

"He's got a great…a great…" He faltered, his attention captured by a squirrel gnawing at a seed in the garden.

She shook his hands to draw him back. "A great what, Will?"

"A great wooden trunk," he said, following the squirrel with his eyes. "Next t' the bed."

"And what's inside?"

"A coat. A' old red coat," he answered, jerking his hands free, and he ran, brandishing his stick, for the squirrel.

A coat, she thought, disappointed. There was nothing remarkable in that, unless there were other, more telling things inside the trunk. The cone of sugar was almost gone, and she wondered how much more she could extract from the boy before there was none left for so much as a pasty. She pestered him off and on for the remainder of the day, but Will could reveal only the little he had heard and seen with his own eyes: that Thomas had fought against the Old Charles during the English war and that Thomas kept the wooden trunk at all times near the place where he put his head at night. She finally gave up her questioning when he began to look at her as a goose regards a butcher who is standing with a sprig of parsley in one hand and a small ax in the other.

She lay in her bed that night, turning over in her mind the few things that Will had told her, and decided that when morning came, she would question Thomas more directly about his past. Her fingers crept up to the space beneath the pillow and she felt the smooth edges of the red book there. She had not yet been able to tear out the pages as she had intended to do, the pages where she had deposited her troubling thoughts. The book seemed to her to be an integrated, almost animate, thing. It had a spine and a hide and within the coverings were stiff, rustling pages that moved the air about like the wings of a bird. Ripping out the glistening paper would be like plucking the white feathers from a goose while it yet lived. It came to her that she would soon have to hide the book from the prying eyes of others if she could not bring herself to blot out the clandestine words.

At first light, upon the last of the breakfast dishes put away, Martha announced to Patience that she would go to the river for leeks and that Thomas should accompany her.

When Patience raised a brow at her, Martha said, "There may be Indians."

"God help the Indians," John mumbled, handing the older man the flintlock.

Martha gathered her shawl around her shoulders, and without looking behind her to see if Thomas followed, she walked purposefully towards the river. When they reached the embankment, Thomas walked ahead of her and she fit her shoes to his footprints, sunk deeply into the soft, loamy soil, up the steeply angled hillock towards the river, which lay in a depression on the other side. Halfway to the crest, he motioned for her to sit on a fallen log and wait. He disappeared quietly over the ridge, moving with caution through the undergrowth, using the barrel of his flintlock to prod his way forward through the tangle of maidenhead ferns.

He was gone for a short while, but she soon heard a low whistle and saw him at the ridge, farther south this time, waving for her to come on. She climbed with some difficulty the last short distance to the top, pulling on roots and jutting rocks to scramble over the peaked ridge, and saw the river running fast and clear below her. Carefully hitching up her skirt, she sidestepped down the far embankment to the water's edge. The boggy ground was chilled, but she felt warmth on her upturned face through branches of willow and beech. She smiled in surprise at the colts-foot growing like borrowed sunlight along the shaded dimples at the river's edge; and on the opposite shore she spied columbine, its red blossoms stirred into motion by hummingbirds.

Thomas had propped himself against a beech, crooking one foot up on a jutting root, and was looking to the right and the left, scanning the bank and the stream for any movement. His silence was of a belligerent sort, like a guard dog gone mute, so she turned her back on him and began pulling up the tender shoots of leeks, which yielded easily in the damp earth.

She soon had a small sack filled, the wet green stalks soaking the coarse linen, their sharp odor staining her hands and apron. But she was loath to leave the spot and decided to look for wild onions as well. When she caught him, through the reflection on the water, looking at the back of her head, she said in an offhand manner, "I am told you have been as far as London."

There was a long silence as she picked through the plaited shafts of river grasses before she heard him say, "Aye." She waited for tale-telling or bragging of some sort, but the silence stretched into minutes. "Well, then," she prompted, "you must now think Billerica flat and rude." She turned to face him, her expression challenging.

He abruptly swept away the small battery of flies hovering below the brim of his hat and answered, "There's good in it. Here 'n there." He met her gaze and stared long past the point of courtesy.

Finally dropping her eyes, she fussed with the linen bag and said, "Will was told you have been a soldier."

He shifted his weight restlessly against the tree and lowered his chin in the way she had come to recognize as a defensive stance and exhaled heavily, compressing his mouth for a moment into a thin, tight line. Then he inhaled slowly and said, "When I were a boy in Wales, the first thing I kenned from my father was to look out across the land to tell the dry ground from the wet."

Martha waited for the story to continue, but after a silent pause, she said, "I don't understand your meaning."

"It means, missus, that the world is a very large place. Full of mean marshes and moors, as well as meadows an' streams. And if you don't want to bog down and drown yourself, it's keen to learn where to step lightly an' where to tread not at all."

He pushed himself away from the tree and was soon climbing back up the hill to the crest, never looking to see if she would follow. Martha stared after him gape-mouthed before she quickly picked up her skirt and scrambled after him.

"Wait…wait," she called and he paused at the crest until she joined him, breathing heavily for a moment and struggling to speak again. "I meant only…to know that which is…" She stopped with a flush of uncertainty when he turned to face her. "I meant only to learn that which is proper as to who you are and… what you are about."

He studied her for a moment before saying, "I were born near Carmarthen. In the uplands." He balanced both hands on the barrel of the standing flintlock, crossed at the wrist, in a prac- ticed way.

"So then, you were a farmer?" she asked, and suddenly to her own ears she sounded tight-lipped and sour.

"No," he answered, looking to the middle distance at the clearing where the Taylor house sat, sending long plumes of dove-gray smoke from its chimney. "My father were a farmer. The year I were born, in 'twenty-six, the winters were so cold that the hand froze to the hearth back. My father had thirty acres of grazing and five for planting. He had four cows, two bullocks, one horse, fifty-two sheep, and a family. He lost most of it that winter and spent his whole life trying to catch back the past. When I were fifteen I left."

"Did you...were you close to anyone?" A quickening breeze blew, uplifted from the river, and a piece of her hair floated across her eyes, momentarily blinding her.

He slowly reached out and grasped the hair, carefully rolling each strand around one finger. "I had a brother who died at seventeen, elder than me by three years. His name was Richard." He rolled the strands again in the opposite direction, like unspooling yarn, and carefully tucked it back behind her ear. "He could run. By God, he could run. He ran every race in Carmarthenshire and won every prize. But the Welsh uplands have a temper all their own. And the very crags and heath that made him fast took away his heart at the end." He dropped his hand and said softly, *"Ni edrych angau pwy decaf ei dalcen."*

She shook her head, confused. He said, "It means, 'Death spares not the fairest forehead.' I held tight to my father's farm in my brother's stead for one year. And then I walked away for good."

She stared at his solemn mouth and at the dark stubble on his cheeks, growing like a crown of briars surrounding the pale and weather-worn flesh that were his lips, and unthinking, she placed a cautious finger to the deeply recessed hollow at the base of his throat and felt his pulse strengthen under her touch. His eyes darted to the side and his head followed quickly, looking over her shoulder, and grasping her arm, he began to pull her roughly after him down the hill towards the settlement. He whispered to her, urgently, "Don't talk. Don't look back until we are safe within the house. Say nothing to the missus."

She tried to crane her neck around to see what lay behind them, but his loping walk caused her to run hazardously down the hill, and she stumbled in her effort to match his long strides. He whistled John from the barn and whispered to him urgently, gesturing towards the river, and placed a silencing hand over John's arm when the younger man's eyes went big and round. Once inside, Thomas bolted the door, posting himself at the open window. When Martha came to stand next to him, he pointed back to the embankment where they had talked moments before. She observed nothing at first and then she saw a slight shifting of the landscape at the crest; dun-colored shapes moving in concert, heaving subtly as though the earth itself had learned to crawl.

Patience, seeing the men returned to the house, served up the midday meal, a thin ladle of soup with dried deer meat and the last of the bread baked days before. She chatted on happily about the leeks brought from the river and the fineness of the weather, of her absent husband, and of the seedlings coming up in the garden, unaware of the guarded looks passing between Thomas and John, and of the alarm that kept Martha rigid and silent in her chair. Thomas sat closest to the door with the flintlock at arm's length and soon the only sounds were of the scraping of spoons against the pewter.

Her bowl finally empty, Patience stood and stretched with her knuckles against the small of her back. She looked at Martha and, frowning, asked, "Are you ill? What's the matter?" Martha's eyes tracked instinctively to the window, and before anyone could stop her, Patience strode to the door, slipped the bolt, and opened it wide. She screamed and staggered backwards, her arms flailing wildly in front of her. Both men stood from the table with such force that their chairs upended behind them. With astonishing speed Thomas pushed Patience roughly aside and stood, his flint-lock raised, at the open door.

Thrusting the children under the table, Martha planted herself protectively in front of Patience, waving her farther back into the house. She felt a rapid, hot breath at her neck and turned to see John standing next to her, quaking and sweating, with a small ax in one hand and a large-tined fork in the other.

Patience, her voice shrill with terror, cried out, "They will kill us, Thomas…" He raised one hand sharply to her to be quiet but kept the long sights of the rifle pointed into the yard. Martha braced herself for the blast from the barrel, but after a moment there was no explosion. She stepped closer to the table, thinking to arm herself with a knife, and from her new vantage point she could see beyond Thomas's bulk into the yard.

A man stood motionless and alone not twenty feet from the door. He was wrapped in doeskin and furs, his chest and arms naked, a club with a knotted head hanging at his side, and on his skin were the angry, festering sores of the plague. The man watched them watching him until the sound of Joanna's voice, frightened and plaintive, floated out of the house. The man's eyes drifted sideways and tracked over the windows and roofline, all the way to the barn, and then returned to stare at Thomas. A racking chill suddenly passed through the man's body and he coughed heavily, pulling his furs more tightly around himself. He extended his arm out for a moment before bringing his fingers up to his mouth. When no one in the house moved, he repeated the gesture.

Without taking his eyes from the man, Thomas said quietly over his shoulders, "Missus, go and put whatever food is on the table into a sack and bring it fast to me."

The beginning sounds of protest from Patience brought a swift black look from Thomas. She quickly pulled the children from under the table and ran for her bedroom, desperately slamming the door behind her. With shaking hands, Martha scooped the remains of bread and meat into a cloth and handed the parcel to Thomas, who walked without hesitation into the yard. Ignoring John's insistent tugging at her skirt and hissing into her ear, "Stay in the house or yer get yerself killed…," Martha moved forward to stand in the doorway. She watched Thomas hold out the parcel, waiting calmly and patiently for the food to be taken.

The man in the yard had not retreated at Thomas's advance. Rather, he had planted one leg behind the other, tilting himself backwards to take in the Welshman's height. The man himself was not tall—Martha guessed him to be in fact shorter than herself—but there was a straightening of his spine and his arm extended outward, fingers encircling the sack with a gentle, almost delicate touch. The sack disappeared inside the folds of the doeskin, and slowly turning without a word or glance, he disappeared into the woody bracken opposite the entrance to the road.

Martha looked back at John standing in the middle of the room, his weapons held aloft. "Oh, for heaven's sake," she said, "put down the ax. Did y'think to cleave him in two and then eat him?" He sat heavily in a chair, placing the fork back on the table.

Thomas closed and bolted the door and took up his post again at the window. After a time he carefully shut and locked the sash in its casing, and she came to stand next to him, waiting for him to speak.

"That Indian was Wampanoag on his way back north, if he weren't to die of the pox first," he said. His breath appeared and reappeared on the glass in veiled patches. "Had they been Abenaki it's likely you and I wouldn't be here talking. They were all with plague or they'd not be begging."

"They...?" she asked, startled. To her eyes there had been only one man in the yard.

"There were half a dozen more in the woods not forty feet away," he answered.

She pressed her nose closer to the glass and scanned the woods for movement. "Will they come back?"

He shrugged and passed his hands over his eyes. She studied his profile, the darkened flesh trenched beneath his eyes and the scar that split one brow in two. "Am I Gelert?" she asked. He turned to her, and she asked again, "The hound killed by his master? You said the tale was about me."

"No," he answered. "You're not Gelert." His breath was moist in her face, scented with wild river onions, green and pungent, but he soon turned back to watch the woods and he didn't speak to her again for hours.

THE MAY WINDS brought rain from the direction of Boston, the air sharpened with the taint of salt water, and Daniel Taylor appeared on such a morning through undulating currents of dampened air, his canvas coat turned black and heavy from the wet. He arrived as Martha and Patience stood in the yard, quickly gathering in the washing that had been hung to dry earlier that morning when the sun had burned free of the clouds. The women had mistaken the crashing and rumbling of the carter's wagon as approaching thunder until they saw the barrel-chested gelding appear steaming and straining over the crest of the road.

Patience covered her face with her apron and sobbed at the sight of him. At his first embrace he said to her, "Now, now, my own little wife, I am home. Come see what I've brought you." He carried into the house bundle after bundle of cloth as well as hides, tools, and foodstuffs: two barrels of small beer, a firkin of ale, one large keg of wheat, two cones of sugar, and a caged cockerel.

He proudly pulled out crates of woolens and linens for new shifts, caps, and aprons, smiling at his wife's delighted surprise. In a friendly hug, he yanked up a startled Joanna, frightened at the appearance of this strange, unshaven man, but she quickly smiled when Daniel showed her a corncob poppet made, he said, by a Carribee slave. Seeing Will standing alone and frowning at his own lack of presents, Daniel set Joanna down and soberly gestured for his son to approach. With a serious face he pulled from a bag a tiny ax and presented it to the boy, as though the gift were the rarest of finds. Will yelled a full-throated cry and ran from the house, bringing laughter from everyone but John, who said, shaking his head, "Best hide the new rooster."

Daniel sat and called for food and in between bites of his dinner rattled off an account of his travels. "I've been as far north as Salisbury and hope to go even farther on the next leg, perhaps as far as Portsmouth if there be enough clearing of woodlands up past Strawberry Bank. You can't believe the farmsteads opening up between Casco Bay and Kittery. Pelts, timber, fish—more than one man can trap or catch in a lifetime." His round and sympathetic face clouded only once, when he spoke of the whispering up and down the coast of Abenaki Indians chafing at the land and furs taken by the Englishers, and of the raids on settlements lying vulnerably close to the edge of the forests.

"It's the French north of the Eastward," he said, scratching at his scalp still burning from the lye soap he had used to kill the lice he had picked up in some bedstead in Boston. "They're stirring and stirring the pot, making friends with the heathens so they'll knock us about the head and drive us all the way back to England." Patience began to cry again, and with a few words Thomas related the visit by the Wampanoag man and of the plague that had visited both colonist and Indian alike. Daniel made placating sounds, distracting his wife by saying, "Here, look, Patience. Have you seen the bowls I have brought you? Look how bright the pewter is."

Martha made panbread for the evening supper with the new flour, molding a tender blanket to hold the old rooster that, over the protestations of Will, who wanted to try his new ax on the bird, was butchered and dressed by John within the space of an hour. Patience waited impatiently for Daniel to finish his portion and retire with her to bed, but he didn't leave until he had generously shared the new ale, not twice, but three times with John and Thomas. When he finally took his wife's hand, she led him off to their room saying, "Oh, Daniel. It's been such a struggle managing all by myself."

John hid a creeping smile, draining the dregs of his ale, and Martha threw him a warning glance, snatching away his cup. The children had been sent to her bed, and when she crawled under the blanket, fitting her body carefully between their huddled shapes, she was surprised to see that Will was still awake. His eyes turned in the direction of the wall where the rhythmic sounds of the creaking bed ropes that supported his mother's bed drifted through the thin walls, and he began to cry. She shushed him and, placing her hands over his ears, pulled him tight to her own body until she felt him go lax and heavy in her arms.

In the morning, it was clear to Martha that the bed ropes weren't the only things squeaking during the night. Prompted by Patience, who dug a sharp elbow into his side, Daniel cleared his throat and announced that a Reverend Hastings, newly appointed minister of Billerica, would be coming to dinner within a few days. He droned on at length about the minister's qualities of piety and of his recently acquired status as widower. Martha had been wiping the bowls clean and felt pulled into the sudden cessation of talk as a clod of dirt into a tunnel of wind. Seeing the expectant looks of her cousin turned in her direction, she realized Daniel had been speaking of the reverend for her benefit.

Casually, he rattled on about the trading he had recently done with the minister, the frugal nature of his habits, the austerity of his bearing, the dignity of his house. Martha brooded on whether the Reverend Hastings would be like the reverend from her child-hood; the man who, despite her best efforts, entered her thoughts at times like a clot in sour milk. If so, Reverend Hastings would have no apparent vices of his own to make him humble or soft in his opinions of others who had sinned. He would be dry and sharp and, worst of all, full of purpose. He would carry within the folds of his cloak the breath of winter and peer at everyone with pale robin's-egg eyes, uncovering and revealing every speck of unlawfulness in moral conduct, and his hands would make a punishment of every caress.

Signaling to John to begin the morning's work, Thomas stood up and walked out the door, shading his eyes briefly in her direc-tion, as though he had come upon her naked. She turned away, suddenly angry, snapping the cleaning rag aggressively across the boards of the table, spraying the floor with remnants of corn-meal. She said to no one in particular, "I'll not be trussed up and bundled off to the first man, reverend though he may be, who comes sniffing around. By God, I'll not."

For the first time in days, persistent thoughts of hen feathers filled her mind. Ripping the apron off her waist, she threw it to the floor and fled from the house, keenly aware of the astonished looks traded between her cousin and Daniel.

She walked in circles around the yard until the pumping in her chest slowed. Daniel soon emerged from the house and, awk-wardly gesturing an apologetic hand to her, began to hoe weeds in the garden. He threw himself into the work as though he would, in a single day, make up for all the time gone, and Martha thought she had never seen a man flail himself so at a task. Every limb was at odds with every other, elbows flying, knees bobbing, face as red as autumn cranberries, until, she thought, he would wear himself into the very soil. She looked at him critically for a while and then turned towards the barn, her arms crossed, regarding the shadow of Thomas passing back and forth through layered columns of sunlight from the open hayloft above.

In the barn she found Thomas running his hand over the flanks of one of the milk cows. The cow had been bawling fitfully for days, moving back and forth in a disquieting motion as it shifted its weight from one front hoof to the other. Thomas didn't turn at her approach, but she knew he was aware of her presence. To make conversation she thought to ask him if the beast had stones in the belly, even though she knew it was a blocked hind stomach. Thomas had once remarked in passing to John that if a Welshman knew nothing else at all, he would know about sheep and cows and, for all their great size, the delicacy of their inner workings. She moved to cradle the cow's neck in her arms, scratching at its cross-grained hide with her nails. It lifted its head, thick upper lip twitching, and Martha breathed in the smell of sour grasses fermenting in the maw behind the animal's grinding teeth and knew from this that it was not fatally sick. Thomas knelt down, pressing his hands gently into the cow's underside, shielding his face from Martha with the brim of his hat.

She sat down next to him and played with the straw between her fingers before asking, "What's a Swedish feather?"

He turned to her, startled, with raised brows, as though she had asked him to jump off a cliff.

"John says I have a tongue like a Swedish feather." She had asked the question in all earnestness, but when he moved to hide a smile, she bridled.

He straightened his mouth and answered, "It's a weapon. A short pike with a steel-pointed blade. I say so as I have had necessity to use one."

"And where," she asked stiffly, "would you have had use for such a one as those?"

"Most times, missus," he said, standing, "between the eyes and the belly." He walked to another stall but soon returned with a flannel cloth and a bottle of oil. He uptilted the bottle onto the rag and commenced gently rubbing the cow's hide, darkening it into circled, glistening patches. "I've been a soldier." He looked at her significantly. "And I believe you know on which side I fought." He set the bottle down, balancing it into the straw, and began carefully pressing his fingers into the cow's soft underbelly, expertly probing the length of the entrails through the tightened, distended skin. "I were a pikeman, so I had use for such as a Swedish feather."

"And did you live in London, as Will says?" she asked, and she was all too aware that her mouth had fallen slightly open, like a girl who is starving, fed with a very small spoon. She had once heard her sister's husband, Roger, say that there was no greater place than London, or more wicked, as men walked with less reverence into a church than a tinker and a dog into an alehouse.

"Aye, I lived in that place. I left Wales, suddenlike, and by sixteen I were a man-at-arms." He nodded for her to hand him the bottle again and he oiled both hands, rubbing them briskly together, warming them. She watched his splayed fingers moving knowledgeably over the cow's hide, and when it bawled again in pain, he called to it chidingly, *"Bod dawelu,"* as though to a child protesting overmuch to a dose of physic. "You may reckon London a palace with streets of pearl and ivory, but they had cows and sheep there as well, the kind that stand on their two back legs. I lived in that cesspool until the war, called by my own conscience to fight." He moved to help her from the straw and draped one long arm over the cow's back. He looked at her evenly before saying, "And now I've told you enough to bring me trouble."

She ducked her head, feeling his gaze raking the top of her skull. "Why do you tell me this?" she asked defensively.

"Because...I believe you know what it's like to carry the weight of something hidden that can't be spoken of. Not to friend, nor ken, nor to the closest partner of your bosom."

As he spoke, she had placed her own mirroring hand across the beast, making an unlinked arc of both their arms. She couldn't look at his face, unnerved that he would know she had secrets to keep; instead, she intently studied the knotted joints of his hands and the calluses that shielded the pads of his fingers. She willed herself to think of the wooden trunk set next to his bed, and the red coat Will had told her was nestled within. There came to her then the stories that her father had told her of the long and bloody civil war in the old England thirty years ago; of the red coats of Cromwell's New Model Army, an army that was, in its day, one of the best and most disciplined to fight in the known world.

She met his eyes and asked, "What could I possibly have to hide? I've never been anywhere, I've never seen anything." A note of bitterness had crept into her voice and she tamped it down lest he think her shrewish. His hand, still coated in a fine membrane of oil, crept over her own, the calluses rasping and unyielding across her skin; but there was no proprietary feel to the touch, and he didn't move his body closer to hers as a preamble to some coarser action, and there were no whispered words as a ploy to reach and grab.

"And the women of London. Were they lovely?" She regretted her question as soon as she asked it and waited for him to deride it as vanity, most certainly what the Reverend Hastings would have done.

There was a slow shifting of weight as though he was considering the best way to answer. "In London," he began, "just before the Great War, fishwives and housewives stood cheek by jowl with great ladies. You could see the mayor's wife pulling up her skirts against the muck like any oysteress. You smile, missus, but it's the truth. During the days before the war, the women of that time were infected with the same fever as their men, and they matched them brick for brick in building the ramparts to shield the city against the king and his army. It was a fever we held on to because to cure it meant to wake again to tyranny. You ask what makes a woman comely?" He tapped one finger lightly against her temple and said, "Thoughts, missus. It's thoughts that make a woman so."

She had opened her mouth to speak when John shuffled noisily into the barn, calling out, "Missus, there's a journeyman come for you. With a letter." John had turned away slightly, and she colored to think he had come upon them having a conversation which had moved beyond the health of the livestock. She quickly buried her chin in her shoulder, hiding her expression, until John had left again. Slipping her hand free, she moved away reluctantly, saying, "You know a lot, for a farmer."

As she passed him, Thomas's head tilted back, eyes narrowing as though to focus better on something wavering and indistinct, and he countered, "Enough to know you'll never be settled with some parson."

As she stepped from the barn, she shook the folds of her skirt into order, all too aware that anyone seeing her then would think her a wanton emerging from a toss in the hay: bothered, flustered, her backside covered in straw. But she found the entire household gathered around the journeyman already being fed at her cousin's table, a man so thin his shanks would have whistled in a high wind. He wiped his hand on his trousers and, handing her a folded piece of parchment, went back to stuffing his mouth with the remnants of cold porridge left over from breakfast.

Martha quickly opened the letter, written on the back of a fragment of a pamphlet from Boston trumpeting the arrival of ships from England, anticipating some homely bit of news about the Toothaker settlement ten miles to the north. She sensed Patience move up close to her and felt a flash of irritation that her cousin would seek to rob her of solitary discovery of news from her sister. The letter, in Mary's hand, was brief; she had lost the pregnancy in her seventh month and was much taken down through the disappointment of her husband, Roger. She had written simply, "Please come."

"Disappointment of her husband," Martha muttered resentfully, remembering bitterly how ill her sister had been at the previous miscarriage. From the first she had laid eyes on her brother-in-law, she had always believed him to be a husband by convenience, and a father by accident. Her hand holding the letter had no sooner dropped to her side in a shared sense of grief than Patience asked, with alarm, "What's amiss? Has anyone died?"

"Mary has lost her babe," she answered and saw Patience grab instinctively at her belly. "And her son, Allen, is ill. I must go straightaway."

The journeyman, finished with his meal, shook his head vigorously, saying, "Large bands of Wabanakis have been seen moving through the forests 'cross town. There's no doubt they be on the path to malice. Stay armed and stay sheltered. I myself am staying in the next settlement until they have moved on."

Patience grabbed at her husband's arm, pleading, "Daniel, let John take Martha. We need Thomas here. To help protect us and the children." Joanna, catching the near-hysterical tone in her mother's voice, began to cry, and Martha picked her up, smoothing her hair out of her face.

With all eyes turned expectantly to him, Daniel looked unseated, thrust so quickly into making a decision beyond what to bring from the cellar. Blinking rapidly, he said, "Very well, but you must wait a few days, Martha, maybe a week, until we know the road to your sister's home is not the road to disaster." When Martha opened her mouth to protest, Daniel gathered himself up, saying, "Now, that's enough. I...that is, we have decided." He turned hopefully to his wife, and when she nodded encouragingly to him, he added, signaling an end to the conversation, "Am I not master of this house?"

The journeyman hurriedly left and the settlement became a fortress. Shutters were closed and nailed into casements. Doors were heavily cross-barred with oak, and vigilant watches were kept by the men by day and by night. The women placed buckets of sand and water under the eaves to put out fires set on the roof and the children were kept indoors at all times. The ample supplies brought by Daniel replenished the fearful watches and, as the week diminished, so, too, did the keg of strong ale, sipped sparingly but steadily to counter nerves brought to a fiery temper through waiting.

On the fourth day after the journeyman had left, a "hallo" from the yard showed a mounted constable come to spread the word that the Indians had moved on. But with them they had taken cattle, horses, and a young girl named Elizabeth Farley. A child eleven years old, she had gone out to empty the morning slops, and when she did not soon return, her mother found many footprints leading westward towards the Concord River. Townsmen followed the trail but lost it in fording the river and so had to give up the search. A day after the doors and windows had been thrown open again to the spring winds, Martha and Patience went to Goodwife Farley with food, to sit with the recently widowed woman, childless, alone and grieving, a mantle of ashes in her hair scraped from the cold remains of her kitchen hearth.

THE DREAM HAD left Martha terrified and shaken, with a sensation of suffocating, of drowning in mountainous, overwhelming drifts of feathers. Upon waking, she jerked herself upright to sitting, knees bent with hands clenched tightly over her stomach, and stifled a cry. Joanna moved restlessly next to her and she felt her way in the dark to the end of the bed, crouching on the floor, her hands over her open mouth.

It was the Reverend Hastings's visit the night before, she believed, that had sharpened the memories of that other black-frocked man she had not seen in over ten years. The Taylors' supper had not gone well and it was close to a certainty that the reverend would never again come to call at her cousin's with a mind to wooing. From the beginning, Reverend Hastings had shown himself to be exactly as she had imagined him to be, judging the quick and the dead with harsh alacrity. He had quoted Ephesians to her when she had proven herself to be insufficiently humble on the subject of marriage: "So man is to God, so must woman be to man." To which she had retorted sharply, "And does not Colossians say, 'See to it that no one takes you captive through hollow and deceptive philosophy'?" The table had sat in uncomfortable silence until the reverend said, in barely repressed anger, "The contract of marriage is God-ordained and is like any other necessary, required, and enforceable contract..."

As he spoke, his words droning on and on through tightly pressed lips like coarse line through a too-small fishing hook, Martha had begun to feel the familiar stifling dread building behind her temples and she clutched at the table for balance. She could feel Thomas's eyes on her, and he abruptly said, "By mutual consent." Baffled by the interruption, the reverend stopped midsentence. "What's that you say?" he asked. Thomas, methodically mopping up the end of his soup, swallowed the last of the bread before answering, "It's the *covenant* of marriage, Reverend. Not a contract. You're not tradin' for livestock." John quickly bowed his head, snickering, and Martha herself felt a hysterical urge to laugh out loud, fully and rudely, into the parsimonious face that looked to his hosts in wounded indignation. Thomas held her gaze boldly for a moment and then, excusing himself, left for the barn, John trailing closely behind.

She had gone to bed in a jubilant mood, only slightly sorry that her cousins were put out by the abrupt departure of their guest. Reverend Hastings's diminishment by Thomas had, it seemed for a time, excised some of the feelings of debasement and shame, long held from the eyes of the world, brought about by a fellow man of God.

A deep-limbed sleep had come as soon as she had pulled up the quilt. She had dreamt of herself as a girl again in the home of the Ipswich parson and his family where she had been placed at nine years of age. In the dream, she stood in the chicken coop, her face to the wall where she had been turned and told not to move, or speak, or resist; the back of her skirt up around her shoulders as brutal encircling hands held her immobile. Thumbs, like two vises, pressing cruelly into her flesh, beginning at the ankles and proceeding higher and higher up her calves, to her knees and then onward to the inside of her thighs. Higher and higher like a Jacob's ladder into the inner tender parts that were covered to the eyes of scrutiny in the brightness of day, places that were hidden even from herself as she dressed for the night in a sweet-smelling night shift scrubbed clean by the parson's wife. And all around her, in the dream, the hens are fluttering, shedding feathers that drift like snow over her face, covering her eyes and nose; feathers that can't be brushed away because to move would be to invite a beating.

And when she woke she remembered fully the reverend of her childhood. The man who had called her "daughter," patiently teaching her to read and write excellently and to commit to memory the whole of the testaments, for to be left ignorant of these things would have reflected badly upon his tutelage. A man who was loved and admired and looked upon for counsel and who only ever once was confined to his bed, shortly after the time that she awoke from her turpitude and, taking his manhood into her hands, twisted it nearly off. She was quickly returned to her own family as being recalcitrant after three years spent in Ipswich and soon took to her own bed with an illness the town surgeon had called "unwholesome." She wept then, remembering, too, that it was Thomas, and only ever Thomas, who had seen, who had recognized, the stamp of a pitiless secret held like a poisoned abscess in the deepest part of herself.

In the morning, she took a needle and thread and sewed the red book into the casing of her pillow. She would keep the pages intact and alive within their covering but hidden away. And if her cousin asked her the whereabouts of the book, she resolved she would tell her it had become corrupt with mold and had been discarded.

CHAPTER 10

THE RAT, TO his own knowledge, had never been on dry land. The ship had been the sum total of his world, and had he gone blind, he could have found his way by touch and smell alone from the bottom of the hull, stinking of pig iron and refuse, up to the forecastle, where the teeming seamen hoisted or lowered the square-rigged sails, and aft again to the raised deck where the captain stood, and never wavered, never stumbled, as though his feet had been nailed to the planking.

The captain rarely asked questions of the Rat, and even if he had, the boy could not have answered in words, being mute as he was. But the Rat was quick in his other senses, and the captain had seen fit to have the first mate give him lessons a few hours every Monday in seamanship—navigation and sextant use— and in languages, the written form at any event: English, Dutch, and a smattering of French. Understanding the other languages in their nautical sense was of practical use in case of a quick decision to board another, less agile merchant ship packed with raw goods from the Americas. The captain's ship was a pinnace.

Dutch-built, fast, and shallow in draught, whereas an English ship of a comparable size would need thirty men, the *Zwaluw, The Swallow* in Dutch, needed only ten able-bodied seamen to rig and maneuver the sails. Every man on the *Zwaluw* held a cutlass close at hand and could have been called a pirate but for the British royal license to "reconnoiter" other ships perceived to be hostile.

The captain was known to be of Dutch origin, owning the Dutch-sounding name Koogin, and though he could speak the language like a native, he had no accent and spoke English like every other member of the crew. His success in trading with his clients, English and colonial alike, gave testament equally to his indifferent loyalties, his willingness to traverse the Atlantic during the most unfavorable seasons, and his ability to hold his patronage in the strictest of confidence. He never interfered with another man's livelihood where it didn't intersect his own interests, so there were no questions asked when five men from London boarded the ship at Plymouth port with passage for Boston.

First on deck from the transport wherry was a man named Brudloe, certainly the group's leader, and as densely muscled as a pit cur. He grinned tightly at everything, an unpleasant lifting of the lips, expressing mirth that stopped well below eyes that were pinched and distrustful. His gaze shifted restlessly at all times, as though assessing every portal and expecting trouble.

Next on board climbed a tall man with a pallid face and a set of slightly stooped shoulders. There was something menacing hiding behind his soft chin and pale skin that made the Rat suck in his breath. Once Baker caught his eye and slowly winked at him, and it was like watching a great northern shark closing its inner lid before feeding.

After Baker came a man as large as a Lebanon cedar. He clumped noisily onto the deck, already unsteady on his feet though they hadn't left port, carrying a boy who was only slightly older than the Rat. This older boy looked dead drunk, or drugged, and was quickly conveyed belowdecks.

The last man to climb over the railing was a fop, wearing a shirt with more flounces than a woman's and a velvet coat. He was called Thornton, and he answered every hail and every instruction with a silent sneer. Whether at rest or in motion, Thornton had a grace and a barely suppressed energy that might have, with enough experience, made him a superior seaman on the bucking deck of a sailing vessel.

Once the ship was under way, the four older men would often come up to the deck to desperately gulp at the air. But the boy, never; he was always left belowdecks.

The Rat frequently grinned to himself, thinking how quickly the London men's swagger left them once the ship headed past the Isles of Scilly and the headwaters of the Channel. He often stood in the webbing of the bowsprit and watched impassively the four landies hanging over the sides, their eyes bulging, expecting to see their shoes coming up through their mouths. He himself clung effortlessly to the ropes like a monkey, impervious to their curses and threatening gestures, laughing silently at their distress, and waving extravagantly to the forlorn outcroppings of the Isles to show the Londoners that there would be no more sightings of land for many weeks.

The Rat had heard the captive boy crying from the Londoners' section of the hold. There were no barriers or separate cabins in the hold, but the four men had hung a blanket for privacy, and when the boy went on sobbing for too long, the Rat could hear first the thud of a swinging boot to the ribs, and then the groan before the captive was kicked into silence again.

The Rat knew, of course, about impressment. The seas would dry up before the practice of kidnapping a man off the docks onto a ship would come to an end. But those who were captured were usually grown men, most of them seasoned on at least one trip on a ship; otherwise they would prove useless, especially on such a small craft, where every sailor had more than one duty to perform. This captive, he was sure, had never before been on a ship and couldn't have been taken for ransom, as he was ragged beyond simple poor. He had the ground-in dirt of a river urchin, a lifetime spent in the sucking muck of the Thames up to his knees, grubbing for barnacles or bait or a ha'penny accidently dropped into the reeking tidal wash.

One day he heard an odd, repetitive moaning, like chanting, coming from the captive, and he realized the boy had been mindlessly singing to himself. The boy's voice had a high-pitched quavering sound, like a wounded bird, or like a man stuttering out his prayers as he's swaying, storm-ridden, on the yardarms, his fear giving desperate music to the pleading.

The Rat crept beyond the blanket when all the Londoners had gone topside, and crawled to where the boy lay bound with his hands behind his back, his knees drawn defensively up to his belly. He sat awhile looking at the older boy sleeping fitfully, noting the bruised, tender-looking swelling over one eye. As though feeling the Rat's presence, the boy opened his eyes, which were not brown as the Rat had surmised but the blue of an island shoal. The boy's brows knitted together, pleadingly, and he opened his mouth to speak. But the Rat heard the ponderous, slapping footfalls of the men returning, and he darted away into the shadows. From behind stacked barrels of powder he watched the men's shadows thrown up by lantern light against the curved ribs of the hold.

The Londoners talked amongst themselves of plans and schemes, their voices getting louder the more rum they drank. They bragged of their fights and the prodigious pay for their robberies and murders, conversing at length of the man in the new England they were sent to capture or kill, or die trying.

Baker, the soft-spoken man with the eyes of the dead, talked of the plague ten years back and of the numberless bodies stacked in the pit at Houndsditch. Frequenting the Pye Tavern hard by the burying grounds, Baker would place winning bets on the exact number of dead piled onto the passing carts, like guessing the number of beans in a bottle.

But as the days went on, the ship heaving and creaking through stiff westerly winds, the men grew silent. The group lay on the floor to sleep, to be battered and rolled about, instead of hoisting a proper hammock. Eventually the men left off even dicing and playing cards, spending more and more time topside, leaving their captive alone, seeking through drink to numb their misery only to wake to a rebellious stomach and a throbbing head. In a way, the Rat thought the most pitiable was the oversize Cornwall, who drank the most but could not eat, spending his entire day amidships, his meaty hands grasping at the ropes for balance until he was chased away by the seamen seeking to trim the sails.

As the Rat worked on deck cleaning the chains, or with tar and oakum patching cracks in the deck, he would watch the captain watching the men, the captain's expression carefully neutral. At one point, Thornton, his fine shirt soiled, the neck lace limp with seawater, approached the captain for a discourse. Without offering the Londoner so much as a "by your leave," Koogin abruptly turned away, retreating to his quarters.

At the steersman's strike of eight bells, the end of the middle watch, the Rat woke and lay in his hammock, which swung in a deep pendulum, following the yaw of the ship. He could hear the seaman next to him wake and deftly roll from his own hammock. There was a rustling of a shirt quickly tugged on and then retreating footfalls as the seaman crossed to the ladder to the open deck. Soon, the man he replaced at watch swung himself into the empty hammock and within the space of ten breaths was snoring gently.

It would be another half hour before the Rat had to begin his duties with Cook, and he took his time thinking of the boy, and how it would be to have a true companion. One who could serve as the Rat's voice, whispering or howling his way through the oft-mapped lines of latitudes and stellar declinations like a singing fish through an invisible net. In all the years spent in the company of seamen, he had never had a shipmate even close to his own age.

The Rat would gladly, if only given the opportunity, share with the boy all his own hard-won knowledge of the ship, not just the trimming of sails or the climbing of the yards, but the listening for the gunshot sounds of a breaching right whale, or the

sighting at night, midsummer, of the green glowing ribbons dancing in currents of water so deep they could never be plumbed.

He remembered with a growing anxiety the previous night,
when he had overheard the four landsmen arguing over where and
when to throw their captive overboard. He had been standing just
behind Thornton, coiling a rope, when Brudloe caught sight of
him and landed a quick kick to his side, sending him sprawling
against the deck. The Londoner glared down at him, the white
channel of scars in stark contrast to his weather-burned face, and
all motion ceased for the briefest of moments, the seamen poised
and wooden in their rigging.

The ship's boatswain, directing the halyards, roughly brushed
passed Brudloe, hauling the scrambling Rat back up to his feet.
He bent down and whispered hoarsely, "Maggoty pie." The Rat
grinned widely behind his hand and nodded. He was to change
out that very morning a fresh fish for an old one on top of the
flour barrel. A dead fish, with its rotting flesh, was used to bring
the maggots up out of the flour. He would later take the worm-
ridden, stinking carcass and roll it into Brudloe's blanket.

The Rat wasn't certain if the captain knew of the plans for the
bound boy, but he had felt a growing tension in the captain's
demeanor, like a rogue wind pulling a sail tight against its
rigging.

After his morning duties with Cook, he stood on the open
deck and happened to see the captain leaning down towards him
from the halfdeck, a deep furrow between his brows. His eyes
flicked ahead to the cresting waves, peaking at fifteen feet or
more, and then back again. "Boy," the captain called to him. He

motioned for the astonished Rat to come up the ladder and stand beside him. The wind whipped stingingly at them on the raised deck, and the two swayed in unison for a moment in silence, each hunching into his own shoulders for greater warmth.

The captain brought out his compass, the thirty-two-point placard that rotated magically beneath the true needle, like the single rose the boy had once seen in the captain's quarters floating in a bowl of rainwater. The captain's eyes then raked over Cornwall, clinging miserably to the grating over the weathered deck, where he had fallen moments before. The forecastle of the ship plunged into a trough as the ship came about for the tack, spraying the struggling Londoner with frigid seawater.

"Do y'know what signals a good seaman, boy?" the captain suddenly roared, looking pointedly at Cornwall. The Rat cocked his head to show he was listening. "Knowing best when to cut a bad line."

He then dismissed the Rat, but called after him in Dutch, *"Het donderend geluid, jungen!" Thunder comin', boy!*

LATER THAT NIGHT, the Rat learned from Cook that the captain would be inviting the four landsmen to eat in his quarters. In addition to rum, the Rat was told, the captain would be offering a bottle of Madeira steeped in wormwood.

"Which will, Rat," the cook barked, "give them fuckin' landies a long sleep and a relief from the pukes, and afterwards, a fuckin' head from Hell." The cook laughed, but then quickly frowned, pointing belowdecks. "It's a shame, that. What's goin' on below."

The Rat nodded his head in agreement, sadly staring at the boards below his feet.

At four bells on the first dogwatch, the four landsmen drew straws for who among them would be declining the captain's invitation, staying behind in the hold. It would have taken a cretin not to know that it signaled a long walk on a short deck for the bound boy that night. The Londoners had been too puffed up and careless in talking of their plans of ridding themselves of the boy and taking his share of some unspecified bounty for the entire crew not to have heard. A blind spot between the masts, a moment's distraction, and the bound boy could be shoved over the railings in the blink of an eye. And who was to prove it was not an accident?

The Rat had not heard the boy crying the whole of the day and he suspected even the captive knew his time was drawing to a close. He also suspected the landsmen were unaware of the battering storm beginning to bear down on the ship.

Soon the three passengers Brudloe, Thornton, and Cornwall, led by the Rat, were groping their way aft across the open deck, leaving their companion, Baker, behind with the captive. The wind had taken on a new, shrieking quality, tearing steadily from port-side, as the three landsmen struggled into the rear galley for the captain's meal.

Brudloe, the first blown into the aft quarters, cast his eyes immediately on the open decanter of Madeira skating across the tilting table, and said, "Damn me, Captain, if it's not a vicious blow."

The captain looked at the huddled three, damp and reeking as doused dogs, and answered carefully, "Yes. It may even come upon us rough tonight." Then he turned his back on the men and, handing the Rat another bottle, told the boy, "Give this to the man below." And then in Dutch, he added quietly, *"Wel opletten dat hij het drinkt, hoor." And make sure he drinks it.*

As the Rat departed, he uncorked the bottle and sniffed the contents. A dark, unctuous smell riding below the sweetness of the wine brought to mind the tar he used for plugging the hull; but deeper still was the odor of a Danish mast, freshly planed, still weeping sap.

He took the bottle and, on his way to the landsman's tuck, counted eight heads: all the able-bodied seamen along with the carpenter. The crew had been sent below, clearing the decks for the worst part of the storm. The only men on deck now would be the steersman and the first mate watching the pattern of the cresting waves.

The Rat found Baker sitting on a weighted barrel with his back and arms pressed into the steeply curved hull, his legs dancing from one side to the other as he attempted to stay aright against the violent pitch of the ship. The Rat saw a bucket close by his feet that held the bile from the man's last meal. Baker's face had taken on an ashen shade of gray, his eyes pressed tightly shut. He was shivering, the air from the more northerly latitudes suddenly cold and saturated with a creeping damp.

The captive looked up at him from his place on the floor. Carefully, but deliberately, the boy's lips parted and he mouthed the words "Help me."

The Rat's eyes quickly darted to Baker's face but the man's lids were still closed, one hand now clamped firmly over his mouth, damming up whatever bit of remaining stew threatened to spill from his gullet. A thought as brief as lightning crossed the Rat's brain: to make a grab for the boy and hope for aid from the crew. But the first rule of the ship was to be deaf and blind to the doings of the passengers.

In that moment, Baker opened his eyes and startled to see the Rat standing there. He spied the bottle of Madeira and, with an unsteady hand, reached out to take the proffered gift. His fingers, uncallused and cold, made the Rat think of the fish on the flour barrel.

"This from your captain?" Baker croaked.

The Rat nodded, gesturing that the man should drink. Baker uncorked the bottle and poured some of the wine into his mouth. He swallowed, shuddering violently, and said, "Boy, give me that blanket."

Crumpled next to Baker's feet was a thin quilt that had slipped off the man's restless shoulders. But the Rat, instead, picked up another blanket, one he had expertly rolled into a tight bolster. As the blanket unfurled, it spilled from its innards the rotting fish that was meant for Brudloe to find. The carcass lay on the floor in gelatinous pieces, a heaving mass of maggots that had gained momentum from the blanket's warmth. The stench rose up and filled the small space like an uncovered burial trench.

A sudden lurch of the ship loosed the bottle from Baker's hand. The bottle went rolling wildly astern, spilling the rest of the dark liquid onto the boards. Baker, cursing, began to retch again into the bucket.

He groaned wildly, coughing and gnashing his teeth. The ship, hit with a wave broadside, juddered massively, knocking Baker off the barrel. He lay on the tilting boards, panting and tearing at his hair. When next he looked at the Rat, all of his former composure was gone. The Rat had seen the look before; seasickness, day after day, hour upon hour, unhinged some landsmen to the point of madness.

At the ship's heaving to port, Baker staggered to his feet, tearing his way through the hastily rigged partition. He looked desperately about, the startled crew, only partially illuminated by the wildly swinging lanterns, remaining silent and watchful.

"Air...I must have *air*..." He was thrown hard against the foot of the main mast, where he steadied himself, tightly grasping at the wooden pillar with both arms. "I must go on deck," he pleaded, his knees buckling.

The carpenter, showing teeth the color of cloves, called out, "There's a storm out there, man. You'll be crossin' an open deck."

Baker, seeing the Rat nearby, balancing expertly against the movement of the ship, jabbed a finger at him and shouted, "Him. He's going to take me up." He tore at the neck of his shirt, raking at his face with his nails. "Take...me...up," he screamed, retching once more onto his shoes.

It was seventeen paces from the waist of the ship to the ladder topside. Plenty of time for the Rat to palm a piece of rope, hiding it under his shirt, so that he could tie himself to the lifelines already strung across the railing. Most men, especially a landsman, not tied fast to the ship would be swept overboard by the storm waves. He nodded to Baker and motioned for him to follow.

The floor around the ladder was soaked from the hatch above, even though the grate was layered over with oiled canvas, and at the next pitch to the fore, they both slid hard into the rungs. Baker shoved the Rat from behind to climb the ladder quickly, and it didn't take long for him to beat the framing loose at the hatchway. The Rat crawled onto the deck and waited an instant for the leeward listing of the ship. Using the momentum, he rapidly slid to the port-side railing and tied himself to the lifeline with a slipknot.

Baker came soon after, pulling himself onto the heaving deck. The wind hammered water into his face, blinding him briefly. The ship in that moment had begun its roll to starboard, and the Rat could already see the man's building terror as he looked through the standing rigging and saw for the first time the towering black water that roiled into collapsing valleys and then upwards to crushing peaks. Baker grabbed at the starboard lifelines in panic.

The spars dipped heavily towards the advancing waves, which crashed over the deck in cascades of stinging foam, and Baker's eyes widened as if with an immediate, savage awareness that there was no end in sight to the ocean surrounding the boat. The horizon, blended into a gunmetal sky, had become a vast, limitless circle wherein nothing of man's designs, nothing of the stationary planes and inviolable right angles of land-bound dwellings held sway or could tame the farthest-reaching vanishing point. He once grasped at the rigging to stand, but he could only crawl on his hands and knees as seawater pummeled over the decks in funneling shocks. The Rat instinctively knew that he would not have much longer to wait.

The ship began its methodical tilt to starboard once more but passed beyond its veering arc at forty degrees, dipping farther and farther away from its vertical axis, seeming to settle its mast into the waves that rushed to drown the deck, spilling over the railings in torrents. The Rat closed his eyes, feeling the immense drag of the waves against his tethering rope, until he felt the vessel righting itself, and when he opened his eyes again, he saw the steersman still straining at the whipstaff. When the Rat cut his eyes to the side of the deck where Baker had last been crawling, the man was not to be seen.

The Rat lengthened out the slipknot and slid across the deck to the opposite side, carefully peering over the railing to scan the waves. He was astonished to see that Baker had managed to cling to the ship, both hands entwined in the standing rigging where it was pinned to the outer hull. The man's fear had given him the strength of desperate action, and he began to climb back up, his feet scrabbling frantically against the gun-port lids and the outboard channel. The man found footing, slipped, then found footing again when the next swelling wave lifted him towards the deck.

Pressed up against the railing, the Rat felt cold metal against his belly, and he remembered a jerry iron tucked into his waistband. The Rat had employed it many times, using its sharp, angled blade to pull old oakum from the seams of planking.

The Rat saw one of Baker's fine, long-boned, even delicate, limbs reaching, clasping the railing. The Rat pulled from his trousers the jerry iron and brought it down fiercely onto the man's hand, separating the large joints of his two middle fingers. Baker howled in pain and surprise as his body pitched backwards into the water that swelled up to engulf him.

His chest heaving raggedly, the Rat lowered himself protectively against the inside railing, almost dizzy with the exultant thought that the captive would perhaps now be safe. Now that Baker was dead, he believed, he hoped the crew would help him to ferret the boy away in some hidey-hole belowdecks, bringing him food and water. He would work all the harder for the crew's approval, making sure the boy did his share of a seaman's work as well. The Londoners, recovering from their drugged sleep, would think Baker had tumbled over the side in the storm along with the captive.

As the Rat pondered all these things, he watched the raging water but Baker never again broke the waves. For a long time after, the Rat would wonder that a man so determined, so self-possessed and dangerous, should not have recoiled to the surface, if only for the briefest of moments.

CHAPTER 11

IT WAS A two-hour journey to the Toothaker house, and Martha and John said hardly a word to each other, both preoccupied and alert for any movement in the woods that signaled more than a deer or fox foraging at the clearing's edge. The morning drizzle had continued for a time and John sat with his shoulders tense, furtively looking to the right and the left at every snapping branch and shifting of wind through the trees. Martha was almost sorry Thomas had given John the flintlock, as she thought he would more likely discharge the weapon at her than at an Indian if they were attacked.

After the first hour, the clouds cleared and the sun shone hot enough to dry the oiled rain canvas, sending steam off their bodies in curling wisps as though their clothes had been set on fire. At the moment they rounded the last turn in the road, they heard the howling of a man in agony, and John pulled back sharply on the reins, almost tumbling off the driving seat in his haste. They saw in the yard in front of the Toothaker house a man sitting in a ladder-backed chair holding on to the seat bottom as though his hands were manacled there. He was grimacing and hissing through his teeth, the muscles of his jaw working knotted ripples along the side of his face, courses of blood streaming down his shirtless chest. Over him leaned another man, slight with dark hair banded neatly behind his head, with a pair of metal tongs, digging at a bloody patch on the man's breast as though he would pull one of his ribs through the flesh. The man with the tongs hailed the wagon with a cheerful lift of his chin and then continued on with his methodical prodding.

When John looked at Martha in alarm, she shrugged and said simply, "My sister's husband."

She walked briskly into the house, leaving John to tend to the cart. She called softly to her sister and wandered through the house, finally finding Mary in bed under a pile of quilts, weeping. Next to her, in a trundle bed, lay her son, Allen, playing with a miniature wagon, his eyes suspicious and watchful, the fever-cut hair bristling from his scalp. He had none of the pleasing roundness of most boys his age, and even as a babe he had been defensive and puckish, as though holding the world away with sharp angles, all bent elbows, knees, and bony wrists.

Martha crawled carefully onto her sister's bed and, as she had done with Will, gently spooned herself into the collapsed folds of the grieving woman's body. They lay in silence until Martha heard Roger come noisily into the house, perhaps looking for his dinner, and with a gentle warning that Mary should stay in bed, she promptly got up and began setting the house to order again. Roger had placed a clay jug of hard cider on the table, no doubt his physician's pay, and from the front door Martha watched the patient as he staggered off to his horse, holding his bound chest protectively with both arms.

As she worked kindling into the fire, she heard Roger recounting to John, whose face twitched with barely concealed horror, the methods of his surgery. "That man is a blacksmith by trade. A piece of iron fired out from the coals and lodged a sliver as long as my middle finger into his breastbone. I worked on him with a probe and a fine saw for three quarters of an hour before finding the last shard. You know, there is a particular muscularity and a sort of…intransigence, I could say, to the material between the ribs, almost like a chicken's gristle, yet a man will bleed an entire basin of blood, or viscous yellow matter, before passing into a swoon."

Martha rapped sharply on the boards of the table, startling John almost out of his shoes, and pointed for the men to sit down to be served.

"I believe now he'll survive the injury," Roger said, smiling, pleased and unconcerned.

Martha, seeing the blood from her brother-in-law's patient still crusting his fingers, set a plate of meat and bread none too gently on the table and said, "Yes. But will he survive the surgeon? I wonder."

Roger smiled tightly up at her. Toying with a piece of bread, he turned to John, asking, "My sister-in-law, being a woman, is not appreciative of my skills as a surgeon; but there is a kind of poetry in blood, don't you think?"

John shook his head distractedly. "To my mind," he said, "the one doin' the bleedin' is not likely the one doin' the singin'."

"Ah, but surely," Roger said, turning his eyes to the clay jug set at arm's length, "you are not too young to remember, say, Cromwell's war and General Skippon's famed cry to his soldiers: 'Come on, my boys, my brave boys. Let us pray heartily and fight heartily and God will bless us.' A song has been made of it."

John shrugged and answered doubtfully, "I know not about that, but had I been older, I would've fought fer Cromwell as my father had done."

"There you see, sister," Roger said, nodding. "Blood stirs a man to poetical leanings, just as naturally as love stirs a woman to tend the pot." He grinned at Martha good-naturedly and she snorted, but she returned to the hearth to begin boiling water for broth. Though her back was turned, she could hear the rasping sound of clay over wood and knew that Roger was pulling the jug closer towards himself. It was so much to Roger's character, she thought angrily, that he would seek to liken a blood-letting to a bard's song while his wife lay unattended in a back room. She moved to stand at the table, her arms crossed, muttering indignantly, "There is no more meat. And this is the last of the bread. It's good that I've brought all for the table or we'd have to send John out with the flint."

Roger rose abruptly from his chair, his color high, and brushed past her, pulling from the sideboard three cups. He set them noisily on the table, and as he scratched the wax from the neck of the jug, Martha deliberately pushed her cup away. Roger poured a measure into his and John's cups and quickly took a sip, closing his eyes to the spreading warmth. Turning to John, he drawled, "John, have you accompanied the cart today because you've a mind to finally marry this one here? Or have you only come to drive the nag?" He placed a heavy emphasis on the last few words while looking at Martha. She slitted her eyes but moved away from the table and into the bedroom where her sister lay.

Mary had fallen to sleep, but the boy turned his head to stare up at her, his eyes pouched and glittering. She sat at the edge of the bed, listening to the men talking, first with Roger's clipped speech dominating, as was common when her brother-in-law conversed. But soon John's more resonant voice gained confidence; the *r*'s rolling extravagantly, his breath eager, the swearing and oath-taking growing through the heat of the liquor. There were short bursts of muffled laughter, as though they hid their mirth in their sleeves, and the rise and fall of queries and answers. The men's voices turned to sniggering whispers and Martha strained to hear more. She stood and moved softly to the open bedroom door, pressing herself against the frame to listen and not be seen. There was a sudden quiet and she froze, thinking she had been discovered, but they had stopped speaking only long enough to fill their cups again.

She heard Roger take a slow, satisfied breath. "It's put about," he slurred, "that your fellow Thomas is a dead shot. A fine counterweight to these yeomen who wouldn't know a flintlock from the back end of their wife's..." He paused a moment, finishing with "broom*ssss*."

"Oh, aye, aye," John said, laughing. "The back end of their brooms, indeed. Thomas is a dead shot, t' be sure."

"I've heard that Carrier fought for the Puritan cause with Cromwell." Roger's voice dropped to a whisper, coarse and confidential. "Although, it is also rumored that he was bodyguard to the first Charles." When there was silence from John, Roger slapped his palm on the table. "Come now, John. We have no fiery leanings one way or the other. I'm a good colony man. I pay my taxes to the king. I've served in the militia. But this, this Carrier, is a one to inspire fantastical musings. I mean to say, just look at the man."

"Hmmm, aye," John muttered wetly, as though still holding the cup between his lips.

"I'll tell you what I've heard, John, and you tell me if it's true. I heard"—Roger paused to drink again, and then belched loudly—"that during the Great War most of the king's men were so ill-trained that they buried more toes and fingers than men. The Royalists were always running away. Ha-ha-ha."

John guffawed and beat the table, saying, "Ha! It's been said in just a way from m' own father."

"An' yer own father fought with Cromwell, did he?" There was the slow scrape of the jug over the table once more.

"My father rode for Sir Will'm Balfour's reg'ment," John said proudly. His words slid over his tongue like heated grease over thick bacon. "It were the first year of the war in…in…sixteen and forty-two. Hard by the village of Kineton, a real be-shited li'l town, or so I've been told." He chortled unevenly for a moment. "They…the Parl'ment men…piled a mountain of severed arms an' legs afterwards. My father found the king's standard boy with his arm cleaved clear through… *clear through!* His hand, lyin' twenty feet away from the rest of himself, still holdin' tight to the banner." He paused briefly to drink. "If not for Thomas, my father would've died fer certain. But…Thomas don't like t' dwell on it." The final words dribbled away into mumbling, and John hiccupped.

"It's the Battle of Edgehill, isn't it? What you're speaking of," Roger whispered dramatically, the words running thick-lipped together. "The first great battle of Parliament against Charles I." He inhaled a sharp breath in awe, and held it in, as though reluctant to speak further; but Martha knew, of course, that he would. A chair creaked with a body settling in for a long story, and Roger said, "I'll tell you what *I've* heard from th' men who were there. It was in winter, the wind blowing hard from the North."

"From the North. Aye, cold, so cold," John said. Martha could hear him sniffling, almost weeping at the memory.

Roger made conciliatory noises and John said, raggedly, "Tell me it. Tell the story, fer I love it well." He hiccupped once more abruptly and groaned.

"Both sides, king and Parliament," Roger began, "were drawn up opposing each other west of the village of Edgehill. The Royals on a hillock, Parliament's men facing them on the lower ground." He stumbled over the last few words and paused to sip loudly from his cup. "The soldiers of each array were in their regimental colors of blue and red and russet, each carrying their standards at the fore, like a field of Turks flowers growing in the snow. The Scots, as was your father, were aligned with the English Parliament. The Welsh and the Cornish, aligned with the king.

"Parliament fired their cannons first but soon the king's nephew Prince Rupert charged with his horsemen straight down the hill and into the heart of Parliament's men, scattering them right back to Kineton."

John's heated voice suddenly erupted. "But the Royalists didn't rally th' charge, the cowardly pricks! They were too busy robbin' th' town blind to wheel 'round and renew their advan'age." He laughed excitedly, pounding the table with his fist. "But Parliament rallied, by Christ, dinnit they?" He pounded the table once more, fiercely, as though Roger had challenged him. "Fer a time after, it were sword-to-sword an' hand-to-hand, with limbs bein' hacked away and blood sprayin' o'er all like a Frenchman's fountain. The king's banner were taken by the Roundheads, but in the tumble of battle my father's horse were killed and fell to the groun', pinnin' him underneath.

"He lay, his leg broken, and saw a horseman comin', a king's man with a gold-hilted sword raised to sever his head right off. He said a prayer, a good...feckin'...Protestan' prayer, when a long shadow fell over him, an' a giant, a pikeman as big as a tree, speared the chargin' horse right through to th' rider. So help me Christ! The giant pulls free the pike, twenty foot long or more, with one hand and with th' other draws out a sword and cuts a bloody swath around my father until he can recover his feet and get on with the fightin'."

There was a pause, and a belch, and a quick muttered oath. A chair scraped loudly across the floor as though someone had moved it suddenly to stand. She heard John moan and then hasty, unsteady footsteps running towards the door. The other chair moved and Roger called out, drunkenly, "Wait, John, wait. I'll attend you. I have a purge that will serve."

Martha slipped into the common room, where the cauldron had begun to boil at the hearth. She picked up the chair, overturned by John's hasty departure, to set it right and carefully laid into the churning water the meat and herbs to make the broth for her sister. She could hear John in the yard, first laughing, then swearing, then retching. She hoped Roger's physic would work so that John would be well enough for work in the morning. As it was, she would most likely be listening to John's groaning the whole day over his thick head and watery bowels.

She flung open the front door and loudly shushed the men, and then pointed them to the barn, scolding, "If you wake my sister, I'll purge the both of you till you're as dry as Lot's wife."

She closed the door and returned to stab at the sluggish fire in the hearth, thinking that a man's storytelling was like a mad-woman's embroidery, plied repeatedly in careful rows that, by themselves, knot by knot, could be neat and pleasing, but that taken together made a larger grotesque image of mayhem, becoming more monstrous with every reworking.

But she knew that women, as well as men, had their own history of blood-letting, their own lust for conflict. In some moments of dire threat, she had desired to run screaming towards the danger, brandishing a knife, with her hair on fire. She had listened, rapt, to John's every rendering of the battle and felt no aversion to the descriptions of carnage, or of the tall soldier of Edgehill, rather, only a taut, vibrant anticipation.

She felt a presence at her back and looked around to see Allen standing at the bedroom door, frowning, his brows knitted together like two geese in a fog. She smiled at him but he turned back into the room and soon she heard Mary calling for her.

THE DAY WAS too hot for Patience to stand over the huge washing pot. The rain had vanished, leaving clouds at the top of the sky, crimped and mottled like the underbelly of a sea turtle. There was no breeze, and dampness hung in the air like in late summer even though it was still May. Martha wiped at the sweat around her collar and lifted, with both hands, a weighted pile of boiled linen with the paddle. Not satisfied, she dropped the clothes back into the water and stood back from the heat.

She heard Joanna singing to herself as she sat, bare-bottomed, on a bucket, her apron and skirt tied up around her middle. The child had resisted all efforts to stop wetting herself, demanding to still wear clouts, and Martha was intent on breaking her of the practice before the new babe came. Martha had warned Joanna not to stand from the bucket until she had passed her water into it. She called encouragingly to the girl, but Joanna crossed her arms and looked away. Martha turned to hide a smile; the child had taken to imitating her habit of crossing her arms, and it brought no end of laughter from Daniel.

She held the stirring paddle out in front of her chest. It was about five feet in length, almost as tall as she. John's battling giant of Edgehill had wielded a pike of twenty feet, or so he had said, making the pike four times as long, and four times as heavy, as the paddle. She tucked it under one arm and held it aloft like a spear. With a sharpened point at the end it could pierce the breast of any oncoming beast, but not clear through to the rider.

She looked around for a longer stick and left the pot boiling to search for branches in the stand of elm at the edge of the yard. A slender sapling had fallen with a storm and with some effort she snapped the lower part from the roots and stripped it clean. After grasping the heavier end, and cradling it beneath her arm, she raised the far end, quivering, holding it chest-high to a horse. Any charging animal would have propelled her backwards and trampled her underfoot, and she wondered what advantage the weapon would be to the men behind the advance guard, crushed beneath the recoiling pikemen.

"That's no way to hold a pike, missus."

She dropped the sapling and whirled around to find Thomas standing in the yard. He walked to where the discarded tree branch lay and picked it up, bending slowly at the waist, his long arms grasping the wood with a practiced grip. "You'd lose an arm with the first charge."

He walked closer to her, standing within an arm's breadth, and said, "First position. You must plant it between your legs and hold it thus." He motioned for Martha to take hold of the pike at breast level, enclosing her hands in his own, pressing her fingers warmly into the wood. He reached forward with his boot to tap lightly at the instep of her right foot, saying, "Second position." He tapped at her instep again. "Wider. You must stand wider or your knees will buckle."

He let go of her hands and moved to stand behind her.

"Third position," he said. "Lower the tip. Lower still, till your arms are straight. Now, brace the end against your right instep and step forward with your left. More forward still. And now you're in fourth position. And now you wait."

She tensed, her knees locked and cracking in the awkward stance, imagining his breath at her neck and his hands coming to rest at her shoulder or arm, but he did not touch her. Rather, he continued to stand behind until the rhythmic sounds of his exhalations became matched with her own.

Moments passed and she stretched her neck against the weight of the sapling. She finally asked, "For what do we wait?"

"Might be anything, missus. It could be a press of men on foot with muskets and pike. Or a charge of men on horse. Or"—he paused, and without seeing his face, she thought he smiled—"a swamp of woodland harpies."

She laughed and shifted the weight of wood in her aching hands and felt the sharp stick of a splinter in her palm. She dropped the sapling, bringing the hand up into her mouth, the nib of the splinter scraping against her tongue, and turned to face him. He reached out, clasping her around the wrist, and lifted her palm higher to see the wound. With his other hand, he lifted the skinning knife that he always carried at his side, the knife he had sharpened evening upon evening, and solemnly passed the small edge of the blade across an inch of her palm. It separated the flesh easily, with little pain, and with the tip of the knife, he flicked out the splinter of wood. Blood sprang up through the wound, and he watched it pooling in her palm before pressing her palm to his chest, letting her blood spread on the linen of his shirt like a bloom.

"You told me before…that I'm not Gelert, the hound," she said, breathing in once and looking up at his face. "Then I must be the infant prince, knocked from his cradle and set upon by wolves."

He inclined his head to her and said, "No." He smiled and inclined further until he felt the slightest stiffening clench of her hand and he carefully dropped his arm back to his side. Her hand, of its own accord, stayed poised on his chest for the briefest of moments before the wail of a child floated across the yard.

"Oh, Joanna!" she cried, and even louder, "Oh, the wash!" Remembering the clothes, in all likelihood boiling to cinders in the pot, she turned quickly and raced away. She did not dare look for Thomas again until she was certain he had left the yard to tend to his traps. Only then did she bring her hand to her mouth, sucking at the wound where the splinter had been, tasting salt and the faint rust of metal.

IT WAS THE last of the month before Martha found the courage to see for herself the great oak chest that sat by Thomas's bed. She had waited until the men had gone out hunting, Daniel tagging along with them, eager as a boy, overstepping the tall grasses with the bobbing knees of a startled deer. Patience had lain down to sleep after the morning meal, her belly growing ever heavier, and the children Martha had sent out of doors, each holding a bit of a sugar teat.

The men's room was deeply shadowed and dank, but she left the lantern unlit, fearful the children would see the light through a crack in the wall and come to question it. She stood at the door, poised to turn back, but the house was silent and there might not be another opportunity for a long while. John's pallet lay closest to the door and she stumbled over it as she guided her hands along the timbers. She balanced herself and waited, adjusting her eyes to the dark, until she could make out the other objects scattered about the room: a once fine, heavy rug thrown carelessly across the boards, a shirt, some bit of toweling. Against the far wall was Thomas's bed, two rope frames with a straw mattress laid end to end, and at its foot rested the chest, the wood mottled dark either from the stain of rainwater through the roof, or perhaps salt water from the passage to the colonies.

She crossed the few steps to the chest and knelt in front of it, spanning her arms across the metal bracing. Surprisingly, there was no lock on the clasp, and she pulled her hands back quickly into her lap. She had thought merely to explore the outside of the chest, never imagining it wouldn't be locked. What of worth, or even intrigue, she thought, could be in an unlocked chest in a home with restless women and prying children. She frowned and leaned forward to stand, resting her two palms on the split seams of the lid.

In that moment, something of weight shifted below the floor-boards. It was not the rattle of footfalls on the cellar stairs or the snick of a latch on a door. The disturbance was not even a thing she had perceived with her ears alone. It was more a vibration, passed through the shoe leather into the balls of her feet. She sank slowly back onto her heels, her hands still resting on the top of the chest, waiting for the movement to come again. But the house was quiet. From a distance, Martha could hear Will's voice taunting Joanna to chase him through the garden, but there had been no creaking bedposts from Patience waking, nor any peevish summoning from her cousin for water and salted bread. A moment passed and there was nothing further to give alarm. Whatever had made the noise had departed; only the growing agitation of being discovered remained, along with an unbearable curiosity.

Without a conscious thought, she unhinged the clasp and heaved up the heavy lid. She had not meant to open the chest when she first entered the room and would have abandoned the action if the covering had resisted, but the hinges were well oiled and the lid was raised to its full open position against the chains without a sound.

The deep well of the chest at first appeared empty. With a breath, she reached down into it and pulled out, bunched in her hand, a pair of breeches and a shirt, both worn and familiar; she had scrubbed them often enough with the rest of the household wash. These she laid aside and reached her hand more deeply into the recess. Her hand touched something of cold metal and she pulled into the light a long, pitted dirk. The head was plaited into a design of serpents coiled together, the edges stained and ragged from years of disuse. It balanced in her open palm like a slender scale and she gripped the hilt, notched cunningly for grasping fingers. She set this aside, laying it carefully on top of the shirt, and reached once more to the bottom of the chest.

Her hand nestled into something heavy and woolen and she pulled free a long coat of faded red with facings of blue at the collar and cuffs. She stood and held it widely in both hands to see the whole of it. Its seams were ragged, the sleeves patched and mended many times, but the wool was as fine and tightly woven as she had ever seen, the color at the folds still resolutely scarlet. She brought one sleeve up to her face and smelled the heavy scent of aged oak.

A pale bit of falling paper caught the light, and she saw at her feet a tightly rolled bit of parchment, wrapped in stiff oiled yarn. Realizing it must have fallen from the other, dangling sleeve of the coat, she bent over to pick it up, and as she lifted the scroll from the floor, a flattened piece of wood, about as long and half as wide as her forefinger, fell out of it.

Draping the coat over the lip of the chest, she regarded the slender piece, trying to place what it might be. Too small and fragile to be a dowel of any useful sort, it was too large to be a needle. Perhaps it was a gaming piece, she thought, and reached her hand forward to examine it more closely. As her fingers grazed the wood, she froze. Her fingers curled reflexively away and she quickly stood again, her clenched hands crossed defensively over her chest. An aversion as strong as anything she had ever felt unfurled its way down her spine and she stepped back, knocking into the chest. She imagined fully and vividly, had she touched the wooden piece with her bare flesh, it would have brought fresh blood from the wound in her hand, the wound Thomas had opened with his knife to remove the splinter; first seeping, then pulsing, then gushing like a town pump. She saw, in her mind's eye, the red bloom on Thomas's shirt, the stain from the cut in her hand, spreading over his breast until it fell in torrential drop-lets to the ground, the linen too saturated to absorb the blood more fully into its fibers.

In her alarm, she had dropped the scroll, and she hastily retrieved it from the floor. Wrapping her hand tightly in the hem of her skirt, she raked up the wooden piece and dropped it back into the parchment. The scroll was slipped into the arm of the coat, and then, carefully, she repacked all of the things she had removed from the chest. The lid was securely closed, the clasp fastened, and Martha stepped from the men's room, rigid and blinking.

The children had moved to the far end of the garden, and she could hear their voices as wavering patterns of sound as though they ran chanting, weaving in and out of the planted rows. Patience still slept; there was no movement or stirring from her bedroom. Martha sat at the table, staring at nothing, her breathing evenly paced. But as she had done with her tongue, running the tip of it over the ragged splinter in her hand, her thoughts pulled against the memory of the small wooden piece, no larger, or seemingly more significant, than any sliver of wood carved by man, smoothed by handling and subject to the laws of time and use. She listened intently for any shifting sound coming from under the floor-boards, but the space below her feet was voiceless.

CHAPTER 12

EDWARD THORNTON, HIS gathered lace nightshirt soaked through with acrid sweat, shifted his swollen legs more comfortably on the bed, and began the letter to his mother.

Dearest Madame,

I cannot say for truth that you will be glad of receiving this letter, sent to you from Boston Harbor; whether for news that I am yet alive, as of this, the 8th day of May, or gladder still for the knowledge that I have, by the time you read these words, passed out of this world altogether. It cannot give you much comfort either of ways, as I have been the source of most, if not all, of your misery and distress these four and twenty years.

His fingers, made awkward by the poison, lost their grip on the quill, and it dropped onto the parchment. Even if his mother agreed to the reading of the letter, he wasn't sure the words he had so painstakingly written could be deciphered, so great was the pain in his hands. A cup of water had been placed on the mantel opposite the bed and he desperately wished for a drink but did not have the strength to cross the floor. The head pains that had plagued him for so many weeks had taken on the quality of heated nails pushed slowly through his skull. He closed his eyes and rested for a moment, listening to the cacophony from the streets.

When first arriving in Boston with Brudloe and Cornwall, he had often come to this garret to visit with Verity, a maid to his innkeeper, Mrs. Parker. Verity had caught his eye within the first few days in port. A lovely girl of sixteen, with pale skin and dark wavelets of auburn, she soon, with only a token struggle, became his frequent mistress. She would not take coin from him like some common whore, but she seemed to delight in little gifts bought from the streets: ribbons, a peacock feather, a pair of earrings made of cut glass.

He would come to her often those first few weeks in Boston, spending afternoons locked together with her in her narrow bed. Later, he came to be nursed by her, having symptoms of dizziness and gut cramping, which worsened by the day. Verity's rented room was on the north end of town, close to the wharves, and had he screamed his loudest, even in the hours before dawn, the shipyard sounds would have drowned him out. Of all the places he had come to inhabit, of all the risk-laden ventures and squandered resources, he had never imagined making his death in a girl's trundle bed, fouled with his own waste.

He grasped again at the quill and, spilling only a little of the India ink from the bottle, continued to write.

Having borne such a wastrel, and borne in good patience and earnestness
the repeated disgrace of creditors hounding you on my account, until you

have spent all but the barest remnants of your good husband's fortune—I
will not shame his name by calling him Father as I have no good reason to
claim any but the Devil for my patronage—you must at least rest
assured that I am most wholly and pitiably sorry for my actions and will
beg you to remember some part of me that was good. Take comfort that you
will never hear the worst of my deeds as the men whose company I have
kept will soon, I have no doubt, pass on their way behind me.

It seemed to him, upon reflection, that the trip to the colonies from the very beginning was darkly favored. Their mission's decline had begun before they had even left England with the torture and killing of Sam Crouch, Blood's former associate and double-dealer. Crouch had died cursing them and their passage westward to Hell. He had gone to his end raving from Ecclesiastes: "Receive deceitful men into thine house and they will estrange thee from thine own."

Their numbers had dwindled again when two more of their group had been washed away during the storm. He smiled, exhaling bitterly, over the apt name of the ship, *The Swallow*; it had certainly swallowed both the eel boy and Baker like a rapacious beast, leaving no trace. So witless had he been on the ship, by the action of the sea and the shrieking of the ocean wind, that he sometimes thought he heard the eel boy's voice, coming from belowdecks days after he had been washed overboard, singing some fragment of lamenting song.

He thought he had known what true sickness was when they first landed at the docks, still miserable from the crossing, but within hours, it seemed, of coming to the colonies, he and his two remaining partners had had bouts of a great malaise and loose,

spotty bowels, along with hours of retching into basins and buckets provided by their landlady.

These periodic incidents had not dampened his pursuit of
pleasure, though. Boston had inns enough, the Salutation Inn and
the Ship Tavern among them. Though there were a few discreet
bawdy houses, sheltering women in drab dresses and with little, if
any, paint on their faces, he soon abandoned these dens in favor
of Verity's company.

And Verity, though young, had been no stranger to the pleasures of a bed. She had the downy skin and unclouded eye of a
virgin, and there was a sweetness to her that moved Thornton in
a way he had not been moved in a long while. She had had
her belly stuffed with child by a Royalist soldier who had abandoned her, the child subsequently dying. When she told Thornton, as they lay under a homespun quilt, of her lost infant, she
cried bitterly and he had tenderly rocked her, soothing her with
kisses. He had told her he knew what it was to suffer such a loss,
although he did not tell her when and how these things had taken
place.

He began to come to her every day, and she would feed him,
and couple with him, bathing his forehead when he sickened,
solicitous in the extreme. They would stroll together on the public square, along Bell Alley and Garden Court, and once, on a
Sunday, sauntered into the North Meeting House. There they
heard a preacher with the impertinent name of Increase Mather,
who preached a sermon "Woe, to Drunkards; the Sin of Drunk-
enness." He and Verity had snorted so loudly, giggling and gesturing irreverently, that they had been asked to leave by one of the
meetinghouse Elders.

Thornton had begun to believe that, after they accomplished their mission, he might even stay in Boston, making his way in land speculation or merchant trading, keeping Verity in comfort in a town house. Maybe even marrying her in a quaint New World ceremony, joined in a pastoral setting, the girl's hair bound up in a wreath of daisies or some such prosaic flower.

He looked down at the parchment and saw he had been crying, his tears streaking the ink on the page. He struggled with the quill for a moment, resolved to put his last thoughts on paper.

You may not be surprised to hear that once I left your home, I did follow my baser instincts into gambling and vice but made good my honor, for a time, by venturing into the earlier Dutch wars six years back, where I hoped to gain again some semblance of note in the company of Gen'l Vauban at the siege of Lille in France. Under his good tutelage I forswore drink and conducted myself in such a disciplined manner as would, I believe — I pray — have satisfied even your husband.

Whilst there, I married a good and honest girl from Lille who bore me a son, and for a time I made good my reputation by being husband and tender father. But to my eternal shame I abandoned them upon becoming reacquainted with the vagaries of the French court that followed upon the siege, and have seen since neither my wife nor my little son.

Early on, he, Brudloe, and Cornwall had made a foray into Salem to meet their contact, a miller by trade who told them the most likely towns and villages to search for their fugitive.

Brudloe had waved off the miller's cautioning words about the dangers of tracking these wanted men, some of whom had experienced disciplined fighting during the English Civil War.

"How hard can it be to track down one great beanpole of a man?" Brudloe had asked.

The miller had looked at Brudloe, his jaw moving beneath a creeping smile. "Oh, it's harder than you might think. To find men of stature in this place, in this hard wilderness, one has only to stand on a Boston wharf and look westwards."

The men had been confident in their plans, but as soon as they returned to Boston, they all became suddenly ill again.

A rending spasm in his gut made him cry out. His hands clenched, crushing the parchment, and his knees drew up reflexively to his chest. He had within the past hour begun to bleed from his rectum, and he could feel a renewed warm trickle of blood seep onto the sheets. When the spasm had passed, he lay panting, his teeth clenching and unclenching. He had spilled most of the ink onto the mattress, but there was some yet in the bottle and it would serve for his purposes. He had only a little left to write.

In battle I have been the slayer of men who begged me, on their knees, for mercy, and the spoiler of women who have done the same, and have done things besides, regarding which I cannot put pen to paper. You must, then, endure the role as my confessor, as I have no priest to make clean my soul.

He could hear Verity's footsteps coming up the stairs to the garret and he paused, looking towards the door. Her step was usually quick and light, but today her tread was more deliberate. It was she who had told him that morning, after she had fed him his cup of chocolate, that she had been poisoning him all along,

along with his partners. She had straightened the sheets and smoothed back his hair as he looked at her in horror. She had explained to him patiently that he was yet one more in a line of Royalist bastards who had killed and whored and burned their way through the colonies: corrupting good women, impressing good men, seeking to murder capable farmers because they had fought against some long-dead king. When he had pleaded with her to send for a doctor, she had shaken her head, saying, "It's too late for that now, Edward."

He had then begged the girl to allow him to make his will, and it was she who had given him the implements to write it. He garnered a last bit of strength, smoothing the rumpled parchment below his palms, and managed to bring quill to paper.

I leave to you my sword, for whatever you may take from its gain, the hilt alone is worth fifty guineas, and some small coins besides. Take this as my amends and know that I will die trusting that you will send something to Elisabetta Daumier of Lille, my own true wife.

Your son, the 17th, and penultimate, Earl of S.
Edward Thornton

It would take another two hours for him to die, alone; Verity not returning again until late that evening. So he couldn't have seen her first read the letter and then burn it in the small hearth, along with the bloody sheets, still warm from his body.

CHAPTER 13

THE FIRST WEEK of June, Daniel returned to his carting, the gelding plodding slowly past the burgeoning fields, shaking his tufted head against the heavy leads to the wagon. Martha stood with Patience at the door as Daniel waved cheerfully, exuberantly, to his wife and children. She passed her arm supportively around her cousin's broadening waist, whispering to her all of the choice things Daniel would bring back to them—a bit of lace, a brace of pewter bowls—but five days would pass before Patience stopped sulking and soaking her pillow at night with tears. Martha could often hear her cousin's indulgent weeping as she lay in bed trying to find sleep, and most nights Will would creep into Martha's room, poking her with a finger until she relented by making room for him within the hollow of her arms. Daniel had promised to be home by the middle of July to see Patience through her birthing. Martha never spoke to him of her nagging fears about an early and difficult lying-in, thinking that to speak of such things would give substance to unhappy possibilities.

On the sixth day, Martha looked at her cousin sitting mournfully at the table, eyes glazed with tears and frowning into the palm of her hand, and said abruptly, "Right, then. I've never seen a woman more in need of a potted cheese."

Patience furrowed her brows. "What?" she asked, dropping the hand from her chin.

"To market, cousin," Martha said, smiling, wrapping a cloak around her shoulders. "And I'll give you a quarter hour to comb your hair and wash your face or you'll disgrace us all."

Within the half hour, the cart rattled from the yard, Patience sitting next to John, her face for the first time bright and hopeful, while Martha sat in the back with Will and Joanna. Thomas had come out from the barn to watch them go, his eyes settling on her at the last. She at first averted her eyes, jerking her chin away, but then, pressing her lips together, she met his gaze full-on. She knew he would think her turning away a kind of modesty, a maidenly recoiling from the memory of the night before. She had come upon him in the barn, scraping the hide from the crippled calf he had slaughtered that afternoon; the animal's malformed legs jutted out at odd angles, wobbling in a kind of ghastly dance with every jerk of the skinning knife against the dangling carcass.

His back and shoulders were bared and she had stood in the shadows watching the cording of the muscles under his skin, damp from sweat and pale as death, as white as lime dust next to the reddish brown of his forearms working to strip away the hide from the twisted flesh of the calf. Sensing her, he turned around, but before he could speak, she had spun away, rushing back to the house, hiding the flush of her neck with her hands. More disquieting than this, though, and the true reason for her turning away, was the knowledge that she had willfully, and shamelessly, plundered Thomas's great oaken chest.

He followed slowly behind the cart for a short distance, his long legs keeping pace, until they turned onto the north road. He stood there, in the cascading dust from the cart, until it had risen up and over the crest, following the snaking of the Shawshin River.

As they rolled above the water's course, trumpeting breezes blew the topmost of trees, whipping branches fully green in unpredictable patterns against the untainted blue of the sky. At the quarter mile Martha told riddles to the children: "At night they come without being fetched, by day they are lost without being stolen....No, not candles, nor yet are they fireflies. *Ah, yes, stars!*"

And John sang a London street song:

> *"I was commanded by the Water Bailey,*
> *To see the rivers cleansed both night and daily.*
> *Dead hogs, dogs, cats and well-flayed horses,*
> *Their noisome corpses soiling the water's courses."*

Both the children and the women squealed in delighted protest.

Patience had been good as her word, giving Martha two of her piglets for trade, and Martha regarded them, their snouts straining wetly through the wicker cage, thinking they would bring enough for a new winter cape and a mirrored candle holder. She had spent most evenings stealing a few moments to write in the red book before bed. It had begun with entries of so much wheat kept in the cellar, so much corn, so many seeds, all matters of the Taylor house. But more and more of her musings had turned to Thomas, recording not only the things he said to her, which were more often like the riddles she had told the children, but how he looked at her, much like a starving man looking at a pasty, as though he would devour it whole. Or, she mused, like a man on campaign, long used to depriving himself, warily wakening to the knowledge of his own hunger.

Within the half hour, they had entered the town green, the meetinghouse of Billerica situated on the northern end, its gray boards neatly patchworked with darker, newer planes of wood. The cemetery, already spilling from the front of the yard, spread like a stone curtain, first to its western edge and then to the back of the meetinghouse. To the eastern side sat the Reverend Hastings's home, the minister she had turned away from Daniel's table with her combative words. The house was small but with a wooden fence fortifying a generous house garden. A girl, perhaps seventeen, gracefully tended the garden, and Martha's mouth twisted with the halfresentful thought that, though she was no doubt aptly servile as the minister's likely wife, she was also quite young and lovely.

There were a dozen women on the green sitting close together, some with their willow-shoot baskets of early sprouts from their gardens, others with brooms or herbals. Apart from them sat or stood the men, coopers and potters, mostly idle as the harvest of summer grain had not yet begun but talking as noisily as the women. As John pulled the wagon up close, all talking ceased. The clump of villagers seemed to Martha like a hive of stinging insects, each contending for the highest position in the honeycomb, each with a stinger for a tongue. But unlike bees, which could sting only once and then died, these goodmen and good-wives could inflict the poison from their tongues again and again, like wasps. The buzzing ceased only so long as it took to scrutinize the new arrivals, and then the hissing was taken up again, no doubt, Martha thought, to the detriment of every visitor's moral constitution.

Helping Patience from the wagon, Martha situated her cousin among the townswomen and went directly to the weaver, a stout man with bowl-cut hair. She was soon disappointed, though, to see only a few coarse blankets from the weaver's own loom laid out on the ground. When she told him she was looking for the goods to make a new cloak, he smiled and beckoned her to his wagon, where he removed from a sack a bolt of English wool. She brushed at the covering of dust lying like a second skin over the surface and saw that the cloth had an almost glistening sheen, the color of slate after a heavy rain, and when she tested the weave with her fingers, she knew she must have it. But he would not take only one piglet for the woolen, and she would not readily give up both, as she had in mind to acquire a new lantern as well. Martha held up two fingers covered with grime to show the man she knew the cloth had long been in the wagon, too dear for any local villager to acquire it; and so it had rested there, perhaps for many months beyond the sea passage from England.

"But look here," he said, "I have waited near eight months, *eight months,* for this cloth." The weaver frowned, shaking his head. "Look at the weave. Feel the weight. Why, the shade of it is a mirror to your own eyes. Look here, missus, do not ask me to come so far down."

"No," she said, pinning him with her eyes, responding *no* to every one of his entreaties and proclamations of sacrifice in giving her back coin as overage on the second pig. Martha had seen enough of her father at bargaining to know when to stand and when to walk away. She shook her head and, giving the cloth over to the weaver, turned around. After twenty paces the weaver called out, "Very well, missus, I will give you back your sixpence, but it should be you and not I who tells my good wife of her newfound penury."

Smiling, Martha accepted the cloth and the coins and pointed the weaver to the wagon to collect his pigs. When she asked him to direct her to the tinsmith, she was dismayed to see him gesture in the direction of a small outbuilding next to the reverend's plot. The young woman in the garden had finished her work and had gone back inside, and Martha quickly walked to the small shed, hoping the minister would be in the meetinghouse and not at home. She knocked softly on the closed door and waited for the clopping of heavy footsteps of the tinsmith coming to let her in.

She heard the sound of jeering laughter coming from the far side of the green, and when she turned to look, she saw a small knot of children, and a few older girls, taunting something obscured by their swaying bodies. She shook her head, thinking how often a gathering of idle children meant the misfortune of some other child, or animal, smaller than themselves. A girl shrieked in gleeful malice and Martha's face turned grim, remembering that children can often be sweetest before they turn bad.

The group parted, scattering into differing tribes of girls and boys apart, and she saw what they had been tormenting. A woman, bolted fast in the stocks, her head pointing towards her toes, cried loudly and bitterly to be freed. She called for water, and for pity, but the children had moved on with their games and no one else on the green gave her any notice beyond a nod of annoyance. Martha turned back to the door, and with her hand poised to rap again, it swung widely open, revealing a slight man in well-worn but clean linen and vest, and with the milky eyes of the blind. His chin pointed beyond her shoulder but his head cocked as though following the sounds of her breathing. "Good day," he said formally. There was a slight pause, and he added, "May I hear your voice? To place you, you understand."

"I'm here for a lantern," she answered, casting one last look at the woman in the stocks.

"Ah, yes, of course," he said and stepped aside, allowing her to enter.

The room inside was as shaded as a cavern, and she realized, as she moved hesitantly over the threshold, that he must work in darkness, as there were no discernible windows set into the walls, the only light coming from the fire pot close to the bench, faintly glowing with copper soldering fragments. He promptly closed the door and she stood in the blackness in uncertain silence. He walked confidently to his workbench and bent over the fire pot, lighting a short taper which he fit into a reflecting lantern.

The startling light revealed a workroom, well swept and orderly, with lanterns of differing sizes pegged to the walls. Baskets fronted the walls, some with cups and long-tined forks, some with smaller workpieces not easily identifiable. The bench was filled with tools, in exacting rows, from the most brutish-size pliers down to smallest, hair's-width dowels and punches. The smith stood at the desk, fingering the tools gently, as if to assure himself of their placement. She stared at his hands, fascinated by their restless creeping, as though the fingers, long as alder whips, had been fashioned with too many articulating joints.

"I do not know your voice." He had waited to speak, talking only when she had drawn in a breath to inquire about the lantern.

"I am Martha Allen," she said, beginning to feel the acrid burn of the soldering pot behind her tongue. The smith raised his brows expectantly but said nothing.

"I would like a lantern. For evenings." She had added the last foolishly, as if he would not know a lamp would be useless in daylight.

There was a slight pursing of the lips, and the man's eyelids fell more heavily towards closing, making him appear at once disappointed and yet self-satisfied. "For evening reading, perhaps? Or for the keeping of *personal* writings?"

At his insinuating tone, she stiffened, remembering the red book sewn into her pillow casing.

He moved assuredly to the wall with the lanterns and asked, "Which one would you choose?"

"I would have something that gives greater light than a candle might. For the writing of accounts, you see. A reflecting lantern, like the one on your bench."

He clasped his hands together, the long fingers dangling loosely at his groin. "Ah, the pity is I have only one, which, as you can see, is mine own." He placed the slightest pause before the word "see," tilting his head to the opposing side, and waited.

"That is a pity," she said after a moment's hesitation.

"Well, then. I thank you.... My cousin Goodwife Taylor waits for me..."

She turned to leave but he surprised her by saying, "If you wish, I could sell you mine." He returned to his bench, his hands encircling the base of the lantern.

"I have only sixpence to pay for it," she began. The large, mirrored lantern on the tinsmith's table, she knew, was dearer by far than the coins she held in her apron.

"Well, the lantern is old. Stay but a moment and I'll grease the hinges and polish the mirrors. Come sit while you wait." He motioned to a stool next to the bench, his manner suddenly solicitous, his smile seemingly ingenuous.

His warmth disarmed her, and despite being disquieted over his initial aloofness, Martha walked to the stool and, balancing the woolen cloth over her lap, sat down.

"I did not realize you were family to the Taylors," he said. He took out the candle that had been burning inside the reflecting lantern and placed it in a simple brass holder close by. He began to dismantle the lantern, laying the pieces carefully on the workbench. The lack of reflected light from the single, guttering candle diminished the scope of the room, crowding the corners into shadow again. "You are, I think, daughter to Goodman Allen of Andover."

"You know of my family?" she asked.

The tinsmith pointed his face towards her, one corner of his mouth curling into a half smile. "I am blind, missus, not deaf. There is very little that escapes my attention. Mind you, I have never traded with your father, but I have heard enough to know the measure of Goodman Allen." There was the faintest hint of mockery in his voice, but he had turned away to breathe moist air onto one of the mirrored panels. He rubbed it vigorously for a time with a cloth before asking, "How is it, your time spent with the Taylors?"

"It is all well enough. They are good to me." The smoke from the fire pot had suddenly made her sleepy and she stifled a yawn.

"You do not find Goodwife Taylor a bit...a bit...how shall I say..." He paused and pointed his eyes towards the ceiling as though deep in thought. "Parsimonious?" He beamed at her broadly and she smiled in return, ducking her chin with the urge to laugh out loud.

With exaggerated seriousness he said, "I should not say such to you, as she is, above all, your cousin." He smiled overly long at her, the opaque surface of his eyes unblinking, and, unnerved, she glanced away.

"The Taylor household is well turned-out, so I have heard," he said, returning his attention to his work. "There are two landsmen on the settlement, are there not? One a Scotsman, the other a Welshman." He paused a moment before adding, softly, distinctly, "Morgan by name."

Martha looked up, surprised. "No. His name is Carrier. Thomas Carrier."

"Carrier? Then perhaps I am mistaken. Though..." His voice trailed off and he shook his head once.

"Though...?" she echoed.

He leaned over the bench towards her, dropping his weight onto resting elbows, his face close to hers. "It's been said that the Welshman got on the boat with one name and stepped off the boat with another. It's common enough. Many of the first families have done it. Just after the Great War, when they had need of safe haven in the colonies."

"Safe haven," she said, her voice turning sharp and wary. "From what?"

The tinsmith's lids came down, half-mast, over the pale, marbled surface of his eyes, his lips pursing suggestively. "The king's justice, of course. He hunts, even now, for his father's killers. All have been pardoned. All but those whose hands signed the death warrant, and those whose hands wielded the implement of death." His fingers brushed over the tools, coming to rest on a small, needle-like screw turn. With a few exacting twists, the trap hinges on the lantern fell free with a clatter, making her jump. "Surely you know that Cromwell's confederates yet live here, hiding in *plain sight?*"

His mouth twisted for a moment bitterly. "If I may use such a common phrase. There has been offered a generous bounty for the capture of these accused men. As you are not native to this town, you may not know that Thomas Carrier has long been suspected of being Thomas Morgan, the man who, for love of Cromwell's cause, swung the ax, taking the life of an anointed king. It is said that after the blade came down, he held up the royal gourd for all to see."

He waited for her to speak, and when she didn't respond, he extended one arm over his head to demonstrate, adding, "He was chosen because he was so tall, you understand, so that when he reached out his hand, holding the still-dripping head, even those pressed to the very front of the platform could gaze upon it." He dropped his arm and shrugged. "But this is only rumor. Perhaps, as you are a woman, I should speak no more on this…" One side of his mouth curled up, his voice trailing into silence.

A sudden recollection of the flat wooden piece in Thomas's oak trunk was followed with the vision she had had of his shirt, stained and running with blood, and she felt a panic building in her head like mercury rising. She sensed the tinsmith listening to her quickened breaths, perhaps waiting for her to press him into revealing more about the regicides, questioning him about rumors that must have wafted through the workroom like smoke from the fire pot.

From her childhood she had heard stories, told as frequently as the coming of tides, from her father, and his cronies, that Cromwell's cousin and son-in-law had long been hidden and fed by local Massachusetts farmers. The glories of the civil war, and Cromwell's decadelong reign between the executed Charles the father and the restored Charles the son, were often burnished and constructed anew at night in secret when the fire was banked and the doors locked. It was a source of deep-seated pride to the New Englanders that not one man, woman, or child had taken the king's bounty in arresting Edward Whalley and William Goffe, Cromwell's kin and fellow regicides, and others besides, who had fought against the first Charles. The colonists were a thorny, resourceful, and resistant lot when it came to betraying one of their own to the Royalists, and they held a perverse pride that common men, for the sake of common rights, had had the temerity, and nerve, to pull down a king.

"Gossip is like a poisoned soup," she said, the tension in her voice making her sound waspish and scolding. "Delicious at first but deadly over time."

He had started reassembling the pieces of the lantern, but he put the tools aside and said, "Well, then, we will not drink of the poisoned cup. We will speak only of cordial things. To my mind, it is a winning trait when a woman does not sup on gossip. It means she can keep an intimate confidence." He leaned forward on his elbows, his nostrils widening, breathing in some scent that inhabited the place where she sat. "You have a deep voice for a woman, but for all that, it is pleasing. You are not yet married, I believe." She dropped her gaze away from his sightless stare, drawn again to the play of his fingers, searching the air like the eye stalks of an insect.

Repressing the longing to jerk the stool farther away from the bench, she gathered the cloth closer to her chest and said, "I must leave now."

His tongue flicked absently at the corner of his mouth. "But I am not yet finished."

"Then I will come back another day." She rose, scraping the stool against the floorboards, and walked swiftly towards the door. Before she could grasp the latch, the tinsmith blew out the candle. She stood for a moment in complete darkness, trying to calm her unreasoning fear that he would come upon her from behind. She groped to find the handle, taking first one step and then another, until she touched what she hoped was the door. She ran her hands searchingly over the wood, feeling for the latch, and when she found it, she tugged hard. The door would not open and she realized he had bolted the lock when she first entered.

She slipped her hands up along the frame, frantically searching for the lock, listening for the sounds of approaching footsteps but hearing nothing. When her fingers touched metal, she slipped the bolt and fiercely tugged open the door.

As she rushed over the threshold, he called to her sharply, "Missus." Reflexively, she paused, and he said, calmly and clearly from his place at the bench, "Ask *him* about the *Prudent Mary.*"

Leaving the door ajar, she hurried past the rectory and, looking up once, saw the minister's face at the window, starkly assessing her panicked flight towards the green. She willfully slowed her pace, matching her breathing to the reflective chanting of the unfamiliar name given to her by the tinsmith: *"Prudent Mary, Prudent Mary."* John beckoned to her from the wagon, and Martha could see Patience and the children waiting restlessly for her to join them.

She was flushed and shaken, but Patience was too satisfied with her afternoon of trading and preoccupied with a crying Joanna to take note. As John pulled away from the green, Will slipped his hands, tightly closed into two fists, onto her lap and asked, "Butter or cream?" He tapped at her legs until she faced him, and he asked again, "Butter or cream?" It was a guessing game they often played where a treat was hidden in one of the asker's hands; left was "butter," right was "cream." If the guesser picked the correct hand, the asker must give over the treat. Martha studied the boy's dirty face, stricken with childish concern for her inexplicable distress, and she smiled, tugging roughly at his hair with her fingers.

"Butter," she said, tapping his left hand. He grinned with relief and opened an empty palm to her. "Go on," she prompted, and he quickly shoved into his mouth the bit of damp sugar that had been clenched in his right hand.

As they rolled past the now-silent figure in the stocks, the woman craned her neck to the side and stared up at Martha with accusing eyes. Rage had replaced the shame of being pilloried, and her piercing look came like a mother's slap, and a mother's warning. The woman's eyes, the palest of blue and clouded with the beginnings of elder blindness, craned and looked at the wagon until it had pulled out beyond the town marker.

THE MOWING OF the common fields began upon the cresting of the sun. The entire town of Billerica had come out to harvest the green and fibrous grasses, sawing at the wind in nodding waves. Each settlement would share in its deserved portion, the largest homesteads getting the largest share of fodder for their farm stock. Well before dawn, men and women on foot and in carts, carrying scythes and rakes and pitchforks, had joined the road winding north beyond Loes Plain. They came together in banded groups, families by blood or marriage, or in camps of common-minded neighbors, eager to give or receive news and gossip of the recent births and deaths in a neighboring village, or the vagaries of trade in a marketplace that lived or died much as the people did. They spoke in quiet undertones, calling to one another in hoarse whispers, as though the sun were a living thing that could be frightened away by the sudden remonstrations and shouts of people.

Martha had chosen to walk the few miles rather than ride in the wagon with Patience and the children, her pace joyfully rapid, keeping time with Thomas's loping stride. The air was cool on her ankles, bare from lack of stockings, and she could have walked barefoot if not for the presence of men. Will got down and ran for a time back and forth between them, teasing and chanting, "Catch me, catch me, catch me," until Thomas grabbed him up and tossed him shrieking over one shoulder. He was carried aloft for a while, dizzy and excited to be able to see ahead to the main group of villagers moving inexorably forward. Well beyond Fox Brook on a hillock, Thomas tossed Will back into the wagon and let it roll ahead, motioning for Martha to stand for a moment alone with him. As the wagon descended the far side of the hill, Patience turned her head around to watch them thoughtfully, her eyes guarded and questioning.

Thomas pointed west to a crooked bend at the Concord River where a deep pool formed, bowered over thickly with cattails and river fronds. He said to her, "In a year's time, that's to be our land. Mine and John's."

Her throat tightened at the beauty, the possibilities, of such a place, and a desire as strong as despair twisted in her chest. The rising sun flared off an eddy on the river, and she turned to watch Thomas, the flat planes of her face catching the biased light. She had never seen a man at rest who could stand so resolutely still; the absence of movement fooled the eye into believing the tall, angular Welshman at his ease was somehow less threatening than he truly was.

He had an economy and a surety of movement to everything he accomplished, never giving more energy to a task than was required, allowing the impetus of a tool's own forward momentum and the pull of gravity to move rock and earth. And yet, at the behest of a neighbor who had no gun for butchering, she had seen Thomas fell an ox with a hammer so forcefully that the brains of the beast had been found in its throat. For all his native strength, though, he had yet to be proclaimed best man at the reaping.

Every man in Billerica with hair on his face worked a scythe to harvest the feed grass, hoping to be the last villager standing in the newly cleared field. Most times, completed within the span of a day and half a night, the scything would have a tinge of desperate zeal to it, a kind of battle. The men would attack the grass, mowing it in ever-expanding patterns, never stopping, except for a brief swallow of water or pocket bread, until exhaustion overtook them. One by one they would drop out until one man remained alone, a corn king, a prince of reeds, upright on the ground littered with broken stalks. Made much over by women and men alike, he would be fed the best meat, given the best ale, deferred to, listened to, sought after. For three years running a townsman named Ezra Black had been proclaimed the winner. Looking at Thomas in the strengthening light, she instinctively knew that he never took the honors as he had nothing to prove to these farmers of Billerica. He simply worked to fulfill his needed allotment of grass, leaving the contest to those yeomen whose reputations, and pride, depended upon such a small and circumscribed ritual.

Within the half hour they had joined the encampment of townspeople at the edge of the field, and upon the completion of the blessing by the Reverend Hastings, the men commenced the reaping. Moving in a northwesterly direction, their long-handled blades swinging in wide arcs, they opened up swaths between the long grasses. The stalks, still wet and clinging from the morning dew, lay crossed together in disordered patterns, turning hour by hour from dark green to yellowish brown. The women and children, some as young as Joanna, followed behind the men spreading and turning the grasses with rakes, gathering them into windrows to dry under the sun. Forty-odd men worked the fields, and they had cleared almost five acres when the drum rolled, calling them to pause for the noon meal of meat and bread and cold water drawn from the river.

Earlier, Patience had pushed a sharp elbow into Martha's side, pointing out Ezra Black with her chin, remarking, "He is not yet married, cousin, and must marry soon or be thought a scandal." She raised her eyebrows significantly, and Martha turned away before she betrayed her impatience. There had been a lustful buzzing around Ezra from the outset as first one young woman and then another found reason to drift close to him, to bring him water or to pull her cap aside to show off a small but immoderately straying curl. He was powerfully built with immense arms, thighs, and calves, but with bandy legs and a head full of dark ringlets that looked suspiciously oiled. Martha could have guessed without being shown who the cock of the hour was.

Patience pressed into Martha's hands a large joint of meat and gave her a push in Ezra's direction. As she approached him, he grinned widely, his squinting eyes disappearing behind the high mounds of his cheeks.

"You are Martha. Your cousin has told me of you," he said, wiping at the sweat on his face. He crossed his arms and looked her over like a mare. "She told me you have been saving something for me." He grinned even wider and winked his eye at her.

She blinked twice and felt the small of her back go rigid. At the setting of her face, there was a slight faltering of confidence in Ezra's eyes, but he pointed to the joint of meat and winked again. Martha could sense the men and women watching them, waiting for an exchange of words. She handed him the meat, wiping her hands on her apron, and glanced at Thomas, who was drinking from a dipper of water, his eyes thoughtfully on Ezra.

"Well, there is no need for excitation. After all," she said, looking down at the crease in his pants, "it is such a small joint."

Ezra threw his head back and bellowed, gazing at her with nodding approval. "It's not so small as you might think. Why," he said, rubbing at the side of his nose, "there is plenty enough to feed the both of us."

Despite her best efforts, she smiled, stifling a laugh, and after gnawing a bit of meat off the bone, he moved in closer. "You hold the rest for me for a short while. I trust it will be warmed in your lap and then I'll claim it again. As best man." He grinned at her and picked up his scythe as the drum rolled again, moving away with the tide of men returning to work.

The breezes which had cooled the fields that morning grew slack and then stopped blowing altogether, the sun shining uncensored in a cloudless sky, sparking off the newly sharpened edges of the working scythes. It wasn't until the light had begun to shift beyond the forests of Chelmsford to the west that the older men, distressed by the heat, began to waver, stumble, and then quit the field, helped along by their women to places in the shade. The spent men rested, boasting of their performance in years past and guardedly laying odds on the last man standing. The women and children labored on, raking and gathering, until close to ten acres had been cocked and loaded into carts and wagons to be taken home, the farmers looking with a sharp eye to every other man's apportioned share.

At sunset, the lowering rays painted the stalks to a golden red and soon John returned breathless and exhausted, dragging his scythe like a ruined toy behind him. His face was pinched with the heat and he wiped at his neck with a sleeve, saying, "I'm finished…cooked to a goose." Propping himself sitting against the wagon, he doused his head and neck with the water skin, drinking deeply. Martha came to stand next to him, shielding her eyes with her hands, anxiously scanning the fields. She asked, "Is Thomas yet reaping?" When there was no answer she looked down to see John studying her, one eye squeezed shut against the sweat still pouring down his forehead.

He took another long drink and answered, smiling, "Ezra Black is a dead man."

Two hours past sunset, there were only five men left in the field, and the villagers sent their yawning, limp children into the blackening shadows to take water to the reapers and to bring back word of who thrived and who faltered. Soon nothing could be seen beyond the cook fires, but the voices of the still-working men could be heard calling back and forth, encouraging, taunting, challenging one another to stay or give up and return to the warmth of a fire and a well-deserved rest. Within an hour's time the calling ceased and there was no sound from the field but a distant whooshing noise of the evening breezes sweeping and bending the remaining shafts.

Martha sat feeding the fire with dried grasses and watching the children, delighted with the little leather-winged bats that flew above the flames, chasing the sparks as though they were fireflies. Patience, resting hunkered on the ground, had begun nodding drowsily into sleep when a man approached the circle of firelight asking for Goodwife Taylor. He had the ruddy face and breadth of shoulders of a farmer, but his shirt was of a better quality than those worn by the other village men, and though it had been soaked with sweat, it looked decently clean. Patience roused herself and, gesturing for Martha to help her up, rose awkwardly to face him. Straightening her apron down over her swollen belly, she said, "I am Goodwife Taylor."

"Goody Taylor, my name is Asa Rogers, recently come from Salem with my brother. I've heard from some here in Billerica that you've land which lies fallow on the river." He pointed southerly towards the Concord and continued, "I am here to propose a fair price on the land. More than fair, in fact." When she didn't answer, he added, "A quite generous offer."

"Who has put about that the land is unclaimed?" Martha asked, realizing with sudden alarm that he spoke of the plot promised to Thomas.

He cut his eyes briefly at her, and she saw a hard shrewdness far beyond the simple cunning of a farmer at trade. "As it so happens, it was Edward Wright, the tinsmith." He turned back to Patience, his voice reasonable and reassuring. "Goodwife Taylor, I'll be building a mill and need land seated on water. Whatever arrangements have been proposed, if there is no binding contract and no coin proffered, the land is yet in your possession, to be disposed of at your will. And to your gain."

"My husband is not here...," Patience began uncertainly, flinching as Martha's grip tightened painfully on her hand.

"That land is promised to another," Martha said, noting the barely concealed flash of irritation crossing the miller's face.

He took off his hat, slapping it twice against his thigh. "What if the land was promised in good faith but accepted under false pretenses?"

Patience frowned and opened her mouth to speak when Martha tugged at her hand to remain silent.

"Very well," he said after a moment's pause. He nodded to Patience. "I'll speak to your husband about this when he is returned. I stay with the Reverend Hastings if you have a change of heart. Good night." He flashed a final hooded look at Martha and walked away.

As the stars pinpricked their way through the sky, there were only two men left in the field. Martha wrapped some bread and meat in her apron and let Will lead her to the place where he had last seen Thomas working. Martha could see from a distance his broad-brimmed straw hat towering above the whispering grasses, reflecting the faint nocturnal light as sharply as a sail under the moon. She wordlessly gave him the food and drink, and when he had finished, she felt his hand slip warmly around her upper arm. He kneaded the flesh, his fingers gripping her tightly. He released her and stepped away to resume his reaping, careful to keep the swinging blade from cutting her or the child. Close by, she could hear the rhythmic swish of Ezra's scythe, his breathing beginning to sound burdened. Will took her by the hand, and she followed him back to the cook fires blazing close together in defensive clusters.

One by one, as midnight passed, the villagers and their children drifted off to sleep, the fires wasting down to embers. The breeze turned cooler and Martha lay down under a blanket, Patience at her back, the children huddled together for warmth nearby. She closed her eyes but sleep would not come. Like a plague carcass, the tinsmith had thrown at her the unfamiliar and dangerous-sounding names of *Thomas Morgan* and *Prudent Mary*, and a hot, new resentment towards the man pricked at her, knowing that he had pointed Asa Rogers to the land on the river promised in good faith to Thomas. "Accepted under false pretenses," Rogers had said. She twisted under the blanket, restless and anxious over what this might mean, and Patience muttered impatiently for her to lie still. Martha slid a lingering hand up the sleeve of her own dress, mimicking Thomas's grip on her arm, and for a time allowed herself to imagine the weight of his arms around her waist.

She woke when the sky was lightening, the stars gone, and she sat abruptly and rubbed at her eyes. A small band of men had walked into the field some distance away and stood motionless looking in the same direction. She quickly rose and walked to where they were gathered and saw that another five acres had been mown through the blackest of night, the grass lying cropped and flattened, as though a monstrous mill wheel had been rolled across the ground. Two men reaping could be seen afar in the newly made clearing. One figure had stopped and leaned heavily on his scythe handle, swaying gently as though balanced on a rending ice floe. The other figure continued in a slow and steady pace, hacking through the stalks with a dulled blade, step and sweep, step and sweep, until the smaller man stopped his weaving and crumpled onto the freshly cut hay.

The fallen man was carried from the field, and there was no clapping on the back or welcoming draught of ale for Ezra Black, only the amazed and wary looks from the waking men and women now running into the field to stare at the victor. Their incredulous faces looked to the tall man, relentless and poised, holding his scythe with a firm and steady hand, as if the roaring pendulum of God had come to sever the life strings between Heaven and Earth.

He walked the few miles to home, refusing to be carried in the wagon's bed on top of the soft and fragrant mown grasses, and Martha walked beside him, slipping her hand into his at the quarter-mile marker.

CHAPTER 14

BRUDLOE SETTLED THE palms of his hands more securely over the pillow, leaning closer to Hammett Cornwall, who sat next to him on the bed. He studied Cornwall's large, mournful face, his downturned mouth, and impassive eyes floating wetly within pouches of skin still tinged with gray. He had begun to worry about the big man, the way he now often stared at the bedroom walls by the hour, never speaking unless responding in grunts to Brudloe's questions or directives. Brudloe observed the pallor, the tinge of mottled scarlet around Cornwall's lips, remaining like a stain, and knew they had both escaped death only barely. The sickness had come upon them quickly, and ferociously, after leaving the ship at Boston Harbor, and if not for the ministrations of the kind Mrs. Parker, their boarding mistress, they both would have been buried with their young companion, Edward Thornton.

"Along with all his fine clothes. And with him an earl. Much good it did him," Brudloe muttered out loud.

The bed under Cornwall heaved and shuddered briefly, and

with an exasperated sigh, Brudloe brought his weight down more firmly on the pillow under his hands. "It's takin' forever for this bitch t' die. She must've found a pocket of air in the down."

Cornwall remained silent, and Brudloe signaled with his chin for the larger man to settle his considerable weight back more firmly over the bulge under the quilt.

The movement under the pillow was growing fainter and he breathed out, "About fuckin' time."

Mrs. Parker, the owner of the inn on Water Street where they had landed after the crossing, had been a pleasant diversion once he had recovered enough to plow her well-trod fields. She certainly seemed willing, crawling right into his bed the minute his eyes had lingered on the upper swell of her bodice, chastely covered with a muslin scarf. She had the breasts and thighs he preferred, soft and malleable like undercooked bread. She was enthusiastic and unguarded in her mounting, riding him topside like a weathervane on a pole but, and this was the thing he found the most exciting, with the withholding, almost modest, puckered kisses of a little girl.

She had nursed the men beyond an illness of almost two months, seeing them through the retching and watery bowels that had killed Thornton after the first few weeks. Following the unexpected deaths of Baker and the eel boy, both seemingly washed over the side of the boat in the storm, the captain of *The Swallow* had kept the three of them, Brudloe, Cornwall, and Thornton, comfortable in his own quarters for the remainder of the journey.

Upon landfall in Boston the captain had led the three of them to what he declared was a reputable inn, clean and no questions asked. Recently, however, Brudloe had wondered about the timing of their illness and the indisputable fact that since his partner's death, the serving maid, who was also Thornton's slut, had disappeared.

A few days earlier, Brudloe, still weak from illness, had gone looking for ale and came upon the constable and Mrs. Parker whispering together in the common room. He had thought at first that the constable was another one of Mrs. Parker's lovers. But she slipped the man a packet of letters with the dry, assessing look of a trading partner, certainly not the face of a woman in the grip of passion, and when the man in turn handed her a bag of coins, Brudloe began to suspect that she might have another business besides innkeeping.

He began searching her bedroom when she went out to market and found buried in a wardrobe letters from a man named James Davids from New Haven, Connecticut. They were instructions, some of them numerically coded, to closely follow the actions of her boarders from England; "pigeons" he had called Brudloe and his fellows.

James Davids was suspected by those in the informing game to actually be John Dixwell, one of the judges who sentenced Charles I to death. Davids had lived in the colonies for years, marrying, prospering at his practice in the law, a confessed confederate of the other regicides as yet to be found and brought back to England for trial and execution. His network of spies was said to be crawling all over New England, and if Davids knew of Brudloe's plans in coming to Boston, so did everyone in the New Englander's pay.

Brudloe had let Mrs. Parker go on thinking he was her pigeon for weeks. Her coy questioning, her spying, her passing of notes to the constable and others continued unabated until he was sure he had convinced her of his and Cornwall's intentions to go north along the coast up to Portsmouth instead of to towns more inland, where Brudloe suspected his quarry to be. They could have just slipped away one evening while she slept and none would have been the wiser. But last night he had heard her weight on the floorboards at the door while he and Cornwall talked of leaving for Salem again, and he knew he could not leave the woman alive.

After supper, he plied her with drink and led her to bed, sticking as close to her as fur on a dog. He enjoyed her not once but twice, and in the morning while she sat across from him as he ate his breakfast, he let her chatter on and on, one slipper dangling archly off one toe, her smiling, dimpled chin cupped in her hands. Then he had taken her hand and led her back to bed, laid her down, and put a pillow over her face. She had fought harder than he had expected, scratching him, gouging the flesh with her nails, until he had called for Cornwall to pull the blanket up over her arms and legs and sit on the damnable whore. It had taken both of them to get the job done and a part of him had to admire her fight.

The lump beneath the quilt was finally still, and when he pulled the pillow away, her eyes were staring blankly, her doll's mouth open and glistening. He fell back against the wall, nursing his scratches, and looked once more at the morose Cornwall. Something about the expanse of the wilderness at the near perimeter of Boston had unnerved the larger man. The port town was a ragged dock city like any other, with porters and thieves and doxies strolling the wharves at all hours, albeit with considerably less noise and swagger than in London. But there, beyond Fox Hill, over the Roxbury Flats, grew a forest without visible end, with roads disappearing into a limitless, rolling expanse of thickets and green impenetrable undergrowth mirroring the jade green wall of the ocean that had almost drowned them.

Brudloe had seen with his own eyes his large companion kill three armed footpads with an ax when they had tried to rob goods that Cornwall himself had only just stolen. It enraged the big man no end to see his hard work come to naught. And yet here he sat like a cropped gelding, meek and soundless.

Brudloe said confidingly, "You need cunny, my friend, and right quick. Your wastin' about's frayin' my patience."

Cornwall looked at him, expressionless, and shrugged. The sound of a fist on the door below made them both startle, and Brudloe held out a cautioning hand to his partner, who had begun rising from the bed. Brudloe stepped to the window and looked cautiously down to the street.

"It's the constable," he whispered, gesturing for Cornwall to stay where he was. The sound of pounding began again, more forcefully, and Brudloe ducked behind the casement as the constable backed into the street, peering upwards to the second-floor windows. The man banged once more on the door, calling out to Mrs. Parker to come quick, but soon he mounted his horse and clucked to it to move on.

Brudloe turned back to Cornwall only to find the man observing Mrs. Parker's silent form with something akin to sympathy, shaking his head as though he had come upon her lifeless body by accident.

With any luck it would be another day before their minder was discovered, and there would be no mark on her body to bespeak imposed violence in the event of their being detained and questioned. Brudloe had pointed the trail northward, and by the time their pursuers discovered their error, both he and Cornwall would be well hidden, and provided for, by their contact in Salem. There they could rest and plan for the killing of Thomas Morgan. He had often, on their miserable voyage overseas, relished the idea of hog-tying Morgan and slowly peeling him like an orange. But now he was tired, too tired to wrestle with the man; he could be happy with the criminal's head alone. He had once gone to see the embalmed, desiccated head of Oliver Cromwell, kept on a pole outside Westminster Abbey, bits of flesh and hair still clinging to the skull. He imagined with satisfaction Morgan's head like that, slowly drying to bacon in a salted barrel.

And then they could quit this sweltering, pine-boxed outpost at the arse end of the world.

CHAPTER 15

A BAG OF GOOSE down lay opened on the bed, the curling, delicate quills startlingly white against the dark gray sacking. There were other things as well, carefully positioned and repositioned next to the bag: four buttons carved from the tiny bones of a squirrel, a cloak pin for the English woolen bought at market, shaved from the pointed splinter of a stag's antler, a doeskin throw, supple and warm from being cured in the sun. Martha sat, picking up and setting down again each thing, one by one, regarding the treasures that Thomas had left for her almost daily since the mowing of the fields, leaving them in places he knew she would go; shyly, stealthily, without any show or stated expectation for return of favor.

Patience had said nothing of the gifts. She would merely, with a disapproving glance, turn away with a cautionary exhalation of breath as though the frequency of the offerings was suspect, even though Thomas was as ever steadfast in his work on the settlement.

Martha picked up the red book and painstakingly recorded each offering, noting with satisfaction the growing list. It was only recently that she had begun writing again in the journal. Each morning or evening, whenever she could be alone, she would carefully tear open the seam in the pillow casing, make her few entries, and then carefully sew the book back into its hiding place. It was the only thing that she could hold completely, without the prying eyes of others, to herself. Patience had not yet asked her about the book. Her cousin was too preoccupied with her own fears about the coming labor pains to think on that which held for her no great worth.

Martha turned back a page and read the entry from the day before.

Monday, July 7th

Patience gave us a fright on the sabbath for in the meetinghouse, while we sang our hymn, she let out a great gasp and grabbed low at her belly. Ezra Black, the bandy-legged reaper, stepped forward to lift her up and gave hate-filled looks to Thomas and me, as though he would cinder our hair to ashes. We carried Patience from the pew but the pain passed away and by evening she was well and begging for sweet cream and calf's-foot jelly. As we had none, Thomas stooped for hours to pick mushrooms for her. For me, he has brought purslane.

Thomas had wordlessly upended the green and glistening clusters on the table to dry, their red stalks pointing up towards the ceiling. Like tiny advancing pikemen, she thought. She knew he had picked the purslane for her because she had said in passing that she hungered for it. She stuffed a few of the leaves raw into her mouth, savoring the stringent, almost bitter taste, and held the rest back for a stew for Patience.

Her cousin was becoming more and more knotted over with worry about the birthing, which Martha was certain was soon to come. The pregnant woman's ankles were swollen, as were her hands and the skin under her eyes. At least her appetite was good, the retching now all but gone. But there was still a disturbing lack of movement within Patience's belly, and she would often grab at Martha's hand and place it over the mounded flesh, pleading, "Martha, tell me you yet feel the flutterings."

This morning, before the sun grew too hot, Martha would go with Thomas to scrape enough slippery elm to make a poultice to ease the passage of the infant through the birth channel. She had wanted to go days earlier, but Thomas had put her off, saying it was not safe. He had for the past week been frequently gone, searching out the scarce game that hid from the heat, and had told her that between the pox and the Indian raids, life was of late never more the width of a blade's edge.

She closed the book and quickly stitched it back into her pillow. She then took up a short curved knife for peeling the elm branches and tucked it into her apron. Joanna had been sitting at the hearth, practicing writing her name in the ashes with a stick, the letters floating canted and disconnected like sprigs of rosemary in soup.

Martha bent down and kissed her head, the girl's hair smelling of acrid smoke and lavender, and admonished her, for her mother's sake, to be at least quiet if not good.

As she walked from the house, John grinned at her and

loudly sang, "Now is the month of Maying, when merry lads go playing…" She scowled, her face reddening, but secretly she was pleased, and John laughed and sang even louder, the words of the song following her across the yard.

Will waited outside with the stubborn pout she had come to know as the desperate disappointment of the man-child, forever being left behind when an adventure away from the settlement was under way. She waved to him as she and Thomas walked south, but Will stood, his arms crossed, his narrow hips thrust angrily forward, glowering at them until the view to the path was veiled by the branches of low-hanging trees.

They walked for a while, not talking, Thomas's pace deliberately slow for her benefit, but there were no glances, and when he didn't soon reach for her hand, she moved nearer. He stopped once and hunkered down, gesturing for her to do the same, and pointed into the shadows of the bracken. It took her a long time to see the deer, twin mottled shapes, their heads bowed in sleep over each other's backs, motionless except for the delicate, almost imperceptible motion of their ribs. He gripped the barrel of the flint, upright like a staff, but never moved to fire it.

They stood quietly and moved on, the building heat creating crescents of sweat under their arms. The birds stopped their morning rustling, settling into sporadic calls and answers, and Martha's hand brushed the carapace of a grass locust clinging, with serrated arms, to her skirt. She swept it away and looked once more at Thomas, his brooding face framed from behind by the powdery dust kicked up by his boots.

She became more discomfited by the silence, by his withdrawn, distracted air, and she burned to ask, *Are you Thomas Morgan?*

Instead, she pulled at his sleeve and said, "I thank you for the gifts." He stopped, his chin pointing towards the road in front of them. "Thomas...," she began. It was the first time she had uttered his name in his presence and she was suddenly desperately shy, as brittle and insubstantial as the locust she had flicked away into the grass.

He took her wrist and walked her to the side of the path where a small boulder was planted firmly into the earth and lifted her in one motion, setting her feet on the flattened edge of the rock so that her face was closer to his own. He swept off his hat, gripping her arms tightly as if to keep her from falling off a great height.

"Martha," he said. She waited for him to speak further, but he dropped his chin and looked away. She knotted the linen of his shirt in both her hands and tugged at the cloth until he looked at her again.

"There are things," he began, "which must be said."

"Nothing needs to be said now, except for those promises you are willing to give."

"No," he said, his hands tracking the distance of her arms, coming to rest over her fingers still gripping the front of his shirt.

Through her palms she could feel the rhythmic pulsing beneath his ribs, and imagined his heart as large as a waterwheel, churning his warming blood through the length of him. His breath expanded and contracted in moist waves around her face, and a half smile rimmed his lips. "The wolf skin would've been better suited to you than the doeskin."

"Is that how you see me?" she asked. "Like a wolf? Is that who

I am in your tale of Gelert? Am I the wolf?" Her face was defensive and half-fearful, like a child expecting punishment.

He leaned closer, bringing his lips to her ear, and asked solemnly, "D'you still not know?" She shook her head, and cupping the side of her face with his hand, he said, "You are the deer shot through with arrows whose heart grows cold for want of being taken."

He looked at her, his mouth solemn, and her eyes filled with tears. He held her, speaking to her in his own tongue, the guttural sounds fractured and sweet against her cheek. "Branwen," he called her, pulling off her cap to crimp the black hair in his hands. He whispered into her neck, first in Welsh and then in English, the tale of the myth-woman Branwen, with cheeks the color of raven's blood and the body of snow. He kissed her mouth, encircling the backs of her thighs with his arms, pressing her against him. Tracing upwards with his fingers the bony prominences of her spine, he rested his palms beneath the hollows of her arms and he slowly pulled her away. He lifted up her apron to show her she should wipe her face, streaked and glistening. He helped her by brushing the creases of her eyelids with his thumbs and smoothing back the knots of hair from her forehead.

"Sweetheart," he said, kissing the hollow of her throat.

By measures her tears dried, and after lifting her from the rock, he took her hand and led her to the grove where she set to work with her curve-bladed knife, gathering the sap from the slippery elm. The insides of the trunks were still soft, the hidden bark light-colored and strong-smelling, and she scraped at it vigorously, the sweat from her face burning her eyes like lye. After a time, she gathered the shavings into a small bag and watched

Thomas scanning the path and the woods for movement, his form grown restless and agitated.

After a while he said, "When you take up a man's name, you take on his history. I'm nigh on fifty years. D'ye know that?" She nodded for him to go on. "I've had a wife before. In England."

Her grip on the knife handle tightened, but she kept her eyes on the bark and the rhythmic scraping of the blade.

"She died when I was a soldier fightin' for Cromwell in Ireland. I were his man in all things, Martha, and you should know it before you tie yourself to me."

His eyes searched the length of the path from the opposite direction they had come, as though he expected someone to appear. She anxiously peered into the woods, looking for something hidden in the shadows, but saw nothing alarming. He glanced up at the sky, the sun at midpoint, and then, nodding, turned to her. "I'd tell you all, here and now, but for the others."

Others? she thought, wiping away a limp strand of hair with the back of her sleeve. She saw him look sharp to the road and she stood up, following the direction of his gaze. A man walked towards them, his arms swinging easily in counterpoint to his rapid stride. He was dressed in a leather jerkin and full breeches like any farmer, but with the confidence of a man used to certainty of action. Lacing her fingers around her eyes against the noon glare, she looked up at Thomas and with a jolt realized that he knew the man, that he had been waiting for him. As he walked nearer, she saw that the man was tall, only a head shorter than Thomas, with a few days' growth of heavy beard, as though he had been living hard on the ground. His footfalls made explosions of dust as his heels struck the path, and the long barrel of a flintlock, strapped with leather to his back, gleamed dully over one shoulder.

He came to stand in front of them, placing a familiar hand on Thomas's shoulder. There was nothing said between them, merely the nodding of heads in casual greeting.

"Here is my friend Robert Russell." There was weight in the word "friend," but Thomas offered nothing further.

Martha looked at the man, unsure how to place his name or face. He was a stranger to her; she had never heard Thomas speak of him before today. Robert regarded her closely, scrutinizing her face, and she wondered if her eyes were still red and swollen from weeping. She self-consciously wiped her slick palms on her apron and waited.

Suddenly he grinned, displaying an alarming array of strong white teeth, and said, "You look confounded, missus. But that is to be expected, as you know little of me, and I know so much of yourself."

His speech was not like Thomas's, but neither was it accented as it would have been with a whole life spent in the colonies. She crossed her arms and said, "I know nothing of you." Uncertainty had made the sound of her voice strident but, rather than taking offense, he smiled wider at her and cut a look to Thomas.

"That is why I am here, missus." Robert reached into a bag at his waist and pulled from it an apple, a perfect globe of pale red and green, and extended it out to her like an offering. "It is from General Gookin's orchard."

"I don't know General Gookin either," she said. She paused a moment before reaching out and taking the apple.

"Walk with me, then," he said, "and I will tell you." He gestured off the path, towards the stand of trees. Thomas took her arm and they walked the short distance to the shaded places. Standing, she propped her back against a slender trunk and held the apple briefly up to her nose, breathing in its rolling perfume, roselike and tart. She looked to Thomas for some guiding word, but he stood apart from her, staring down at his feet, lost in his own thoughts. She clasped her hands under her apron, tense and expectant, knowing that good news never would need such a courtship of words.

"General Gookin is known to both of us, Thomas and me, from the Great War. He fought like us for Parliament. He is now here, in the colonies, and has great tracts of land: orchards, fields, and men, of which I am but one. Thomas and I made the passage on a ship with the general." He paused and looked expectantly at her, as though he had run a great distance ahead and waited for her to follow.

Unaccountably, she remembered the instant of fear when the tinsmith blew out the candle, the blackness, the scrambling to find the lock. And the name he had given her when she crossed the threshold to leave. "*Prudent Mary,*" she said. "The ship on which you crossed over was the *Prudent Mary.*"

Robert dipped his head in assent.

"And there were others," she said, using Thomas's word. "Others who came with you, because to stay in England would bring… danger."

Robert laughed, throwing his head back. "That's putting it prettily, missus."

Thomas held up a cautioning hand and said, "Martha." When she looked into his face, she saw that he was afraid for her. "It was

General Gookin who found us shelter, and he watches over those who made the crossing with him, as best he can. All our fates are tied together. So one goes, the others may follow. I would not burden you with a name that'd mean prison, or death, if you didn't know the truth."

He moved in closer, grasping a branch above her head. "Robert an' me, we sleep with our backs to the wall. One loose word about any one of us, and some village newcomer, and all his grandchildren, would have coin enough to live like princes."

Her hands, hidden beneath the apron, squeezed tighter together, her nails piercing the skin of the apple. She turned her back to Robert so that Thomas alone would see her face, and asked, "Why could you not tell me this, Thomas? Do you not trust me?"

"It's not for lack of trust, Martha. It's our way. It's for our safe-keeping, and for yours. If I should be taken, Robert would do his best to protect you."

"You needed to see my face, and I yours," Robert said, pushing himself away from the tree where he had been leaning. "Though it is better truth to say I am more the advantaged by having seen yours."

Thomas led her back to the path and she followed him haltingly, her head filled with the knowledge, and half-knowledge, of his life before coming to Billerica; that he had had a wife and had fought across two countries with the Great Protector, Cromwell, now proclaimed a criminal throughout England and its colonies. Yet the one question she burned to ask had not been uttered.

Thomas waited for her in the sandy loam of the path, Robert at his side, the afternoon light filtering in columns through the dust of a midsummer's drought. They looked at her solemnly, waiting for her to step from the lip of the meadow's edge onto the road. If she turned away now, she could walk through Fitch's settlement, following Bent Stream all the way to the Taylors'. There she could take up the hoe and hack away at the vines overtaking the corn until she had worked herself through the choking runners, clearing neat channels of earth, row upon row upon row, in endless successions of soil and rock and sand, until she in turn was planted in the dirt.

Instead Martha asked, "Are you Thomas Morgan?"

There was the slightest pause, his hesitation not one of deception, but rather of a man careful in handing over a thing of staggering weight. She felt the falling away of fear and in its place flared the dreadful excitement of the battlefield harridan, the woman who follows after soldiers, hopeful of gain at the end of a desperate fight. In her mind there was a quick succession of images: the embattled waves of tramping men, the sounds of iron on leather, the trumpeting of dying horses and men. The poetry of blood.

And then he answered, "Aye."

Robert turned and walked the way he had come with no goodbyes until he had swept up the path twenty paces or so. Turning briefly, he called out, "I'll be about, missus. Rest easy on that."

Later, Martha would halve the apple, twisting it in her hands, and hand the largest part to Thomas, who ate it in two bites, skin and core, swallowing whole the bitter pips, the seeds that would always endure beyond the fruit's demise, the hard and reluctant carriers of secrets.

*　　*　　*

FOR DAYS AFTERWARDS Martha rarely spoke to Thomas yet often found ways of standing close to him, the air between them discouraging even the simplest intrusive demands of others. John laid off his teasing banter, quietly leaving the common room or barn whenever they were near. Patience, worried over the impending birth, stayed close to her bed, saying nothing to Martha about her solitary time spent with Thomas, giving out only a succession of peevish requests for food or to move her pillow this way or that.

On the eighteenth of July, the true pains of labor started for Patience. Her water broke in a thin stream while she was at the wash, and John was quickly sent in the wagon for Mary, who would help with the birthing. In a scrap of note, Martha wrote for her sister to bring black cohosh, as the cramping had begun sluggish and weak. She knew that Patience would never willingly take the cohosh — "squaw's root," the pregnant woman had dismissively called it — but Martha would sneak it into her broth if her cousin didn't have the strength to bear down through the final stages.

Patience, greatly relieved that the pains were so light, was full of high resolve and friendly chatter as Martha walked her about the yard, through the common room, around the bed. Patience speculated aloud when Daniel would return and what he might bring back for her. She questioned Martha endlessly about what name she should give the child if it should be another boy, dismissing every name Martha suggested, finally deciding on the name Daniel; if it should be a girl, she would name it Rebecca. Will, agitated by the sudden tension and nervous vulnerability of his mother, marched back and forth through the yard, a stick over his shoulder like a rifle, challenging hordes of invisible attackers. Wave after wave of invading bands were subdued, until he knocked

Joanna down, making her scream, and Martha used the stick on the back of his legs.

At four in the afternoon, Martha laid Patience down on the bed and examined the crown of the birth channel. The pains had begun to come more frequently, less than every half hour, but the crown was not opening sufficiently for the infant's head. The plug had not been completely dispelled and Martha was loath to puncture it as she had known other midwives to do. Often, it nicked the tender part of the babe's skull, or allowed a pustulance to start in the womb, causing fever and death. She decided to wait and heaved Patience up again to walk her around the garden once more.

For six hours the women walked and rested and walked again. Martha brought a pan of warm water and helped her cousin squat over it, her shift pulled up around her breasts, allowing the steam to open up the womb. Finally, close to midnight, the pains stopped altogether and Patience fell into an exhausted sleep. Martha lay down next to her, prodding Patience's belly gently with her fingers, but felt no answering kick; an hour later Martha closed her eyes and slept.

Martha dreamt of the wolves trapped in the pen and jerked into consciousness at hearing the high-pitched scream of a struggling animal. She woke to a blackened room, Patience writhing in agonized spasms next to her. Martha quickly rose, feeling her way to the hearth to light a few candles. When she returned to the bedroom with the guttering light, she saw a dark stain of liquid on the mattress, her cousin's face open-mouthed in the extremes of fear and pain.

"Patience, your water has fully come. This is good news, cousin. Hush now or you'll wake your children." Martha heard padding footfalls behind her and saw Will and Joanna standing, staring wide-eyed and frightened, at the bedroom door. Behind them loomed Thomas, his body in the helpless stance of useless men, and she waved him out of the house, into the barn. She led the children back to bed, giving them each a piece of bread to suck on, and quickly built up the fire, adjusting the iron pot to boil water. She shredded into the pot lavender and chamomile, and carried back into the bedroom the slippery elm paste covered in a wet cloth. She sat on the bed with a candle, positioning herself to examine Patience, satisfying herself that the womb was beginning to open, expelling the child.

Within a few hours, though, Martha was dismayed to see her cousin beginning to tire, unwilling to bear down with the cramping pains that left her scrambling up the wall behind the bed, her arms and legs flailing, as though she could leave her distended belly behind to do its own work.

With much coaxing, Martha roused her and set Patience on her lap in a chair. She encircled Patience's belly with her arms, pushing down whenever the pains came, whispering encouraging words over her cousin's frantic protests that she couldn't, wouldn't, bear down anymore.

Dawn had fully come before Martha heard John returning with the wagon. She rushed into the yard, anxious to greet her sister, but was dismayed to see Roger climbing from the wagon as well. His eyes were veined with red and he scowled, on the back end of being in his cups, and she knew he was the reason for the delay in her sister's arrival. Saying he had long been with a patient and needed sleep, he quickly found his way into the barn, and Martha hoped he would sleep through until Patience had been delivered.

Mary followed quickly into the bedroom and, with only the briefest of examinations, whispered for Martha to begin feeding Patience the cohosh. They dosed Patience every hour for three hours and Mary was soon satisfied that the roof of the womb was finally opening sufficiently for the head. With the birth pains coming every few minutes, Patience shrieked and cried, and Martha knew that she herself would be coming undone without the soothing presence of her sister. She watched Mary's assured movements, admiring her calm, but Patience's face had taken on the color of old ivory, with black bands underlying her swollen lower lids, and when Martha caught Mary's eye, she saw the press of wary concern on her sister's face.

Mary took up the slippery elm and applied it with gentle fingers into the birth channel, all the while encouraging Patience with how fine her son would be, how proud would be his father. Martha crawled onto the bed behind Patience, raising her up into a sitting position while Patience thrashed her head from side to side with increasing violence screaming, "No more, no more, no more…"

Mary said quietly, "Martha, we need to dose her again."

Patience went suddenly limp and still, a look of renewed panic growing on her face. Through cracked lips, she croaked, "What's that you say? What's that?" She looked first at Mary and then up at Martha bending over her shoulder, and whispered with rising hysteria, "You're poisoning me. You're killing me! Murder! Murder!" Her eyes rolled towards the door and she pleaded, "Help me, they're poisoning me!"

Martha followed Patience's gaze and she saw Roger standing at the door. He said, "Christ on the cross, but you can hear her out to the barn." He paused, regarding the women unsteadily, and offered, "She needs to be bled and heartily."

Patience reached out to him with grasping fingers and shrilled, "Yes, let him take it. Open my veins and take this pain from my head."

"Husband," Mary said quietly, "you are tired. Rest more and let us do our work."

He paused for a moment, assessing the pregnant woman on the bed, observing her pallor, her swollen limbs. He asked Martha, "How long has she labored?"

"Since yesterday morning late." Martha wiped at her cousin's face with a cool cloth, clenching her teeth. Roger's answer to everything—every bruise, every pustule, every boil—was to aggressively bleed the patient until the sufferer was as white as lambs' wool.

"She is phlegmatic...," he began.

Martha clapped her hands over her cousin's ears and snapped, "She is not phlegmatic, she is exhausted."

He shrugged, but before walking away, he said to Mary, "I have brought castor oil, if it comes to that."

Patience covered her face, sobbing into her hands, saying she would surely die, and Martha held her in a rocking embrace. Castor oil was tricky and vile; it was certain to bring on powerful labor, but too much of a surgeon's distillation, the castor beans having been soaked in the oil for months, and the laboring woman would indeed be poisoned. Mary put her ear to Patience's belly, listening for the sounds of life within, and when she raised her head, she said urgently to Martha, "Help me get her up."

It took the two of them to lift Patience out of bed and they

eased her down squatting onto the floor, both of them holding
her arms, pleading, exhorting, bullying Patience to push and push
and push again. After another few hours, Patience began a shuddering fever, her body lathered in sweat. When Patience began to
rave incoherently, she was eased back onto the bed with pillows
propped under her head. Beckoning for Martha to follow, Mary
walked into the common room. They found the men eating a
cold midday dinner of day-old porridge and meat, their faces
strained from the sounds of a woman's agony. The children sat on
a bench, their hands interlocked in terrified silence.

Mary beckoned to Roger and, when he stood in front her,
whispered, "She has no more strength left to labor. If the babe is
not pushed out of her womb very soon, they both will die."

He walked to his saddlebag and sorted through some bottles
until he pulled out a small brown vial. Lifting the stopper out, he
carefully poured a tiny measure of the syrupy oil into a cup of ale.
Pausing a moment, he added a drop more. Swirling the mixture
in the cup, he said, "She must drink it all at once."

"She'll not do it willingly," Martha warned, wondering how
they would pry open her cousin's jaws to swallow the oily drink.

Carrying the cup, Roger followed them back to the bedroom
where Patience lay panting, her hands gripping at the torn sheets,
her eyes fixed on the ceiling. Advising the two women to hold
Patience down, he leaned over the bed, saying, "You must swallow
this down, Goodwife Taylor. It will help you in your labors." He
said it pleasantly, matter-of-factly, but when she began to shake
her head wildly in refusal, clamping her lips more tightly together,
Roger reached out, pinching his fingers over her nose, and waited.
She soon gasped for air and he poured the liquid over her tongue,

quickly palming his hand over her mouth, forcing her to swallow or be drowned.

Before he left to resume his dinner, he gently stroked Patience's hair, cooing to her that all would be well, that the babe would now soon come. Patience smiled up at him and Martha marveled that for all of Roger's weaknesses, his passion for drink, his carelessness with his wife, he could at times show kindness. She admonished herself to have more charity where her brother-in-law's shortcomings were concerned.

The action of the oil worked quickly and within a few hours, Patience, howling and bucking, had been delivered of a boy, his forceful passage soaked in a spill of blood and water running in rivulets over the mattress onto the floor. While Mary worked to clean up the afterbirth, washing Patience with practiced hands while she slept, Martha swaddled the infant and held him close to her breast. He was the most perfect infant Martha had ever seen, each finger, every toe creased and rounded in rosy flesh, the nails crescented and silvery. His head was gently domed, neither flattened nor marred, despite the many long hours of the labor. She examined the infant skin, looking like cream and marigolds, stroking the cheeks, full and dimpled, the lashes still dark and segmented with the fluid from his mother's womb, the lashes that would never crimp or dampen with crying, the curved and protruding lips that would never part with laughing, for he had been born without a breath to waken him, and with never a breath he would be lowered into the ground.

CHAPTER 16

From the Private Journal of John Dixwell
Catalogue XXIII
New Haven, Connecticut, Anno 1673, 28th day of July

In primis: the following code, dated 19 July, was received this morning by courier from my agent in Boston and is hereby re-created from the original:

301227262227102225301627221 8

31213521152218103016143321111310112127233 4

3121192710181228131024192310112110131614342313

2722231927111611141024211323 2111

12183216132210121118102722303510311911181 3

The cipher translates as follows:

Parker expired. Followed pigeons north 4 days but no sightings. Returning Boston. Advise and replenish funds.

Faciendum: a courier should be sent to the constable in Boston with funds for the Boston agent in the amount of fifty shillings, to include remuneration for Mrs. Parker's burial, along with directives to friends in Woburn and Haverhill to observe and report, taking no tumultuous action against Brudloe and Cornwall, *pro tempore*. It may be our English pigeons have misled us about their going north up the coastal roads.

However, the courier from Boston has informed me that, as there is plague in Springfield, the post road towards Boston is now barred, as well as ships coming into Boston Harbor, to keep contagion and death from entering the city. My agent must make his way home from Boston as best he can, with no word soon from me. I fear the foul wind of sickness may have already settled in New Haven, as my wife has been downed with a troubling fever. I have bled her three times, but the fever rises with the hours.

Further to this difficulty there are Indian raids to the west. Seven people have been murdered, their bodies hacked into suet, at a settlement in Danbury thirty miles from here and we are left for only God to defend us, as our stores of powder have been neglected, our garrison only basely built.

It may be weeks before we can alert our Massachusetts friends who have for so many years lived in our care and under our watchful eye. It is for me only a little thing, sitting and watching and cawing like an alarming parrot, repeating and passing on those communications uttered by careless and odious Royalists—some of whom have meant to do harm, others who've merely loved the sounds of their own voices—when those I seek to warn have sacrificed so much for the sake of common good: they who have given up land, family, and the most modest of pleasures to keep on living; they who are now only a few and who have, from the first instant of the Struggle, done what others were not willing to do. And though I may count myself a part of that struggle, it is doubtless not so great a sacrifice having affixed my name, one name out of many, to a king's death writ, when others have taken up the mask, the rope, and the ax.

If any in our care are captured and brought back to England as traitors alive, here is what awaits them upon judgment from the king, this purveyor of ancient justices and charitable acts: they will be taken from their place of imprisonment, bound and dragged on hurdles, to the place of execution at Tyburn or Charing Cross. There they will be hanged by a short rope for only a little while, just shy of death. Then will they be cut down and dragged again to a long table where the executioners will saw off their privy parts and throw them to dogs to be eaten. A long cut will be made in the bellies of the newly hanged; the entrails spooled out slowly upon a rolling pin. *This in full sight of the sufferer* who screams in agony to a crowd of leering subjects fed by oranges and sweetmeats provided by the king's men. Each organ in turn will be pulled out and burned and, if the executioner is practiced and skilled, the dying man will not go to his end until he has smelled the charring of his own tender flesh.

I have lost close to a dozen confederates in just such a manner, myself escaping the noose of betrayal and capture solely by God's Grace and the advantage, at times, of only an hour's head start.

Those in our care have damned themselves to their native country, and have given up their own unfettered liberties for the right to go on breathing; a few even now hide in cellars and attics as though they were thieves. But a new country, and a new people, baking in the slow fire of brutish energy and stirred with the infant zealotry of practical idealism and independence, have claimed them.

In these late days, I am often reminded of the lament of Dante in his sublime *Paradiso,* who knew full well the torment of the exiled: *Tu lascerai ogne cosa diletta più caramente; e questo è quello strale che l'arco de lo essilio pria saetta.*

You shall leave everything you love most; this is the arrow that the bow of exile shoots first.

CHAPTER 17

MARTHA SAT ON the threshold, fanning her face with a dampened apron. The heat had become burdensome even at that early
hour, but there was an eastward breeze which would last until
midmorning, and she watched the men moving through the fields,
testing the grain heads with their fingers and teeth, preparing for
the summer harvest. She had come outside to escape the Reverend Hastings, who had been with Patience, still confined to her
bed weeks after the burial of her infant, praying for hours. His
visit had started gently enough with a passage from Romans: "If
God is for us, who can be against us?" But then he moved on to
the book of James and the sick, who should "call upon the elders
of the church night and day until evil is cast out." And finally, he
raked her over the coals of Deuteronomy, wherein "sinful, unrepentant men, women, and children perish and are cast into the
sulfurous pit."

Before the reverend had barely climbed off his cart for the
visit, he had taken Daniel solemnly aside and mouthed a few
words into his ear, no doubt, Martha thought, encouraging

Daniel to begin the plowing of his wife as soon as was seemly, giving her another babe to forget the one only recently lost. As John passed Martha on his way to the fields, he had murmured, "By God, I know lowland Presbyterians more cheerful than that one there."

Daniel had returned to them a week after the delivery and truly mourned for his dead son. But his concern now was for his wife, who lay in bed, refusing most times to eat or drink, ignoring the demands of her two living children. At night Will and Joanna kept close to Martha in bed, despite the suffocating heat, Will twirling strands of her hair around and around his fingers into ever-tightening coils.

Martha's concern was for the anger she saw in her cousin's eyes whenever she looked at her. It was not an open hostility, but the creeping kind of resentment that could, over time, build into a rage: blameful stares, sour words, implacable silences. Patience became especially agitated whenever Martha and Thomas stood close together, as though their happiness, guarded as it was, mocked the loss of the infant. Mary and Roger had waited to leave until after the burial, and it seemed to Martha that her cousin saved the greatest portion of blame for her.

Ten days following Daniel's return, Asa Rogers appeared at the door. Thomas and John had gone away hunting, and when the miller smiled tightly at her, his gray teeth showing through thin lips, Martha knew he had been waiting for an opportune time to resume his press for the land. He gave his condolences to Patience, sitting forlornly at the table, and briefly restated his case to Daniel.

"Goodman Taylor," Rogers began, smoothing the lines of his

jacket into order, "you are an honorable man to keep your promises. But I have it on good authority that the man who works for
you is in fact a criminal."

Daniel looked unhappily at Rogers, raking his hand through
his hair so that it stood spiked like a cock's comb. "Thomas has
ever been honest, hardworking. I have never heard word from any
man that he is other than what he shows himself to be."

"No doubt he is a workhorse, but from Salem there is rumor…"

"Rumors, aye, and spiteful gossip from the tinsmith." Martha
rose to stand behind her chair, her hands twisting forcefully at
the joints.

Daniel held up a quieting hand. "It is a harsh accusation to call
a man criminal, sir. What mean you by it?"

"That he is a regicide, sir." Rogers turned to Martha with
raised brows.

Daniel took a steadying breath, saying, "There is not a farmer
here in Billerica who does not have, by marriage or birth, family
that fought against the king. But the king in his grace has pardoned all, sir."

"All but those whose actions have directly brought about the
death of the first King Charles. I have heard such stories from
Ezra Black, who is of a prominent family here in Billerica."

"Stuff and nonsense," Martha said, her voice high and
querulous.

Rogers, looking to Daniel, asked, "Is it your custom to let a
servant question your judgment thus, or the opinions of others?"

Seeing Martha's reddening face, Daniel quickly added, "She is
my wife's cousin."

"How much are you offering to pay?" Patience suddenly asked. She had been sitting with a bent head as though drowsing, and Martha looked at her with astonishment.

Rogers oriented himself closer to Patience and said, "I'll pay two pounds now and another two in one year's time."

Martha sucked in her breath at such a sum; two pounds was an outrageous amount that could only be offered by a man expecting to receive a bounty from somewhere other than his professed trade as a miller. Daniel then stood and escorted Rogers to the door, saying, "I will think on it and give you my answer." Rogers left with a lingering, meaningful look at Patience, as though he would enlist her help, and when Martha glanced again at her cousin, she saw the same calculating look that had driven Patience to haggle with Thomas over the shared bounty of the wolves.

Martha stood at the door watching Asa Rogers ride away, his coat and collar stark and correct, black and white as a deacon's. But his assessing, avaricious glances at the Taylor barn and fields put her more in mind of a crow studying the latch of a corn crib. Her mother while midwiving, at the sight of a noisy flock, used to say, "One crow for sorrow, two for joy, three for a girl, and four for a boy." But the crow, as well as a prophesying bird, was also a ravaging thief, spiteful and destructive when thwarted.

When Thomas returned that evening, they sat together in the yard away from the prying eyes of the house. She told him of Asa Rogers's visit and his extravagant offer to buy the land. Thomas ducked his chin and chewed thoughtfully on a blade of grass but said nothing for a time. A woolly bear caterpillar, reddish brown, tipped with black, bristled past her feet and she watched its slow progress. It was the first one she had seen that summer and was surprised at its early emergence.

"We had such in England," Thomas said, as he prodded it with the toe of his boot, making it curl into a defensive ball. "But there we called it fox moth. He tells of an early winter."

Martha nodded, tenting her apron over her knees. "The winters in England cannot have been colder than this place." She turned her head, studying his profile and the downturned corners of his mouth.

"Aye, the winters here are cruel, to be sure. But the north of England…" He paused, looking up at the stars emerging from the east. "There is no greater cold than wind that blows south from the Scottish moors." He lay back on his elbows, tracking a streaking light crossing Polaris into the northern horizon. "One winter, durin' the war, the greatest river in Scotland froze hard enough for twenty thousand clansmen to cross over and fight with Parliament. They were the hardest men I've ever seen and yet near a quarter of them froze to death. I lived only by crawlin' inside the bodies of the horses I killed for food."

"Will we be taking up house in the milk cow, then?" she asked, meaning to make him smile, but he looked at her starkly, his eyes receding into shadow below the prominent ridge of his brow.

He reached across and, picking up her hand, worked it carefully between his two palms like clay. "Martha, I'm a hard one to put down. And you must know that if it comes to it, I will do what needs be done to protect those dear to me."

Martha had seen enough of his strength to know the truth of it. She had envisioned, at times in a kind of fever-dream, his abilities on a battlefield, and yet how long would brute force last against a warrant of arrest served by a party of constable's men? What hadn't been said between them was that, in marrying him, she put him at risk of being captured. She would dull his wits with her domesticity, with her belly full of child, and he for loving her would never desert her; of that she was sure.

If only all armed conflict could be decided instead by scything a field of timothy grass. Then, she thought, every townsman could return to a whole roof and a waist full of game pie, their champions lying over the windrows of wild weeds and thistles on summer-mown earth, not in tormented death but in comfortable exhaustion. But men, being what they are, could never take the excise of battle without tearing apart the land, pulling the sky and its curtain of stars in afterwards.

"Tell me," she said. "Tell me everything and then we'll bury Thomas Morgan so that Thomas Carrier can live."

CHAPTER 18

From Martha's Diary:
Begun Thursday, August 28th, 1673

These, then, are the words of Thomas Morgan Carrier,
known as the Welshman, who places in my hands through
faith and through trust the whole of his story; inscribed by
my hand alone through his remembrances. Committed in
secret from the eyes of men and the tongues of women and
hidden from the knowledge of the teller himself, I will
commence to make a true record of these happenings.

*I were born in Carmarthenshire during the cruel winter of sixteen
and twenty-six. My father while crossing a crook of the River Towy
heard the Hag of Warning, Goorach uh Hribun, shriek out from down
under the ice and snow, "My wife. Oh, my wife," and by this he
kenned that my mother, who labored even then to birth me, would die.
Runted and puny, I had no name until I were past four months old
and the ground could be dug up to bury my mother's body. The earth*

where I first placed my feet to walk was savage hard and rocky with scarce enough topsoil to fill the hand. But Father was canny and carried inland from the shores of Llandach sea sand mixed with lime and dung. From this he grew barley and oats for his sons and daughters, and fodder for his cows. We bartered our sheep and milk cattle in the lowland fairs for corn and wool culled from the beasts of Tremain. And the Welsh cotton my sisters made of it could have floated a man in the Cardigan Bay, so tight was it woven. The old house, or hendre as it is even now called, was small but cunning-built. And a harp sat in the window, though none of us could play it but our mother, for it was said that a Welshman without a harp had no soul.

The winters through we huddled nightly over the smoking peat and daily whipped the cattle against a frozen sleep. But when spring came, my brother and I would run to the southern pastures and rest in the hafod, the summerhouse of loose rock and thatch. There we would stay until the frosts came again, chasing the wolves from the calves and chasing each other through the hills above Llangadok. I grew to a man swallowing the dust from my brother's feet, for though I stood hands above him, I could never best him in a race. And so we lived our days until my brother died, his heart giving out at the end of a great race between Carmarthen and Kidwelly, a distance of ten miles and more. I was but fourteen, and into that graveyard furrow my keenness for life was also buried, dropping away like sunlight into a well.

I lived that winter through doing as my father willed until the March thaw, when he gave me a bundle of woolens to take to Swansea for tin. I walked two days and a night through fog and a tearing wind but didn't so much as raise my collar against the rain, so low was I. There is a legend in Cymry, which is what the Welsh call their land, of a monster called the Afang which likes the taste of flesh better than cake.

It lives in the bogs and lowlands, swallowing up man and cattle alike, and with the flesh, it devours the essence of its prey. So, too, it seemed to me, following down the River Truch to the sea, that to stay in my father's house would be my soul's end.

When the bale of woolens was boarded onto a merchant ship, I boarded with it, and paid for my passage with the woolens and with strokes of tar and sandstone upon the deck. The three-master was filled with coal and iron bound for Caernarvon and hugged the coast around St. David's Head to New Port and Cardigan, banking the Irish Sea. I slept every night upon the deck because the beams below could not contain my height. But the biting cold up top was nothing compared to the stench of rotting wool over the pale and wormy seamen resting in the holds below. For a day and a night we spied an Irish galley with thirty oars and a square-rigged sail. It was a shallow-draughted pirating ship out of Dublin only seventy sea miles westward and would have overtaken us had a gale not sprung up.

We rounded Badesey Isle in a storm that howled like the dogs of Hell with waves that breached the topmost timbers. Men were blown from the decks and floated like corks in a monstrous vat of ale. On the third day the skies parted and I saw like a crouching giant the gray walls of the Castle Caernarvon.

I made my first night's supper on the wharf, putting my back to unloading ships full of cargo: wheat and barley, woolens and hides, waiting to be shipped to England and beyond. There had never been the likes of this fortress, so I thought, with eight angled towers, thirty feet or higher, braced walls punched through with murder holes, gates, arrow loops, and spy corridors. To look upon it was to know the shame, and the pride, of being a Welshman — shame that an English fort sentineled our fairest port, pride that it had to be built so high and so stout to keep our great-grandsires from overrunning it again.

I made my bed in the shack of an old crippled seaman named Darius in a court off Newgate Street hard by the jail. For weeks I bent my back to loading off bales by the outer postern. I lifted those bales to my shoulders and walked like a mule up King's Head Street to High Street, day upon day. Mornings as I walked to the wharf, I carried the old lame man on my back to the western wall of the castle. At the foot of Eagle Tower he would sit, there to beg the day through.

The soldiers posted in the tower would greet us by calling down, "Look, there is Darius with his Black Dog." For idleness sake, they threw at us roots and stalks and once a bottle which cracked open my skull. Seeing the blood, Darius called up through his fist, "My Black Dog against any two of ye. A shillin' a throw-down, ye damnable whores. Tonight on Market Green."

By that evening I had lifted a quarter ton of iron and a hundredweight of wool from two ships and had walked six miles to a nearby town and back again. The king's men had gathered between the market sheds and the smithy shop when I came walking onto the green, Darius on my back. I placed him on the ground and turned to face them. There were eight gray-coated soldiers, but seeing me up close, they quickly sent for a bigger man. The man they found was near as tall as me, with the bulk of unkind livelihood, but he was spindle-shanked and angled poorly for hand-to-hand. He spit into his hands and made a run for me, grinning, showing the whites of his eyes. There was some grunting and circling about and I would have put him gently to ground, but for the knee he put in my groin. I broke his arm before I brought him to his knees and pounded his skull with my fists. The rest of the men backed off a ways and soon moved, grumbling, on to their suppers. One man stayed, a hardened corporal, a Welshman named Jones, who paid Darius his wager and led us to Green Gate Street for a pie and ale.

Laughing, Jones watched us eat like the starving men we were, and he said in Welsh, "You're a fierce dog, all right. Black Dog is a name the Englishers fear well. It's the stalking spirit of Newgate Prison, a dungeon in London dug deep into the ground and full of horrors. No light, swarming with vermin and other creeping things, the condemned lying like swine on the ground, howling and roaring. And when the Black Dog comes on paws of madness and despair, sweet death is welcome."

The corporal gave us more ale and recounted his memories of London. "It is the fairest of cities to those who have the mettle. It matters not whether you are Welsh, Cornish, or Scots. All are welcome. Even the damned Irish can find a motherly teat to feed their base and ugly natures. The city is like a great forge that takes in pig iron and puts out fine instruments of every kind, instruments of peace and war. It's a fire-filled, loud, boastful place. Hammers beating in one yard. Pots clinking in another. And tumbling bodies of water turned by wheels, rushing through the heart of it. Church bells clamoring at all hours. Wagon wheels beating the coppered streets into an alchemist's dream. Dogs and horses and men braying for dominance. The huzzas of soldiers out for a drink and a piss at all hours of the night.

"And the women, Great God in Heaven, man. The whores are like nothing you've ever seen. Not like these little kitchen morts here, girls who will lift their skirts for the smallest brass mirror. The doxies of London have great silken thighs and breasts to make a man cry for his ma. Even the Welsh milkmaids are game for a proper backwards toss. All a man needs is his infantry wage and voice enough to say, 'After you, my dear.'"

Jones walked with us along Castle Ditch Street to our nightly hovel, Darius falling to sleep as I carried him, snoring wetly against my back. When we approached King's Gate, Jones said, "Here I must leave you, Thomas. I have a mind to billet you into the fort so you can serve the king, and make me a handsome sum throwing to ground every last one of the Englisher bastards. But you are Welsh, as I am Welsh, and I would say to you as a friend — or as a father — might: walk, ride, or crawl from this place and get you to London. Live in this place and you'll die a wharf rat like Darius here, or lose your nose from the French disease got off some dock whore. The king takes into his own bodyguards able men of great height and strength, which, by God, you are such a one. Make yourself known. I will give you a packet for a captain that I've served with in the trained bands. He is Welsh and will be glad for another countryman."

He bade me good night and knocked heavily with his fist on the gate. When the night watch opened to him, he called out over his shoulder, "The world's gone all English, Thomas, and Welsh e'now is but a barley-bread tongue."

By midmorning the following day I had my letter from the corporal and some small coins pressed into my hand. It was in the first days of April when I left the city walls, and at the first mile marker, I peered back through the laggardly fog at the towers of Caernarvon and for a time felt myself to be at liberty.

Past thirty miles, I walked through the great castle of Conwy and then, in a needling shower, pushed my way into the vale of Clwyd. I worked from farm to farm, fallowing and herding, pressing on to the border lowlands in Denbighshire, where I lambed forty lambs for a great lordly house. But I burned to see London and so, not wanting to end my days in Wales, I passed beyond the fair pasturelands of Wales into England.

I made my way among the white chalk downs and gleaming hills of the Cotswold farmers and there my path crossed a brawny, pock-faced man, loaded with the hides of rabbit and lamb. He offered to show me the roads into London if I would stand his guard during the night. By noontide the third day we had traveled down Tyburn Street to the gallows, the westward portal to London.

The Tyburn gallows were three great posts joined topmost with stout beams. They rose up, tall and menacing, from the middle of the road, so that any cart or footman must pass around them. So large were they that three prison carts could have been backed into them at one time. There, dangling from the beams, were three bodies, freshly hanged: a man, a woman, and a boy. A few village women were yet gathering up their baskets of food, lingering long after the last of the struggling feet had stopped. Their children played in and out of the hanging posts, stuffing themselves with nuts and singing, "Hangman, hangman, one, two, three. Hangman, hangman, you can't catch me."

The hides trader took his leave of me at a crossroads and, pointing the way, told me how to find my way to King's Gate. But because I was threadbare, I was then kicked and beaten to the stables, and finally to the king's coal pits behind the Scottish Yard. Because of my size, I was set to loading and carrying coal for the cook fires hard by the Thames. Day upon day I corded wood and off-loaded barrels for the small-beer brewery. I slept crooked in a stairwell under the bake house and fought off wharf rats as great as bull mastiffs to keep what little bread I was thrown.

The bake woman was Welsh and a sharp-tongued gossip, and though she would hardly look at me, she found my silence a midden into which she dropped never-ceasing news of the day. London had become like a body with two heads that strained and tore at itself to go separate ways. One head was the common Parliament, led by fire-filled Puritans whose lay preachers had given themselves such names as Praise-God Barebones. These Puritans knocked down gilded altars, believing they were the stuff of idolatry, and resurrected in their place rude wooden tables for the communion bread. The other head was the king with his Catholic wife and archbishop, who would have every man in England read from a common prayer book of his own devise. The bake woman would spit into the fire and say hotly, "It won't be long now afore the king's wife will have us bakin' the blood of our newborns into the wafers for her mass."

On a morning in June at low tide, the damp stones stinking of the privy pits above, I was kicked awake by a river guard and told to go to the stables to help hang a door.

It was early yet, the fog not yet risen from the Scottish Yard, but at every lodge there were 'prentices and workmen standing in their doorways, waiting for me. And at every station the masons, porters, and smiths grinned and pointed, hiding their mouths behind their fists. Even the master of the beer cellar had roused himself from his bed. The porter's lodge at the outer wall discharged the porter's boy and two guards at a run as they followed me across Whitehall Road, and behind them came a full measure of workmen together in a tide.

To the west of Whitehall Street lay the horse-guard yard, flanked on three sides by the stable. Standing about the yard were six or seven of the king's mounted men in blue coats and breeches, and with them a slant-eyed fool who wore around his neck a riding halter. He was large but with a child's soft looks. One of the horse guards, seeing the crowd, walked towards me with a bridle and bit in one hand, and in the other a short whip.

With a great laugh he said to his fellows, "I'll raise my wager, now that I've seen the Welshman. Ten shillings my fool beats your fool."

He stopped within an arm's breadth and, holding up the bridle, said, "Come, my great dray, bend down your head and take this between your teeth. I swear to you the whip will but tickle your neck if you run apace. Win for me and I'll give you a shilling."

He cocked his head at me, his smile faltering when I didn't move. "Come, come. Take this bit and then give me your hand so I may straddle your back."

Dropping the bridle down to his waist, he gave a great sigh as though deeply burdened by my silence. He flicked the whip at my chest, bringing a welt. "Well," he said, "this one may need gelding." He lowered the whip to slash at my thigh and I grabbed his fingers, squeezing them until they popped. I lifted him up and hung him by his coat from a high hook on the stable wall. Two of his men, weighted down with sword and cuirass, rushed at me, and I put them to ground like stranded kettle fish.

Suddenly, a loud field-ready voice cried, "Hold, hold!" and a stout, middling man with a red-winded face strode into the yard, pulling 'prentices and guardsmen roughly about, and with a great waving of arms made the sentries raise up their pikes. The bluejay I had hung on the wall was rescued and the crowd was soon scattered to their posts.

"Now, then," threatened the stout man, standing on my toes. "What mean you to come and beat my men? I'm Llwewelyn, captain at arms, and I will have your head on a pike before you can finish a prayer. What say you?"

At hearing his good Welsh name I handed him the letter from Corporal Jones and waited while it was read. After a few surprised words, the captain embraced me as though I were a son truly lost and only just found, and I was that day taken into the king's guard.

I drilled with pike and musket that summer through. Fitted with gorget, breastplate, and helmet, carrying a pike twenty feet long, five feet

greater than other sentries, I made a fair impression upon the citizens of
Whitehall. Posted at the palace gates where the stream of traffic was
greatest, I wore a coat of scarlet with boots special-made to lift my
height above seven feet. Men, and not a few women, would come to
King's Gate of an evening to gawk at me.

One night I was placed with a Cornishman, himself seven feet tall,
on the stairs of the banqueting hall for the king's summer's-end feast.
There the Cornishman and I were paired at the north entrance flanking
the great ladies and lords that did pass through. Soon, before us stood the
king himself. A man of smallish stature, not above five and a half feet,
with sad eyes and a tripping tongue, he admired and examined us with
pride. His queen came behind and with her own hand tied upon our
breastplates two ribbons of red and gold. Afterwards, whenever the
king was to go to Whitehall, whether to banquet or bait or receive
men of great importance in his privy galleries, there stood the
Cornishman and I.

We sentried beneath ceilings painted of men and women naked as
newborns, flanked by hangings of silvered thread and carvings of
alabaster and gold. Our cuirasses and helmets were kept from
blackening by the king's own armory squires. Our matched pikes of the
finest ash were tied with the ribbons of favored court women who
traipsed about us like cats in a granary, winking and gesturing for our
notice, vying for a glance and a promising smile.

October brought open rebellion in Catholic Ireland, where it was
proclaimed that British settlers were cut down by the thousands.
Londoners came to call the slaughter the Queen's Rebellion, for it was
she they blamed for encouraging popery and open revolt. There was
bloody action in the streets and even into Westminster Hall from
citizens who feared the king himself was secretly a Catholic, bringing the

well-remembered horrors of the Inquisition back to Protestant England. The king's guards were called out to quiet the town and bring order again.

We broke dissent in Old St. Paul's Church, where Puritan zealots gathered to try to turn away gaudy merchants who had filled the church naves with their goods, using the very baptismal font as a money counter. We chased the riotous preachers from the cathedral into the courtyard, where booksellers sold their wares to every rogue with a coin, and took the good ministers in chains to the Tower. We routed gangs of marching outlaw 'prentices, seeking only charitable pay and a relief from endless taxes which the king's pleasures demanded, into the stinking alleys and public houses, where they sought shelter, and into houses where trap doors and ferret closets could hide a desperate man with a dirk or striking stick.

We raided the fomenting Cradle and Coffin Inn in St. Giles off Drury Lane, bastion of dissenters who wanted no hint of popery in their places of worship. And plucked deserting soldiers, sickened from the misuse of their own, from the Red Lion Inn over Fleet Ditch, and the Blood Bowl near Water Lane, where it was said a man a day was robbed and murdered.

In every public house and shop we searched, there followed offers of money and ale to turn away and look elsewhere. Our exemplar in this regard was the king himself, for he took bribes from every country in Europe to keep his armies from joining one royal dynasty over another. The money, for pride, I would not take when many of my fellows did; but a man will take drink when he is thirsty, and comfort when a welcoming cubby is made under a woman's skirts. It was a short step then from guard to garrison lout, and I made time in gaming, baiting, and cockfighting. There were fairs and shows in every street. Giant

women and dwarfish men were paraded on Fleet Street with baboons
and dancing dogs. At the Eagle and Child Inn a monstrous ox grown
nineteen hands high was shown for a coin.

There were ready fights to be had on any corner or crossroads, as
most men were frayed with the threat of street war. A cap cocked back or
a bitten thumb would bring bands of Catholics and Protestants together,
knives drawn and keen for butchering. The Parliament threatened to
impeach the queen for her Catholic ways. The queen in answer told the
king, "Go and pull those rogues out by the ears or never more see my
face." My post was moved to Commons that winter to keep the
Parliament men in mind of their king.

It was nigh on Christmas on a bright, cold day that I stood guard at
Commons, nursing a head from too much drink. The evening before had
been a pitiful show. An ancient bear, too old to fight, had been mauled
in the Southwark baiting pits by a pack of young hounds. Blinded and
matted with gore, the bear struggled to die on its hind feet but its owner
gave the prod to anyone who would beat it down again so the hounds
could better tear at its flesh. A terrible rumbling had taken up in my
ears to watch that bear shaming every man-jack of them with his
courage and his refusal to die on his back. The prod was in my hand
before I had given a thought to it, and I stripped the bear baiter's
backside to mincemeat before I was held down by ten of my fellows and
hastened from the ring. The roar was still in my head that morning as I
gazed out of blood-hazed eyes at a young woman, standing before our
sentries preaching.

She had come for weeks offering prayers for our blackened souls, and
because she was small and henlike, I had given her not a thought. She
was only one of many women who shouted or pleaded or spoke in
strange tongues of the sinfulness of the king and his men. Newgate

Prison had been flooded with these dour preaching shrills and they were of more sport to the courtiers that came to watch them rant than were the murderous scum waiting to be hanged. The guards posted with me soon made their own sport with her. Ripping the maiden's cap from her hair, they fondled her with their hands, yet she stood upon her little stool, speaking of love and fragrant sacrifices to God. All the while she gave no heed to the men molesting her but looked above their heads to the highest rafters as if to watch a brace of nesting doves. Believing in that moment that no merciful act goes without punishment afterwards, I batted away the men and told her to go home to her husband or father.

She reached out and, placing her palm upon my breastplate, said, "Is not my Father the same as yours?"

The weight of a guard's armor is over forty pounds. It can shield the flesh from jab of pike or disgorged ball from musket fire. Heavy mace and war hammer can break the bones beneath the metal, but it takes a timely, well-aimed thrust between the plates to pierce a man's vital innards. A pain began to sear my chest, as though burned with Greek fire, and for a time, I know not how long, I counted the gray-green channels in her eyes. There was no artifice about her, only her steady gaze which spoke to me like cannon shot that everything I had done, every journey, every effort, every path I had taken until that moment, was worthless.

A guard called out, laughing, "Watch yourself, Thomas. The girl's a witch."

I pulled her hand from my chest and told her roughly to go away or I would chain her and carry her to Newgate. She left that day but she was back again the next. And came every day after, preaching, not to my men, but solely to me.

It soured every pleasure. Alehouses, gaming dens, baiting pits, they were all the same. And truth be told, it had all come to smell of rot. A whore though she washes herself in scented water still stinks of her daily trade. My eyes were now open to good men put in chains, tortured, and hanged. Men who desired only a chance to die in bed and not in a war in some foreign place. Men who wanted to pray without the shadow of bishops peering over them, coming between their souls and God. Men who asked the Court to give them better rights than the dogs that were fed at the king's table. Nights I dreamt of the baited bear and the hounds, and though I kept my eyes from her, I came by measure to listen to the girl with the gray-green eyes.

The winds filled with ice, and though we had a coal barrel at the sentry, she would not share our warmth and chose instead to shiver alone inside her thin woolen cloak. Her words passed through blue, quivering lips, but the weaker her body, the stronger her voice. Odds were laid for when she would fall off and die of the frost, but the men did not impede her and took to calling her Lady Dampen. Her eyes followed my coming and going until I felt them like chainmail around my neck. But her voice was a kind of harp that vibrated in time to my blood. I had seen the faces of dying men in prisons and streets, and in the face of my brother, Richard. And for every one of them, brave, mad, or bad, a corner of fear lived in every eye. But in her eyes there was none; only a certainty of which she spoke.

Once she fainted and I carried her to cover, wrapping her in my cloak. I asked for her name, which she gave in sounds like waves over sand: Palestine. She clasped my hand to her face and said, "This world will soon be swept away."

On a January morn, the king rode to the House of Commons to demand the surrender of five Parliament men who had given him quarrel. His birds had flown, though, and empty-handed he returned to Whitehall Palace, pursued by mobs of screeching women and men, threatening to pull him from his coach. He sent out his royal guards with lance and flintlock to compose the people, but we were pelted with rocks and chairs. Barricades were built and chains pulled across streets and byways to hinder our progress. We were a few hundred against six thousand Londoners made drunk upon the newly born idea that a country can rule itself without the shadow of a crown, and on that day the word "liberty" was on every tongue. The king soon left London, the queen making haste for Holland.

I was ordered to march with the king north to Cambridge. Along the way we passed bands of men lining the roads, calling out to us, "Brothers, come join us! Leave the tyrant behind and become a new citizen." And for the first time, for many of the soldiers in the ranks, it mattered not that we were Welsh, or Irish, or Cornish; it mattered only that we were men who could make our own destinies without the consent of a king. Until that time, a man's only country was that expanse of wilderness large enough to encompass his own clan, his own family profit. But there, on those dirt pathways, just as Palestine had prophesied, were the makers of a unified homeland, a whole England.

The king traveled to the port of Hull, where the gates of the city were locked against us. The royal troops then packed up and went to York, where we encamped until the spring. We were then closer to the borders of Scotland than to London, and with every mile, with every rough conscription, dragging a son or husband from his home or thieving food from poor yeomen, I became more and more resolved to leave the king's ranks. I could not eat or sleep or take a step without the best part of myself rebelling against the base acts of a titled few.

A few good lords, attending the king at York, begged him to come to terms with Parliament. It was there I first saw Lord Fairfax, officer of the field and greatly admired by all the men for his strength and wit in a fight. He addressed the king directly, saying that if he did not work with Commons, a bloody civil war would surely follow. The king gave him his back, and Fairfax, a fiery man for all his good honor, addressed the royal troops, calling them to serve in glory the people of England. And so I, being sixteen and of age to serve in Parliament's army, laid down my pike of ash with all its brightly colored, foolish ribbons and made my way back to London. My friend, the tall Cornishman who had stood next to me at the banqueting hall, stayed with the king, and when next I saw him, it was across a field of battle. He would die at the siege of Basing House, a cannonball his final pillow.

I married Palestine Ross in the last days of June and together we made ready for war. We set up in small rooms off Fetter Lane, close to the chapel where her father preached and where I went to be baptized into faith. The gathering storm was there in that temple and in chapels all through London. The pulpit words were little fires that scorched the hearts of all who listened. And like upright brands, with our heads aflame, we carried the light to anyone who would listen. Those who did not, we put aside in Newgate Prison. At night before sleep, my wife sang psalms and encircled me with gentle arms.

I worked for months in a carpenter's pit, planing timber for Parliament's navy until my arms outgrew my coat. In late summer I took leave of my wife. Giving her what coins I had, I left with Parliament's troops under the command of Lords Fairfield and Essex. Their orders from Commons: to rescue the king from himself.

We were a ragged, out-of-step band of thousands, 'prentices, tradesmen, and untested soldiers. But in two months' time we were drilled and marched and preached into good order. A new pike was given to me, and I learned the facings, doublings, and wheelings of field battle, all the while chanting, "How great be my God."

I fought first at Edgehill at October's end and killed my first Welshman, who, knowing me for a countryman, died cursing me to Hell. His words, spoken in Welsh, worked like acid until I imagined I wore his curses like pagan markings on my naked skin. Then came the killing of Cornishmen, Lancashiremen, Cheshiremen, and again more Welshmen, in countless, endless numbers, and I learned the torment of being known as a traitor to my own country. In overwhelming numbers the Welsh fought for the king, for the royal house of Tudor first took root in the harsh and spirited soil of Wales, and its men would not be severed from their pride except through the biting edge of a sword.

Battles were won and lost and won again. Men less base than I died drowning in their blood while merciless plunderers lived and gained in fortune. For every man that joined the fight, three would creep away under cover of night to far-flung counties. Soldiers gambled on the sly and kept time with the baggage whores that posed as washerwomen. Order slipped from the ranks like water down a chain.

In May of sixteen and forty-three we joined with a cavalry troop at Winceby and broke the Royalists' ranks, taking eight hundred of the king's men. Chief among our cavalry leaders was a tall, wiry man who charged his group of horsemen as though it were one body. His clothes, ill-fitting and coarse, hid limbs of hammered iron. So tight was his discipline that his men were taxed twelve pence for swearing and put in stocks for drinking. And for raping a woman, though she be the Whore of Babylon, hanging with a short rope. His voice, sharp and piercing, carried a mile or more across the battlefield, and it became the tuning gauge to all our rallying cries. His name was Oliver Cromwell.

One black evening, on a night with no moon, I huddled under my cloak as I ate my supper of bread and meat, both gone green with age. A man came out of the darkness and asked if he could share my fire. I knew his voice at once to be Cromwell's and I gladly made room for him next to the warmth of the flames. I had heard his voice earlier as he went from soldier to soldier, stoking courage, giving solace, offering prayer. He was one of the few officers to ever do so and was greatly loved for it. We spoke of humble things: our homes, our wives, the pleasures of a man's work far from the battlefield.

He asked me my age and if my father yet lived, a question for which I, sadly, had no answer. After a time, he rose to go but stood for a moment within the circle of light. He gestured out towards the many campfires filling the surrounding field in the thousands and said, "I know well the horrors of killing a countryman. Prayer and steady fasting give some comfort and yet will only serve to temper the pain. Your agony, which shows clearly on your face, gives the true measure and worth of your conscience."

He nodded and gripped my shoulder fondly for an instant, as he might have done for one of his own family, and said, "Somewhere out there is my own son just your age, Thomas. I would not ask another man's child to risk death and not my own." He walked away, and I pondered on how many Royalists' sons had paid other men, poor and untitled, to fight their battles; and it came to me in that moment that I would have followed Cromwell into the sea if he had asked.

Cromwell's name, and leadership, soon became the banner for victories, and in June of 'forty-five his cavalry joined our infantry for the battle at Naseby, which brought thirteen thousand of our men against seven thousand of the king's. We faced one another across a dry valley of heath, the sky a blue bowl above us. A strong northwest wind rattled the banners and trappings behind us. I was placed on the front line of pike hard by the right flank of Cromwell's men. I could see Cromwell on his mount, his face filled with a savage joy. He was singing psalms and once even laughed. His darting eyes found me, and saluting me, he cried out, "Have you said your prayers, Thomas, for yourself, as well as for your enemies?"

I nodded, proud that he addressed me directly in front of the troops. His horse reared, nervous for battle, and bringing the horse to heel, he exhorted me, saying, "Never forget that God calls those he loves most to do that which is most hard. I remember it always, as should you."

He spurred his horse about as the king's nephew Prince Rupert began the charge and engaged the battle. And though the prince broke our lines first, Cromwell did win the day, capturing three thousand prisoners, most of them Welsh. Within a fortnight they would be paraded in the streets of London, hanged, or jailed. But I was no longer a Welshman; I was of no country anymore but that which embraced Cromwell.

The general had seen my way with a pike at Edgehill, piercing a horse and rider together like a spitted cod, so he elevated me to corporal, enlisting me into his New Model Army. Through town and countryside he fought, taking bread and praying with his common troops. He would always make time especially for me, giving me words of encouragement and, when needed, correction. Once he gave me, with his own hand, a prayer book which I carried under my breastplate, its weight like a shield over my heart.

His was the spirit borne up by the Holy Word after which we followed, like magpies upon the red-tailed hawk. Any Protestant man who had fought for the king but desired to pledge for Parliament was welcomed as a brother, regardless of birth. Those that were popish bred were reformed, or swept to dust.

*We fought until the king was captured and brought to Commons as
a betrayer to his own people. Even from his prison, Charles Stuart
plotted with every foreign land, Catholic or Protestant, taking money,
arms, and men to win back his throne. He went to his trial believing he
had never done wrong, regretting only that he had not first hanged the
dissenters and queried them afterwards. The king was tried as any
common man and sentenced to death, Cromwell's name writ largest
upon the warrant.*

*In sixteen forty-nine, in the biting winter of January, scaffolding
began to rise before the banqueting hall like the shell of a great beast. A
master builder had been paid two shillings a day to build the stage from
which the king's head would fall. Ropes had been hammered into the
planks to tie him down should he resist. The high executioner swore he
would never ply his trade on a neck that had carried a crown, and
the crowds became sullen waiting for Commons to begin killing the
Stuarts.*

*In the blue dawn of January 26th, I was called by Cromwell to
Westminster Palace. I was led through a dark warren of rooms and
found the general alone on his knees, praying. Seeing me, he rose and
gestured for me to come nearer. There was only one candle in the
chamber, but I could see the breath curl from his lips like gray mist from
a northern sea. The man had been at prayer, yet there was no aspect of
Godly play about his face, merely the steady glint of eyes that had long
gazed upon a lock and had only just discovered the key.*

*He studied me from the shadows before saying, "Thomas, I can see
you've greatly changed from the boy who shared his campfire with me. You
have the look about you now of a resolute man."*

I nodded to him that this was so.

"And your wife?" he asked. "She fares well?"

"Aye," I answered, remembering that Cromwell's own beloved wife had been gravely ill for a time.

"It is said," he began but paused, as though considering something of gravity. "It has been brought to me that she speaks openly of her doubts that Charles Stuart should be put to death." His eyes were downcast, his words carefully chosen, but I had no doubt of his fearsome attention in waiting for my answer. For the first time in the years of serving him during the war, through all the battles won and lost, through all the trials and intrigues that placed him as the man destined to rule the new England, I felt the prickling of dread, not for myself, but for Palestine.

I said, "My wife, as ever, keeps with our cause. She is free to reveal her mind, I believe, as we now have no fear of tyrants. Is that not so?"

He stepped nearer so I could see the measure of his gaze boring into me. He asked, "Do you upon your life love your country?"

I answered him that I did.

He moved closer still and asked, "Do you have love for me as well?" Again I answered him, yes.

There was a rustling sound as he gathered his cloak tighter about his shoulders. The room became an empty cave for the beat of twenty and then he asked sharply, "What is it in the field of battle that is both threat and remedy?"

"A man's sword," I answered.

"Yes, a man's sword. Men are like swords, Thomas. We are all instruments of God. Remember you, before the battle at Naseby, I spoke that God will love him best that takes the hardest path?"

A shallow morning light had slipped into the room and with it a kind of creeping disquiet, draping over my head like a cowl. I remembered well what he had told me before the battle. He had said God would call those he loved most to do that which is most hard. Cromwell, who had beaten a royal army through the iron of his will, leading mountains of men to their oblivion, had chosen the hardest path. But he had come to believe that God would love him all the more for it and follow after him, like Cromwell's own legions of troops, spreading glory to the earthly victories along the way.

His face, now lit from the strengthening sun, was quiet, but in his eyes was a question of faith, like the gaze of Abraham upon his son as he wielded the knife over the burning altar, ever willing to make fragrant sacrifices to the Lord. He dismissed me from his presence and I thought then that he had only wanted from me a renewed pledge of loyalty.

In the winter of 'forty-nine, the great hall of Westminster was the place of judgment for Charles Stuart. A man like any other, he walked before his judges wearing no crown and carrying only a silver-headed cane. Fifty judges found him guilty of setting his countrymen to bloody civil war. He was proclaimed a tyrant and sentenced to death.

The king's prison was St. James Palace, where I had been sent as guard with others loyal to Cromwell. Smaller than Whitehall and close to the hall of judgment, it could be better armed with fewer men; and better spied-upon, for the king had once before been spirited away by Royalists, and he never gave up hope for ransom or escape. It was the weakness of the man that he could not see that his great adversary was not of the Royalist cloth: Cromwell could not be bribed or bullied.

I had been placed on the outer parapets as sentry. But on a cold and windy day I was placed directly outside the Stuart's chamber. I stood guard with a man I did not know but who had proven himself at the battle at Naseby. His name was Robert Russell.

We followed our prisoner at every waking hour: at his prayers, at his rounds through the gardens, at his meals, where we stood hard by and counted every knife afterwards. It was at my dawn council with

Cromwell that I was told I would accompany the Stuart king on his final walk to Whitehall.

The few days before he was to die, Charles Stuart accepted his fate and kissed his children good-bye. Once, rising from his prayer altar, he stumbled, and I caught his arm. He thanked me and, straightening his vest, said, "I have known you before, Corporal." He looked me up and down and, gesturing to my sleeve, said, "You were my royal bodyguard once. The coat you wear is the same crimson as before, and yet it comes to me that the lining has changed." He raised one eyebrow, his lips curling. "Yes, yes, the lining is quite changed."

At midnight before the morning of the execution, I was awakened from my sleep by a colonel of the guard and brought, with Robert Russell, to an outer courtyard. There waiting were three other men, soldiers of Cromwell's New Model Army. We drew our cloaks against the blistering cold and followed without a torch to a far door, bolted from the inside. Upon a knock it was opened, and we were led down into the bottommost part of the castle. We gathered in a vaulted room where tapers had been lit, and the colonel left us to stand awhile. Soon two men, cloaked and hooded, came into the chamber and I could see in an instant that the taller man was Cromwell. The smaller man was his son-in-law and fellow soldier, Henry Ireton.

Cromwell swept off his hood, saying, "Every man among you has been tested and found steadfast: in zeal, in loyalty, in courage and godliness. But there is not one man here that does not have blood on his hands. Not even myself. We have fought together, friends, and God has found us worthy. There is but a single obstacle to a final victory, and that is the death of one man." He paused, holding up a finger. "One man who at his death on the morrow will give us the liberty we seek."

The finger, held upright, wavered and in turn pointed to each of us. "But who will be the liberator? Who will be the one who frees us from the tyrant? By God, I would do it myself but for the people saying it would be to crown myself king."

Motioning to Ireton, Cromwell took from his son-in-law a set of small wooden stakes. "Let God decide, then. We will choose in lots as the Testament prophets did. The first to draw the short lot will be headsman."

There was a heavy silence in the room as each man waited to take his turn. Each one of us had in recent days been counseled alone by Cromwell, asked by him if we loved God and England. We had only to look in Cromwell's eyes in the torchlight of that chamber to know that to be loved by him in return was to be forfeit to his cause. The first man reached out with shaking hands to take up a stake, and came up long. And so did the next man, and the next. It was down to Robert and myself, and when Robert reached for the two remaining pieces, he came up short. His face knotted, first in surprise and then in terror. He had killed his share of common Englishmen in battle, but to kill an anointed king was to pull the sun down from the sky, leaving a void for anarchy, bloodshed, and damnation to fill.

Cromwell turned to me, holding the last piece, and waited silently for me to reach out and take it. He clasped my arms in his two hands and said, "I had prayed that it would be you, Thomas. I have often dreamt it so." And with that I offered myself to be Robert's second on the killing platform, and thus it was decided who would wield the ax.

We were sworn to silence and returned to our beds, where we waited for first light. For hours I heard the ragged, labored breathing of Robert Russell as he readied himself to be both the savior and villain of all England, and thus the world. At dawn we were led to Whitehall and secreted in a closet off the banqueting hall, waiting for the time of execution. Charles Stuart was brought to the hall in the morning but could not be taken to the block as Parliament was meeting urgently for a bill banning kingship forevermore. They had only just remembered that after killing the present king, his son could one day seek the crown for his own. It was two of the clock before the king stepped, with his chaplain at his side, before the thousands gathered to watch.

Robert and I donned masks, but the Stuart knew at the instant who we were. And he knew, as Robert stood nearer to the block, that it would be he who would deliver the blow. The king bore himself with steady dignity, wearing two shirts together so he would not shiver and be thought a coward. He spoke to those gathered, citizens and soldiers of London, some words of defiance. Unrepentant in his sovereignty, he said, "I go from a corruptible crown to an incorruptible one." He turned to Robert and asked calmly, "How will I tie back my hair?" His locks, though quite gray, were long to his shoulders and he did not want the headsman to miss the mark.

The moment stretched into the wretched silence of waiting death; the crowds remained hushed and expectant. In all of the dreadful hours before dawn, the terrible imaginings of the execution, Robert never believed that the king would turn and, with studied grace, speak directly to him. I stepped forward and said quietly, "Sir, you must tuck it into your cap." He nodded and did as I directed. Then he turned to face the mob and prayed awhile with his chaplain. When he had finished, Colonel Hacker, the man who had summoned us to Cromwell, motioned for the prisoner to approach the block. Again the Stuart paused and, turning to me, asked, "Can the block be set no higher? I would kneel at the block and not be made to lie down upon the boards."

For all his self-possession, there comes a time when the presence of the void looms too great and a quaking begins in the limbs. I said, "Sir, we have no time. It cannot be made higher."

He nodded and lay prone upon the boards as one would lie down for a long sleep. Robert had not yet pulled the ax from its hiding place, but I could see its blade winking beneath the straw. There was no quick movement from him then as there should have been to pick up the ax; no setting of the feet in readiness to hoist the heavy shaft, bringing the blade down neat and true. A gentle moaning came from the man on the block and a pleading whisper. "For pity's sake. Do it now, do it now."

But Robert, filled with the immensity of the act he was about to do, had turned to standing stone. And so I pulled the ax swiftly from the straw and within five steps was beside the block. For pity's sake, and for pity's sake alone, did I, in one rapid movement, draw back, bringing down the ax with a clean and heavy stroke. And, with no accompanying words of the rights of men or the rule of governments or of wars won and lost, the head that had ruled as king fell from its body and lay staining the harsh and glistening boards beneath our feet.

CHAPTER 19

HAMMETT CORNWALL LEANED against the rock and closed his eyes. He was tired and content to sit awhile, letting the old woman do her work beside him. The long illness and the weeks following, traveling through the unsettled nowheres, had sapped his vital spirits. At the outset, he had had profound reservations about killing the landlady; she had ever been kind and, if not for her bustling care, he was sure both he and Brudloe would have ended as fodder for maggots. But the necessities of clandestine travel had supported it, and he had mostly forgotten her since departing Boston.

The biggest worry plaguing him was that, at some point in the past few weeks, lost and trampling through endless thickets, he had also lost his voice, as though all the puking and retching, first on the ship and then in the sickbed, had stripped him of the instrument of speech. He'd known a man once who'd had his throat cut and lived, but forever after, the man could not utter so much as a word, not even a whisper. The man'd had to gesture and point, like the idiot cabin boy on the ship. The thought of the black time on the ship made his breathing labored, and the old woman made placating noises. He couldn't understand her words, but the tone seemed to say, "Soon, soon."

It wasn't that he didn't want to speak. At first he'd found the infirmity taxing in the extreme; but, try as he might, he couldn't seem to talk. Brudloe had believed it was belligerence that kept him silent, and had berated him and hounded him until he had shown Brudloe his fist, and the smaller man was then quiet. But now the silence had come to be comforting to Cornwall. He was sick unto death of all their straightforward plans unraveling, their repeated blundering into uncertain circumstances. Now, at least for a brief time, there were no expectations, no bothersome queries and laborious decisions to be made; only walking in companionable silence.

Because of their weakened condition, he and Brudloe had briefly considered taking horses when they fled Boston but, being street-bred, and he being so large for even a plow horse, they set out to Salem on foot as originally planned. They had met their contact in Salem and, after a few days' time, were given a map and pointed towards Billerica to take their man, outfitted with flintlock, powder, tethers, and a butchering ax.

It was on the way to Billerica that they had come upon the Indian. Through a stand of tightly cross-grown birch trees they saw a figure of a man standing stock-still. His shirt and leggings were the color of bark, his black hair blending into the shadows. Only a gentle trembling of the leaves in front of his face betrayed his living presence. If he, Cornwall, had not approached the edge of the path, loosening his breeches to take a piss, he never would have seen the savage face-on. He stood astonished, his mouth open, his prick in his hand, staring at the motionless figure as though a tree fairy had appeared. Unable to speak, Cornwall waved his hands in circles at his side, as though swimming through a heavy tide.

By the time Brudloe had seen the man himself, the Indian had drawn his club, bringing it with full force onto Cornwall's jaw. He was knocked down but remained conscious, able to witness Brudloe's panicked misfire of the flintlock and the club smashing against Brudloe's skull, knocking him also to the ground. The Indian had moved, not so much with speed as with an economy of motion that made Cornwall, with all his size, almost envious.

Ululating screams erupted out of sight, and the undergrowth disgorged a dozen more forest men, each carrying a club and knife. The men stood over Cornwall, kicking him, flicking him with their knives, shattering one wrist as he buried himself defensively behind his arms. He could see Brudloe, his head profusely bleeding, thrashing wildly about. Brudloe managed to reach his own knife and, pulling it from its scabbard, viciously slashed at the jabbing limbs surrounding him. He connected with the muscle and bone of a warrior not agile enough to leap out of the way until he was bludgeoned senseless. Brudloe was then lifted and dragged into the brush, and Cornwall felt a noose being fitted around his own neck and tightened until his hands were securely bound with a leather strap. He was herded off the path and dragged a few hundred yards into a clearing.

Cornwall was thrown down next to Brudloe, the noose around his neck tightened still more, so that his breath wheezed through his throat. The warriors hunkered down, examining the flintlocks, hefting the weight of the ax, ignoring their captives as they spoke quietly in their own tongue. Cornwall looked at Brudloe, a blackened knot rising up over one temple, uncertain he was still alive until he saw Brudloe's chest heaving beneath his shirt. Cornwall brought his bound hands up to his chin, gently feeling inside his mouth. Several bottom teeth were loose and they fell, like kernels of corn, into his gently probing fingers. His jaw was cracked, perhaps in several places, and he knew when the shock wore off, there would be pain. His wrist was badly broken, but at least there were no bones showing through the skin.

The Indians seemed content to wait until Brudloe began to stir, moaning and cursing. As soon as he had regained his wits, both he and Cornwall were heaved up and, prodded and kicked, forced along through the woods heading north, following no discernible path. The pace, rapid and unrelenting, brought them across hilly, rough-scrabble terrain strewn with boulders and choked with bracken and dense fern. After a few hours of stumbling progress, Cornwall decided that there was no fixed route to their forced march; rather, their captors were taking, in a crisscrossing, arbitrary fashion, sudden directional changes, as a flock of wary, migrating starlings would do.

They came to a stream, and Cornwall was pushed facedown into the water, which he took to mean that he was to drink. As his hands were tied in front, he could cup the water and take his fill, whereas Brudloe, his hands tied behind, had to lap up water like a dog. They were kicked to the other side of the stream, and Brudloe started up a steady, low cursing that continued angrily for hours until dark, when they stopped to make camp. They were thrown a biscuit each, but Brudloe's demands and gestures to be untied went unheeded, and he had to rely on Cornwall to feed him like an infant. Cornwall then broke apart tiny pieces of the hardened biscuit, which he shoved through swollen lips, dissolving them on his tongue to be swallowed with his spit. The warrior that Brudloe had slashed with his knife sustained a deep gash in his leg, and when he peeled off his blood-soaked leggings, the wound hung open and fleshy on his thigh, like the mouth of a corpse. In good humor, with no grimacing or spectacle, he packed the gaping wound full of leaves, which he took from a bag tied at his waist. Taking up a bone needle and a hair plucked from his own head, he commenced to sew up the ragged flesh. The Indians made no fire that night, nor any night, until they had traveled, to Cornwall's reckoning, a week in a general northwesterly fashion.

The pain of his injuries was terrible, especially at night. But in the daylight hours the rhythm of the ceaseless walking and the studied quiet of their captors, uttering only what sounded to be abrupt, cautionary warnings, brought a kind of settled acceptance to Cornwall's mind. Apart from their initial thrashing, the Indians had not mistreated them, feeding them little, but no less than they themselves ate. After a few days, Brudloe was retied, with his hands to the front, but he was also leashed with a noose like Cornwall's that tightened at the slightest bit of resistance from him. The only burden to Cornwall's sense of ease was Brudloe's ceaseless scheming and raving about escape and how he would murder each one of the "fuckin' black whoresons of Satan." But the astonishing thing, at least to Cornwall, was that the Indians were not black, as he had long believed; they were a golden color, lithe and oiled, their skin flexing over sinewy muscles like eels over rocks. They were in stature small, but as with the fabled cairn people from his own native country, they did not so much travel *on* the land as *through* it, their feet leaving no mortal tracks in the mud to speak of their passing.

Cornwall had heard about Indians from the New World. He had even paid a penny to see one exhibited in the Tower in London a week before he and Blood had robbed the king's jewels. The specimen was dead and stuffed like a partridge, of course, but he looked nothing like the men who walked with resourceful vitality through the forest in front of him day after day. The preserved figure, propped up in a dark, squalid cell, was as short as a child, with opaque blackish-gray skin and a broadened nose with thick lips. The figure was naked except for some rings of brass around its ankles and arms, and its eyes were sewn shut with coarse thread. Their Indian captors spent their time, while not walking, grooming themselves and one another, painting their skin with ocher and red clay, braiding shells and feathers into their forelocks, plucking out or scraping off with an oyster shell the rest of the hair on their heads. He would have considered it womanish if not for the grave, ritual-like manner in their ablutions.

After the first week, small groups would veer off into the bracken, returning hours later with the carcass of a deer or smaller animal. Then the evening fires would be built, spitting cuts of flesh and bone with branches to cook over the flames. The captives were given their portions, and when Cornwall could not chew with his shattered jaw, he thought he would go mad with the desire to gnash the charred flesh between his remaining teeth. One of the warriors squatted down next to him, handing him bits of meat he had first chewed to a soft pulp. Without reservation, Cornwall gratefully accepted the meat, sucking on the juices before swallowing each piece.

Brudloe, grimacing distastefully, muttered, "How can you feed off 'im like that? You'll be wormy in a month."

After another week they came upon a village of conical dwellings made of shingled wood and animal skins, with clustered gardens of corn and beans. They were met and escorted by a guard of young warriors, whooping in triumph as he and Brudloe were led to the largest dwelling. Their fiery escort made Cornwall almost exuberant, and he could not help but smile at the old women and children who walked next to him, examining his clothes and skin as though he were a prized stallion. Brudloe took exception to the handling and kicked out and spat at the people when they came too close.

The young women were exceptionally comely to Cornwall's eye, with the same fluid skin as their brothers', their breasts partially bare, high and mounded, dotted with dark brown nipples. To his dismay, he found himself becoming aroused, and the women good-naturedly mocked and teased him for it when his member tented the front of his breeches.

A man wrapped in a mantle of bleached deerskins stepped from the dwelling and stood blinking at the captives. He had the face of an Old Testament prophet and was supported on both sides by two young women perhaps not past their girlhoods. When the prophet's eyes came to rest on Cornwall, the Londoner grinned, wanting to reach out and touch the leathery skin, exploring with his fingers the striated shells and bones fringing the ancient man's cloak. Cornwall looked around at the glistening, naked children, the old women with their gentle probing hands, even at the warriors painted and poised like exotic birds, and he thought, Fairies. They're like fairies.

The old man shuffled closer to Cornwall and said something clipped and guttural. He gestured towards one of the warriors, who brought him a pipe. The pipe was lit and the old man puffed smoke at Cornwall's shoulders, at his face, his feet and groin, until the smoke had gathered around him like a garment. Cornwall grinned wider, breathing in the acrid, woody scent, laughing in delighted expectation. It was the first sound he had made in weeks and he looked into Brudloe's eyes, expecting to see a mirror to his own mirth. But Cornwall saw in Brudloe's face an expression beyond alarm, something closer to panic.

They were soon led to a small hut, fed and watered, their neck nooses slipped free. And though they were still tethered by their wrists, they were able to move freely about the village. Day by day they watched the gathering in of more warriors, bringing their own women and children, carrying baskets or freshly killed game, and Cornwall anticipated a festival or feast of some sort. Despite Brudloe's ceaseless hissing plots for escape, at times throughout the night — "You hold the guard, I'll slit his throat" and so on — Cornwall had no great desire to leave.

As the days passed, they were allowed to watch the warriors' games: nets on sticks which hurled a ball of rawhide back and forth to opposing teams, and even a kind of dicing with carved bones painted in colors. Once, Brudloe's bonds were cut, and to his great surprise, he was given a knife. He stood staring at the weapon until he realized he was to fight a group of young warriors who called and pointed to him encouragingly to take his ground. When he didn't fight, the blade was simply taken from him without a struggle, and the warriors instead admired the scars on Brudloe's head and face. They later led him to a clearing and painted his forehead and shaved the bristle on his scalp, leaving a patch for a topknot to grow.

When evening came, they were separated, Brudloe taken into the larger dwelling, where the prophet lived, and Cornwall propped up against a large boulder, his restraints tightened. He was brought meat, which the old woman chewed for him like the warrior had done, gently placing the pap on his tongue with her fingers. Even though her eyes were black and slanted over high, angled cheekbones, she put him in mind of his mother. She once grinned at him, her teeth worn down and mulish-looking, and so he closed his eyes, content to rest while she sat with him, whittling pine branches to sharp points.

The people continued to gather, the women bringing wood for the communal fire, piling it close to Cornwall's feet. They addressed him solemnly in a language that sounded to him like the gentle rattling together of beads, and he nodded to them, grateful for their care and for sharing their feast.

The night sky was clear and he watched the stars emerge randomly, untidily. He followed the thread-thin path of a comet racing towards the North Star. His bindings began to chafe his wrists and he shifted uncomfortably. There were smaller fires burning, dotted around the village, and the people began to sing, chanting and beating their feet on the ground, already packed solid with the movement of generations. Soon, he imagined, they would release his bonds and bring him into the large hut as they had done Brudloe, scraping his scalp clean, stripping away the filthy, louse-ridden rags he had worn since getting off the ship in Boston, letting him inhale the perfumed smoke of the long pipe the prophet had waved before his face.

He thought he caught a glimpse of Brudloe standing in the riptide of dancing bodies, his painted face underlit by firelight, but the transformation was so complete, Cornwall couldn't be sure it was he. The chanting had taken on a new urgency, with cries and mimicry of wild woodland things: the leap of stags, the frilled threatening shuffle of badgers. Cornwall shifted restlessly, bringing his arms up to show the old woman he was ready to be cut loose and join the feast. A group of women had joined her, their faces expectant, close to feral as they lit the kindling at Cornwall's feet. He was taken again by their beauty, the sharp angles of their faces shining like mica freshly planed. He suddenly remembered as a young man seeing, on a raised stage in London, a rendering of a fairy folk tale. The fairy queen had been bewitched and fell to lusting after a man with the head of an ass. He remembered how he had howled with the absurdity of it, his laughter carried up with the voices of the other watchers to the uppermost tiers. He guffawed out loud with the memory of it. "Fairies," he said, surprised and elated to hear the sound of his own voice again. "Fairies," he said again and again, repeating the word with increasing desperation as the villagers first pierced his flesh with the pine shafts and then set them on fire, so that like a living flame he ran the gauntlet of warriors wielding clubs; and then with terror as they pushed him into the charred kindling, until he had burned beyond the ability to speak.

CHAPTER 20

MARTHA RESTED IN the yard, its sparse grasses bleached in the sun to jackstraws, with Joanna in her lap. They played with a porcupine that John had fashioned from a pinecone, its eyes and nose made of dried currants. Will had taken it from his sister earlier, taunting her and stripping some of the quills from its back, until Martha had rescued it, giving him a bruising pinch on the arm for his cruelty. Joanna had cried for a while until John came and made faces at her, bringing a smile. He had been digging out a Dutch cellar for the apples and roots they would soon be harvesting, and he came to sit next to Martha in the shade, brushing away the autumn flies with his hat, mopping at the sweat on his neck with the tail of his shirt.

Although the days were still warm, the nights were suddenly turning cooler and Martha had felt of late an earthly gathering in, a compacting together of living things; animals burrowing deeper within their nests at night, fish lying weighted and sluggish in the streambeds and shallow ponds. Even the clouds ran low and stuttering in their early-morning progress, as though seeking warmth from the ground.

Martha watched John's expressive mouth, downturned and moody, gently refusing Joanna's entreaties to recite some silly fragment of song. A pall of worry had settled into his reddish highland face, making him look drawn and sickly. He had, in fact, over the most recent days come to look as miserable as she'd ever seen him, and she wondered if his unhappiness sprang not only from worry over Asa Rogers's suit for the land but also from her own deepening closeness to Thomas.

It came to her in that moment that she didn't know how John happened to be with Thomas. She knew he was not related by blood, and, besides his youth, his actions, quick-witted and foolish at times, were at odds with Thomas's sober and deliberate nature. With ever greater frequency, she had heard John's worried questioning of Thomas about the miller, seeking reassurance that Daniel, if not Patience, would keep to his bargain about the land promised to them. John could not have failed to hear the arguments between husband and wife after they had retired to bed. The entire household could hear Patience's low beseeching tone turn first sour and then loudly demanding as Daniel reasoned with her to put aside her expectations of profiting from another's loss.

In the mornings, Patience would sulk and be cross until Daniel made much of her, telling her what next he would bring from Boston. Patience had always been desirous of comfort, Martha knew, but grief had turned her venal. Her behavior had put all of them on edge, and Martha had begun to feel the pricking of thorny resentment at her cousin's avarice. If Thomas had resentments or worries, he kept them close-handed and hidden; but even he had become more reticent and silent, as though he had been hollowed out from the long, clandestine telling of his former life as a soldier in England. His eyes at all times, though, followed Patience like a man walking in deep brush, tracking the progress of an adder.

Martha shifted Joanna more comfortably on her lap and regarded the distracted frown on John's face. "Your father, does he yet live?" she asked.

"No. My own father's long gone. He died durin' the war."

"How, then, do you come to be with Thomas?"

John smiled sadly. "I was made orphan when my father was killed at Naseby, so I have no memories of him. They were great friends, though, Thomas and he, after Thomas saved his life at Edgehill." He took an apple out of a pouch at his waist and began to peel the skin away in one long curl. "'Twas Thomas who sent a share of his soldier's wage to my kin so we wouldn't starve. I found my way to him in London when I came of age an' crossed on the boat with him to the colonies." He dangled the curling skin in front of Joanna, making it dance. "He has been both father and friend to me."

Placing a hand over his arm, she said quietly, "I know about Thomas. He has told me all." She had spoken softly, almost to a whisper, but John looked at her sharply, suddenly wary. He quickly handed the skinless apple to Joanna, gently dislodging her from Martha's lap. He pointed to the trench he had been digging and said, "There are more in the straw, Joanna. How many do ye think ye can hold in yer apron?"

She skipped away and he watched her sorting through the straw at the lip of the shallow depression, gathering up hardened knobs of fruit.

He turned to Martha and said, "There are men coming."

She looked at him without understanding. The skin under the constellation of brownish flecks across his face had gone pale, his mouth constricted and dry. He cast a searching glance towards the house and whispered, "Two men, Englishers, came through Salem lookin' for Thomas. That was weeks ago."

The skin on her scalp pulled tight, like a drawstring on a sack. "What do you mean, 'men'?"

John breathed out and carefully grasped her wrist. She looked down at the hand and realized he thought she would bolt away in fright. He said, "Murderers, bully boys, paid by the Crown to bring back the traitors. They're not colonists, of that we're sure. The news has come to us from sympathetic men."

Throughout the days and weeks that Thomas had recited to her his story, reeling out history in parceled bits, furtively and in hushed tones, Martha had never spoken aloud the word "traitor," but it lay in the back of her mind like a canker. It had caused her to lie in bed at night, trembling, images of slaughter and mayhem forbidding sleep until she had daylight enough to commit his words into the diary, the quill across the paper helping to empty her head of terrifying thoughts. But then night would come again, and the scraping of branches on the roof became the beetling movement of the little wooden stake in Thomas's great oaken chest, awakened through her touch.

"The thing is, missus, these men, they've gone to ground."

"Gone to ground," she echoed. She anxiously scanned the

surrounding woods, realizing that both John and Thomas had known of these bounty men for weeks. "Perhaps they are lost, or have turned back."

"Or are biding their time," said John. He had been holding on to her wrist and let go only when Martha looked with alarm at his fingers tightening painfully on her skin.

"How will they come at us?" she asked, panic rising to a hard knot in her throat.

"If they're still alive? By stealth. By surprise."

They turned for a moment to watch Joanna, who had been joined by Will. The boy stood listlessly by, watching his sister piling apples into her apron. Behind him in the distance, Thomas had stepped out of the barn for a breath of air. The sun at his back, Thomas's every feature was erased into blackened silhouette, his stance deceptively calm. His head swiveled in a practiced arc, easily scanning the surrounding forests and fields; but Martha knew that Thomas's peculiar stillness was anything but passivity. It was a marshaling of strength towards some pending skirmish.

Will had come to her, peevishly burrowing his head in her lap. "My head hurts," he said, his hands cupped around his ears.

"It's all of your meanness, Will, blocked in your skull." His hair spiked up in dampened clumps and she gave one a playful tug, running her hand absently over the taut curves of his face. She felt the scorching skin on his cheek and quickly she pulled him up to face her. He was flushed crimson, his bottom eyelids pooling with fever tears, and even as she held him, she felt through his shirt the onset of shuddering chills. Martha could hear behind her shoulder the intake of breath and the muttered oath as John saw for himself the sickness in Will's face. Martha grabbed him up and ran for the house, forgetting for the moment the bounty men and any fear beyond death in the form of a spreading pox.

It took three days for the rash to blossom, first appearing on Will's tongue in white sloughing pustules, his fever continuing to rise until he lay alternately sweating and freezing within the blankets twisted between his thrashing legs. The men were sent to live in the barn, their meals carried out from the house along with the news of how the boy fared. Joanna was taken by John to the Toothakers, the child to be kept until the contagion had past.

The women hourly bathed Will's face with cool cloths, forcing him to swallow spoonfuls of water or broth even as he vomited into a bucket at his side. By the fourth day he lay still, his eyes sunken into their sockets, shallowly breathing, so that Martha was forced to stoop again and again to feel his feathered breath on a finger.

Patience had been calm through the beginning crisis, and Martha was grateful that her cousin had rallied her full attention to her son, lovingly holding him as they changed his shirt or replaced fouled linen for clean. But as Will responded less to their commands to drink or eat or roll over, a hysterical note began to creep into Patience's voice. On the evening of the fourth day, Patience burst into tears and, gathering Will into her arms, rocked him roughly while pleading, "Will, be a good boy now. Will, do you hear me? You must get up now. You must get up."

Martha, as gently as she could, pried her fingers from around the boy and laid him back down on the bed. It was the bed that

Daniel had brought to Patience upon their marriage, and Martha knew it would never be shared by Patience and her husband again. If they survived, it would be burned along with the quilt soaked through with Will's fever sweats.

On the morning of the fifth day, Will seemed to rally, his fever and chills subsiding. He opened his eyes, asking for bread, and cried plaintively when he was told he could have only broth. He watched the women moving about the room with glittering eyes, too weak to move, except to swallow the spoonfuls of liquid poured into his mouth. By noon his fever had spiked again, his breathing increasingly labored, and when his mother, sitting at the edge of the bed, bent down to comfort him, he whispered, "I want Martha."

Martha had been standing at the foot of the bed, but before moving towards him, she instinctively looked to her cousin. A stiffening had begun the length of Patience's spine, a lowering of the head, a tightening of the shoulders. Patience, without turning around, said to Martha, "Please get more water." The words were spoken quietly, but rage filled the space like a sickroom smell, and Martha quickly left to fill another basin with water.

She paused briefly at the front door and saw that Thomas had begun an agitated pacing in the yard. Seeing her, he paused, searching her face for some sense of resolution. She shook her head once and turned away, returning to the bedroom door, where Patience was waiting for her.

Martha came up short, the basin slopping water onto the floor, taking in the furied, twitching muscles on her cousin's jaw, the corded muscles at her throat. Patience had placed one hand on the door frame, the other on the door itself, barring Martha's entry back into the bedroom. Patience tried once to speak, her lips trembling with emotion, and, after a shuddering breath, demanded, "Why are my children dying?" She stared defiantly at Martha, then closed and latched the door.

Will succumbed during the night. Martha knew the exact moment of death, even as she sat at the common room table, locked out of the sickroom. Patience had begun a low, muffled moaning, as though she had buried her face in the bedclothes, repeating "no, no, no," over and over. Her voice soon rose in pitch to a shrill keening that went on until Daniel, driven from the barn by her screaming, threatened to take the door off its frame. When Patience unlatched the door, she collapsed at his feet, and Martha staggered to her own bed. She thought sleep would come, exhausted as she was, but she found the porcupine on the pillow that Joanna had left behind, the toy that Will had so gleefully tried to dismantle, and she wept, tearing at her pillow.

At dawn, wrapped in a quilt, Will was taken for burial. Daniel drove the wagon, Patience walking behind him like a penitent. She would not look at Martha and angrily pulled away when Martha reached out to touch her shoulder. After the wagon had pulled out of sight, Martha stood gazing at the pale crimped clouds and the arrow-shaped flock of birds surging south, like the wake from the prow of a great ship, and felt a desire to settle into the ground, resting there for the whole of winter, blanketed by the weight of snow. For the first time in days, fearful thoughts of the bounty men surged in her head, mixing with her grief like a noxious poison.

As she stood in the yard, she felt Thomas's presence, and before his arms could enfold her, she had begun an open-mouthed, anguished sobbing, threads of saliva mixing with tears on her chin. She had shed tears the night before, the bereft and insistent weeping of loss. Now was the futile cry of the wet nurse, breasts still swollen and leaking milk, who had tended and night-watched the dead child of her heart; the wail of the stepmother, the caretaker, whose own cries must not be heard above the din of the helpless parents.

He took her arm and led her stumbling and blind onto the path to the river. They climbed slowly up and over the embankment, their clothes soaked with the heavy dew on leaves of ferns clotting the rise, until Thomas finally settled her on the fronds at the water's edge. They sat close together and for a while Martha wiped at her face with her apron, soon wet through with her tears, and followed aimlessly the course of eddies and shallow pools not yet filled with autumn rains.

"I told you I had a wife in England," Thomas began. He had turned to face her, bringing his arm tentatively around her shoulder. "But I had a son as well. He died along with his mother."

She looked at him, surprised, astonished, and yet she wondered why she had never considered it before. He had been married for years, why would he not have had a child? But the news in that moment had also made her feel defeated and added to her sense of loss. She turned her head, biting her lip, afraid of sobbing uncontrollably again. He lowered his arm and she saw that she had wounded him with her moving away. She drew herself closer, sliding her arms tightly around his ribs, burying her head against his chest. She breathed in the smells of musk and old wood fires and folded her legs next to the long bones of his thighs.

After a while he spoke, and listening to his words within the concavity of his chest was, to Martha, like hearing a mine shaft closing in on itself.

"I had fought for seven years as a soldier for Cromwell, killing my own countrymen; killing a man who had been king. I thought I'd seen every base thing a man could do to another. But in this I was wrong. I was sent by Cromwell to Ireland to help crush the Catholic rebels. Those that threw down their weapons were murdered along with the ones who refused to surrender. The resisting were burned alive in their churches; priests spitted like spring lambs in the marketplace, women raped while lying over the bodies of their children, babes dashed to the stones."

She stirred against his ribs as though in protest but he quieted her, shushing her like an infant, and went on.

"I was sent out to a settlement hard by a town called Drogheda to clear out the miserable hovels there. Not even proper houses but caves dug into hillsides covered over with daub and thatch. From the last hovel a man, wearing no more than a linen shift and felt-tied boots, reared himself from his nest, slashing at my arm with an old clannish dirk. I'd never seen a man so wild in his attack. I killed the man but kept to this day his dirk to remember that a man is most savage when fighting for his home.

"It was then I heard a child's wail coming from inside the cavern. There was no door, but a sheep's hide covering it. I crawled into a chamber, smoked and reeking of death, and spied a small boy, no more than four years old, clinging to the body of his mother. She had cut her own throat rather than be taken by us.

"I have seen harried deer with less fright than was there in that boy's eyes. I sheathed my sword and held out my hand to him. He bared his teeth at me, for he had been told by the Irish priests that the English would eat him. The boy believed I'd tear the flesh from his bones for my supper, and he took the knife with his mother's blood still warm on it, and brandished it at me.

"For an hour or more I spoke to him, of cattle and fields and harvesting grain. And even though I did not speak his Irish tongue, my own good Welsh is drawn from the same well. I told him of my brother, gone from the earth. I told him of my own son just his age, and after a time he crept towards me and fell onto the bread I had offered. When I left the hovel, he followed after.

"From that day forward I thought I was done with killing, and when my wound grew rank and would not close, I was mustered out and sailed for England with others whose limbs could not fester, for they had been hacked off, by Irish rebels or English surgeons. I did not learn of my family's death till I returned to London. They had been dead near three months."

He paused, inhaling deeply as though the air had thinned, settling his chin more heavily on the crown of her head. His fingers dug into her, and she held her own breath, willing herself not to flinch under his hands so that he would go on.

"My wife, Palestine…" His voice thickened for a moment. "My wife died for a man named Lilburne, leader of the Leveller cause, put in the Tower for preaching the rights of men. Petitioning for his release, she challenged Cromwell himself in front of the Hall of Commons. She caught his cloak, calling him to task for killing the king and jailing people of goodwill. Can you imagine it? A man who was like a king himself, called to task by a girl. There was not a man living who dared put hands on the Protector, but my wife dared. By Christ she did." A brief exhalation of air, coarser than a laugh and more prideful, passed through his lips. She felt a lightning stab of something close to jealousy but willed it gone before he could feel it through the crown of her head like a fever.

"It was Cromwell's men who jailed them, taking my wife and son to the Tower. The bastards had waited till I was shipped for Ireland. They meant only to frighten her, to stop her from calling Cromwell to task for becoming a tyrant himself, but the Black Dog had come breathing contagion, and she and the boy died in the filth of their cell."

She tried to push herself away out of the hollow of his arms so that she could see his face, but he held her tightly to his chest. Her forehead rested against his neck and she could feel the working tendons and muscles of his throat constricting, his jaw hinging wordlessly up and down, up and down, as though testing the air for further grief. She reached up and felt the slick of tears in the hollow of his cheek. Placing the flat of her palm over one eye, she gently stroked with her fingers the place where the scar on his brow lay, and waited for him to speak.

"I broke the back of the jailer who had locked my family away, and spent a month in Newgate Prison. From my cell, I heard the outcry of men and women, confined and tortured, attesting to the thing Cromwell had become: a man of treachery who schemed to claim kingship in all but name.

"The Protector himself paid for my release, but I took off the red coat of my rank then and put it in a wooden chest. The Irish dirk, the wooden stake that committed me to being an executioner, and even a parchment note written in Cromwell's own hand were all put away from the prying eyes of men. I took up shop on Fetter Lane as an ironsmith and never again saw the living Cromwell."

He pulled away, encircling her face with his two hands, tracing with his thumbs the swollen lids beneath her eyes. She met his gaze reluctantly, thinking of the time she had plundered the great oaken chest. But she now had a history for everything inside it: the faded red coat, the curious dirk, and the rolled parchment, within which the little wooden stake had been wrapped. She shivered, suddenly cold.

He said, "I yet think on my son as he could have been, were he to have lived. He was tall for a boy and had his mother's love for music. But he is gone from me forever, and though I grieve for him, I cannot wish myself to be in that place where he is. Not yet, not yet." He clasped the back of her neck and brought his forehead to rest against hers. "Children may die, Martha, as will we all. No one knows when that end-time may be. But for this day, we live. So bide with me. Bide with me and take from me what you can, as I will from you. And however long it is that we walk this earth, we can stand for one another and leave off grieving until one of us is gone. I'll not ask you to be mine, for you were mine at the moment my eyes opened to you, fuming and roaring into the mouth of a wolf. I will never seek to blunt the fury in you, never, and will honor your will as my own. What say you? Can you be a soldier's wife?"

She looked at him wonderingly and at length, remembering other women's acquiescence to an awkward suitor's prologue to marriage: girlish smiles and laughter following some artless boy's long-limbed shuffling and shy proposals. In all her imaginings of a sober and practical union, the breeding of children, and the

laboring drudgery of a woman's sphere, she had never dared hope
for the promise of this; that a man would take her knowingly for
all her mannish, off-putting certitudes and canny will, her prickly
refusals to adhere to womanly scrapings, her ferocious and ill-
tempered nature. But how could it be other? To be a soldier's wife
would suit her well.

She kissed him in answer, pressing her body for a while into
his, and, after a time, he gathered her up and led her home.

IT WAS THREE days afterwards that Patience found the red
diary.

Martha had been finishing the hem of her cloak made from
the English woolen for which she had traded the piglets at market, the blue-green cloth that Thomas had said was the color of
the Irish Sea before a storm. She gathered it into folds around her
neck, placing Thomas's antler clasp first at one shoulder, and
then the other, before moving to the small bedroom window to
better see her work. It had stormed earlier in the day, but the rain
had slackened and turned to a rolling fog, settling into dells like
ponds of lambs' wool. She caught herself humming a snatch of
song before remembering the words: *The song of winter becomes like
sleep and drowns the air with a gentle roar; and limbs like fingers grasp the fruit,
into which time doth pour.*

The tune was mournful—it made her think of the inevitabil-
ity, the nearness, of death—but she stopped her humming, guilty
that Patience might have overheard her. Patience had barely spoken to her since Will, placed in a small coffin hastily provided by
a neighboring carpenter, was laid into the ground. Martha had

spent most of her time while indoors confined to her room, sewing or furtively writing in the diary, at times overcome with tears for the boy. Blessedly, no one else in the family had become ill, and John would soon be sent to bring back Joanna.

Earlier, she had heard the unmistakable sounds of an argument between Patience and Daniel coming from the common room. There were suppressed, passionate exchanges punctuated by the sounds of her cousin's angry weeping, and Martha had waited until silence had returned, making her think that Daniel had led her cousin into their bedroom. Placing the cloak aside on the bed, she walked into the common room to build up the fire for the noon meal. She was startled to see Patience standing behind a chair, her fingers tightly gripping the ladder back, and in the chair in front of her sat Daniel, holding in his hands a red leather-bound book.

There was a moment of confusion when Martha simply stared, wondering that there should be a twin to her own singular journal. But Daniel's face was stricken with something beyond grief. A crimped mask of fear had compressed his lips into two white slashes, and he asked, "Is this your doing?"

"Patience gave it me," she answered quickly. "The book is for the house accounts." She heard from her cousin an ugly exhalation of air, and when Martha met her eyes, a prickling band of sweat sprang up around her neck.

"I will ask you again, Martha, is this your doing?" He anxiously palmed the stubble at his chin, and Martha frantically searched his face, trying to gauge the depth of his knowledge. How far beyond the beginning entries, the notations of supplies and homely expenditures, had he read of a regicide's life?

"It was given to me by your wife, Daniel. It is mine." Martha dropped her chin, clenching her hands together. "I thought my property to be inviolable."

"Your property. *Your* property." Patience rapped fiercely on the back of the chair, making Daniel wince. "Everything in this house by rights is ours. The food you eat, the bed you shared with our children. The cloth that came from the sale of *our* pigs…" She stopped for a moment, collecting herself. "I went to lie down on my son's bed and found that… *accounting* book sewn into your pillow, next to where my own child laid his head. In truth it is an accounting book, but not such a one that is to our prosperity. Indeed, I think it is to our ruin."

More than the pity Martha felt for her cousin in that moment—the thought of Patience trying desperately to breathe in the remaining scent of a dead child impressed onto a pillow—she awakened to an overarching terror that she had, through her own playing at secrets, betrayed Thomas.

She met Daniel's gaze and held out her hand to receive back the book. He looked away from her, gripping the book's binding tighter, turning it end over end in his hands. He said, "You will leave today for your father's house until such time as I have reflected on this. I will keep the book and you will not return until—"

"She will *not* return to this house, and as for the Welshman—" Patience began.

"Silence!" Daniel roared. "Enough." Wounded and shaken, Patience gathered up the folds of her skirt and left the room, weeping.

"Martha," Daniel said, "John will take you in the wagon

today." He laid the diary on the table, his palms splayed over the binding as if seeking to hide it. Martha could see the lines entrenched in his face, and she knew his sadness would never find release pinioned against his wife's towering, extravagant grief.

"Daniel," she began. "Cousin, I have never asked you for anything, and have done all I could for your family. But I ask you, I beg you, to burn this book rather than read it more. I would you call me thief and have me arrested rather than harm come to another through my indiscretion." She took a few steps closer to the table. "Cousin, the teller of these words has no knowledge of this book. Think what may come from revealing these pages to others. I, myself, have not told another soul. Please."

"No," he said, taking the book from the table. "You must promise me you will never again speak of this. I will reason with Patience. She is—" He paused for a moment before continuing. "She has faults enough, but she is my wife and will be silent on this if I demand it. You must understand...she had no knowledge..." He stood abruptly, dragging a hand through the tufts of his hair. He stepped closer, saying, "You have put us all in grave danger with this book, cousin."

Martha looked at his red-rimmed eyes and knew in the instant that he had read the whole of the book. "It was recklessness that led me to write it. I see that now."

He clasped her firmly by the elbow and walked with her out of the house, leading her into the garden, dotted with swelling gourds. He stood scanning the surrounding fields, cropped bare through autumn harvesting, and said, "Martha, if Thomas ever knew of this book, it could be the end of the trust he has placed in you." When she tried to speak, to tell him of the bounty men, he held up a hand and said harshly, "Not another word. You must leave now. Speak to no one else about this. I will think on what is best to be done."

Martha searched his face, which seemed to reflect only the flushed and open visage of a simple carter. A kind and generous man who had coddled and spoiled his wife and children alike; a man who could not, though it save his very life, hit the broadside of a barn with a primed and ready flintlock. But she also sensed a forcefulness that he had, until that moment, hidden from her. Or perhaps it was that she had not looked closely enough to find the greater substance in him.

He glanced at the house, the door still open and beckoning, and Martha could see the rings of black under his eyes and the stubble of beard that proved the cost of hiding her secret.

Martha quickly bundled her few things together and, wearing the new cloak, climbed into the waiting wagon. Thomas had gone hunting hours before, or so he had said, but she wondered if his going had been a kind of self-protection. She craned her neck again and again for some glimpse of him, but the wagon was quickly engulfed by spiraling wisps of fog dissipating with the rising heat. John sat next to her on the driving board, his face anxious, his eyes, wide and blinking, fixed on the road ahead.

Midway through the journey John said to her, "Do not worry about the Taylors. I will see to them, no matter what…" He paused, his voice trailing away.

She sat shivering with the cloak drawn tightly around her shoulders, even after the sun broke free, shining hotly on their necks, and a pounding like the threshing of grain began in her ears. She suddenly pressed her hands over her face, her breath exhaling raggedly against her palms, and she felt John's hand go to her shoulder briefly before she turned her head away.

"Thomas will never break faith with you," he said. "Never."

She shook her head, voiceless, searching the familiar pathways of burled oak and elm already washed with russet brown and yellow. She smelled the honeysuckle, made heavy and overripe by the rains, remembering that its scent could foretell weddings. On the day of the summer harvest, Thomas had proudly pointed out to her his plot of land at the bend of the Concord. A place of sandy shale and gray rock pressed firm and flat by rushing seasonal tides, facing the rolling furze of Broad Meadow on its westerly side. Wood and stone, he'd once said, about his house that was to be. It was to stand on the banks above the glistening boulders, settled in sheltering birch and ash, the great common fields at its back, the gold and amber of the setting sun at its front.

Now, in all probability, through the determination or spite of her cousin, the house that stood at the bend would be shackled to a miller's wheel, and the man dispossessed of it perhaps manacled to a prison ship bound for England. There would be no marriage now, in any event, if Thomas believed that she had betrayed him.

John stopped the cart some distance away from the Allen house at Martha's insistence. She climbed weakly from the wagon and stood mute in the shifting dust of the path, unable to say the simplest of good-byes.

She turned and walked across the yard to the house. Standing silently at the open door, without greeting or explanation, she took in the surprised looks on the faces of her father and his two hired men. They had been eating supper and they sat with their

spoons poised over their laps as though she had appeared like a
nymph, come from the woods to haunt them. Andrew Allen
slowly lowered his spoon to the table, his surprise quickly turning
to dismay, and then to suspicion, and motioned abruptly for the
men to leave.

When he and Martha were alone together, he wiped his mouth
carefully with the back of his hand and asked, "Are ye in the family way?"

Setting the empty bowl from her bundle on the table, the bowl
she had taken to the Taylors' to fill by her own labors, she shook
her head, and without a word, she crept to the attic, to her old
bed, and lay down to sleep.

When Martha woke, it was daylight but on which day, she
wasn't sure. She had fallen asleep on her belly, her arms curled
under her chest, and her eyelids felt swollen shut with crying. She
had woken and slept in so many fragmented, half-aware snatches,
she was uncertain which recollections were dreams and which
were taken from actual events. She pushed herself upright, seeing
that someone had covered her with one of her mother's quilts, and
she rasped her fingers across her papery mouth, needing desperately to drink.

Holding her shoes in one hand, she walked carefully down the
stairs, only to see her father sitting alone at the table, observing
closely her unlaced bodice and wild, unbound hair knitted over
her shoulders. He tapped at the table with his forefinger, his
bird's-nest brows rising with alarm, as if to say, "Here. Here is a
thing which needs be attended." But when she didn't speak, staring at him with red-veined, purposeless eyes, he shifted his gaze
away to the window and sighed noisily. She walked to the rain

barrel and drank deeply, letting the dipper spill water over her skirt, and taking a piece of corn bread from the hearth, she went to sit at the table.

"Yer mother's gone with a shroud to Goodman Abbot's." He cut his eyes to her briefly and she realized it had been her father who had covered her in the night.

She toyed with the dry corn bread on the table for a time and, resting her forehead in her hands, bit the tender inside of her lip to keep the tears from coming. She heard the sound of a chair being scraped back and her father saying, "Come with me now." It was the commanding way she had always heard her father speak and, reflexively, she pushed up from the table, following his gesture to cover herself with one of her mother's shawls.

She followed him through the yard, the eyes of the workmen on her, questioning, curious, and quickly she realized her father was leading her to Sunset Rock to the north of the house. They climbed the rock slowly, pausing at times for her father to favor his weak leg, and stood looking over Boston Way Road, empty of all carts or wagons, the air silent except for the distant sound of a pick on a rock somewhere beyond Ballard's Pond.

Her father crossed his arms and asked, "Are ye still...? I mean to say, d'ye still have yer...?" He paused and sucked at his teeth for a moment.

Martha looked at him, her mouth downturned. "If you mean, am I still intact, the answer is yes." She exhaled sharply, muttering, "Much good may it do me."

The wooden sign above Chandler's Inn, a rough-hewn board with the mark of a horseshoe, squealed once in an errant breeze and then hung motionless.

He shook his head and gestured. "Ye look like a madwoman." He shifted his weight from his ulcered hip, taking in the view of harvested fields. "Thirty years I've made this my home." He looked at her as though she'd dispute the fact. "The spring of 'forty-three I came. There were scarce twenty of us between the Cochichawick and the Shawshin. And here, right here on this rock is where I stood to spy my holdings." He coughed loosely and spat off the ledge. "I had a brother lost in the Great War. My brother James."

She looked at him in surprise. He'd never before mentioned a brother in England.

"He took for soldiering with the Solemn League and Covenant for Cromwell," he said. "He died on Marston Moor and I didna' know of it for five years. But I know why he fought. So that a Scotsman wouldna' have to bend his knee to tricked-up vessels and rich cloths thrown up over the altar of Christ like a whore's skirt."

In all her years she had never heard him speak at length about anything other than the determined acquisition of that which increased the holdings of Goodman Allen.

He pressed his arms tightly around his chest and said, "There's been talk. About you and the Welshman."

Martha crossed her own arms and waited. The anxiety she had felt in the wagon on the way to Andover had begun to build again, making the jellied parts of her eyes feel pierced with gunmetal shards. She pulled the shawl tighter around her chest with unsteady hands and stared at her feet, two steps from open air.

She felt the restraining grasp of her father's hand over her arm. "Oh, fer Christ's bloody sake, Martha, I didna' raise ye to be *well regarded*. To be *liked*. Any puny, weak-waisted slut can be liked. I raised ye to be *reckoned* with. To be fierce in the face of others' pridefulness. T'say to those who would be puffed up in their own cleverness, 'Kiss ma backside and the Devil take the rest.' D'ye hear me? I don't know this...slack-kneed girl in front of me." He softened his grip on her.

"I'd rather ye be wed to a wanted man with principle than to a magistrate with the balls of a seahorse."

He took from his pocket a small gold coin and bounced it in his palm. "A coin has two faces, but it's forged from the same metal. That's you and I." He tapped twice at his brow. "We're the same." He reached out for her hand and closed her fingers over the coin. Martha looked at him amazed; she didn't know whether to be more surprised at his holding her hand or the giving up of a gold coin. He turned abruptly and began his descent down the rock.

He threw over his shoulder, "Ye have to ask yerself, daughter. Is he worth a fight?" He stumbled, cursing, then righted himself and shouted, "It's a fair way to Billerica on foot. Best start now."

She gave him time to return to the house and, slipping the coin into her apron, descended the rock on steadied legs. She walked Boston Way Road for a short distance before cutting west at Preston Bridge over the Shawshin and followed Blanchard's Plain southward. The paths were still boggy from rain, veined through with muddy rivulets and carpeted with mottled leaves that clung fast and clammy to her legs. At Strongwater Brook she peeled off her shoes and stockings and picked her way across the sucking black clay, mired up to her knees. On the other side she sat on a stone wall, rubbing hard at her blackened legs with leaves, scraping away the sodden dirt, only just remembering that all her few belongings were still in Andover. She laughed aloud, the sound harsh and challenging, thinking she didn't even have the cloak for a blanket.

The path descended into rows of pines, banked and half-buried by a recent mud slide, and when she came upon Long Pond, she realized she had walked too far west. She floundered through a backwash of branches and fallen trees, losing the path for a time until she came upon Alewife Creek, getting her bearings again. In another hour she passed Nuttings Pond and saw her cousin's house, a thin column of smoke coming from the chimney.

Behind it stood the barn, and she watched it for a while until she was certain Thomas was there. She crept along the shadowed side of the barn, slipping in through the door. She stood quietly for a moment, listening to the sounds of Thomas and John mucking out a stall.

She stepped forward into the light of a hooded lantern and said, "Thomas."

They both startled at her voice, and she could imagine what they were seeing; her dress was torn and muddied, her shoes two stumps of clay embedded with leaves and the bristling eruptions of twigs.

She said again, "Thomas."

Thomas set down the pitchfork and, turning to John, said, "Leave now. Stay gone a good while."

John propped his pitchfork against the stall and walked quickly past her, closing and latching the door.

She stepped out of her shoes, leaving them behind like a chrysalis shedding its casing, searching Thomas's face for any sense of betrayal. But there were no bitter looks, only an alarmed concern as one might give a sleepwalker. She stepped closer, staggering through the straw, and he was there, holding her up briefly, then setting her on a stool. He turned away, filling a bucket of water from the trough, and knelt in front of her. Peeling off her stockings, he dipped his hands into the bucket and began to wash her legs with long, kneading strokes. The water was surprisingly tepid on her skin, as though the huffed, steaming breath of the cows had warmed it first.

He set aside her shawl and carefully washed her face and neck, cupping one palm around the back of her head, running his other hand across the birdlike bones at the base of her throat and the darker skin above her bodice. The water ran in droplets between her breasts, collecting on her ribs like animate things, and she recalled she must breathe. Her hands, lying useless at her sides, were collected and rinsed with water until the pads of her fingers were pale again.

While he washed her he spoke to her calmly, beseechingly, in Welsh and then in English, telling her, "Daniel spoke only that you and the missus had quarreled, and that he sent you for a time to your father's."

"Thomas," she whispered, "through my own carelessness I have revealed to Daniel…"

He held her chin so that she faced him. "Martha, Daniel knows who and what I am. He always has. He is but one of many who has chosen to give safe harbor to men such as myself." Startled, she reflexively pulled back, but he held her fast. "Pots are not the only things he carries in his wagon. His work goes to the heart of his commitments to keep those in hiding from harm. He carts letters and dispatches from here to Boston and back again for a man named James Davids who, to the best of his abilities, watches over those of us wanted by the king for treason." He craned his face closer to hers, his voice low and urgent. "Daniel carries the greatest treasure in the colonies: intelligences, warnings, instructions. Without such knowledge we would be like blind men pursued by dogs."

That Daniel had put himself, and his family, at risk of imprisonment or death made her ashamed she had ever thought him weak. "Has he said more?" she asked. "Why he sent me away?"

He shook his head. "Beyond crossing words with his good wife? Only that he would give you time to reflect on the life you may be choosing." He traced a lingering finger across the prominence of her collarbone.

Relief that Daniel had not spoken of the red book overwhelmed her, and she lowered her chin. She held up her empty palms, like a supplicant, to show him she had brought nothing with her on her arriving, for she had nothing. He pulled her head roughly to his chest, and then he lifted her up, carrying her into the recesses of a far stall.

The hay was newly set, both green-smelling and fusty from the mold of summer. He set his back against the wall and pulled her to him. Her gestures were reticent, shy, and he kissed her gently until she had caught fire and pressed her mouth between his lips. She straddled his lap, understanding that his great weight would burden her, and helped him pull up the bulk of her skirt and shift which then lay like a gray curtain around them. She placed his hand over her breast and willed herself to slow her own motions. She brought her forehead to rest on his, her eyes opened and watchful. There were no whispered pleadings or sentiments offered to justify their actions, but a voiceless question had formed on Thomas's face and she said, "Yes." "Yes," she said to him and settled her hips more insistently on his.

He encircled her tightly, her soft lower ribs shifting under the force, and then he moved to open the cloth of his breeches. He kissed her, biting her hard on the lip, as though to distract her from the pain, the tearing of the small veil of tissue between her legs, the skin straining for an instant, like the belly of a silvered trout, torn on a barbed lure.

After that there was very little pain, only the sensation of dying by slow measures, the blood swimming to the surface of her skin like resurrected bounty brought up from some polar sea. She could feel the beginnings of pressure marks on her arms and thighs, the scalding of her flesh by the uncut bristles of his face. She wound her arms more tightly around his neck, impressing herself onto him, promising to wear the unintended bruises like the flags of a new country.

CHAPTER 21

THE HOUSE WAS darkening, the sky where the sun had set banded with the filtered, wavering red of calamitous fires. George Afton, his face reflected crookedly in the fractured glass of the common room window, looked out once more into the yard but saw no one approaching. He caught in his reflection the broad streaks of soot he had purposefully rubbed onto his cheeks, and the first downy growth of chin whiskers erupting, and thought he had succeeded in making himself appear older than he was.

He hunkered back close to the hearth, feeding the low flames carefully with small, dry pieces of wood, keeping the smoke through the chimney thin and unobtrusive. His job, he knew, was to wait, but the hours spent alone had eaten away at his spleen until his hands trembled on the grip of the pouring ladle, causing the molten lead within to spill. He had been filling bullet molds for hours and had a small pile of twenty or so musket balls cooled, ready to be trimmed.

He steadied his hands, carefully pouring the lead into the grooves in the molds, but the shadows were making it difficult to be exact. He replaced the ladle by the hearth, setting aside the mold blocks. Taking up a knife he began to trim the tits, the extruded tips of lead, from the group of already set balls, and thought about his hunger. The supply of meat and bread was almost gone and his stomach pinched painfully; he had had nothing to eat since that morning. He tried humming a bit of a song, a habit he had long had, to distract himself from discomfort. He was always singing or mumbling a tune, especially in times of danger or stress, and it brought no end of annoyance to his most recent employer.

He pulled his woolen cap farther down towards his ears, causing his hair to form a ragged fringe over his eyes, further obscuring his face. He thought longingly about sneaking a pinch of bread from the remaining hoard of food. The house where he tended the fire had been deserted by a family ravaged by the pox and there was not so much as a speck of flour left in the larder. There were no beds either, or quilts; the house was quite abandoned. But then, that was precisely why it had been chosen: an empty house hidden by dense trees and bracken; an intact roof and a working flue; but most important, within walking distance of the Welshman. Remembering to check the cooling molds, he turned towards the hearth and felt the rustling swell of a breeze at his back.

Wheeling around, he saw a dark form slipping into the room over the threshold. "Jesu!" he shrieked, losing his balance off his haunches onto the floor.

Brudloe stood at the open door, the door that had been greased by George himself into silence. "I fuckin' told you to be alert, boy, didn't I?" When he spoke, his parted lips showed the gap of the two top missing teeth, and he strode to the fire, slinging his flintlock against the wall. "Didn't I tell you?"

George nodded and made more room for Brudloe at the fire. The man smelled of hibernating animals, George thought, the warm, half-rancid odors rolling off him in waves. Brudloe nodded for food, and relieved to have an excuse to move, George went to the oilskin and unwrapped the last of the supplies. He was glad he had suppressed his desire to take some of it; Brudloe would have known, and there would have been trouble.

Taking off his outer coat and wiping the dirt from his hands on his greased leggings, Brudloe tore off a piece of bread sideways into his mouth. His top lip had been split from the attack that took his teeth, and he had an odd habit of distractedly running the tip of his tongue through the opening like a water spaniel.

Brudloe had told George of the raid he had been compelled to join by his captors, a large tribe of Abenakis, against a hunting band of Iroquois. They had by stealth attacked during the hour before dawn, the skirmish lasting less than a quarter of an hour but bloody in the extreme. He had stabbed a young buck as he lay sleeping, but had missed the vital killing spot, and the warrior's hands came up thrashing to gouge out Brudloe's eyes. Brudloe's hands closed around the Indian's throat and squeezed with increasing fury, even when the man under him had picked up a rock, smashing Brudloe in the face repeatedly. He felt his teeth break away, swallowing his own blood and part of his lip, but he kept the pressure on until he felt the gristle of the man's windpipe break apart and collapse under his hands.

After that raid, Brudloe had said, he was considered a *sanoba*, a "true man," and was not watched over as a captive. Soon after, he made his escape, walking for weeks, from settlement to settlement, until he was taken in by French trappers and then carted southward back to Massachusetts by various tradesmen. He said he had been lucky not to have been shot or bludgeoned to death by the trappers as he had worn native clothing, his hair shorn to a topknot. Even now, with the war lock partially hacked off, his scalp looked exposed and mangy.

George realized he had been staring at Brudloe's head when he felt the older man's eyes on his own grime-covered face. Brudloe scrutinized him in a way that made George feel it prudent, while with his partner, not to close his eyes in true sleep without a witness. George turned away, continuing to trim the lead musket balls, and willed his pumping heart to slow. It was in Salem, three days before, that he had been placed in Brudloe's hands as an accomplice to the murder of one man. The Royalist agent with whom Brudloe had stayed had given assurances that George was up for the task: a pack mule who worked on the cheap, and who would keep his mouth shut afterwards. But since then, Brudloe would often look at him as though reconfiguring a complicated, vexing puzzle.

George asked, "Did you see the Welshman?"

"I saw him," Brudloe said. His upper lip parted obscenely and George realized with a jolt that the man, in fact, was smiling. "I watched him for hours. In and out of the barn like a fox in a hole. I could've shot him a dozen times over from where I perched. But he wasn't alone."

Brudloe tossed George the remainder of the bread and, getting up, walked to the window, his back to the room. He regarded the fast-fading light, scanning the yard like a sentry, and said, "Tomorrow, though. Tomorrow's the day if I have to slit every throat in the house to do it."

A wind, shearing up the trees in the yard, blew leaves over the open threshold. Slowly, almost thoughtfully, he kicked the door closed with the toe of one boot before sauntering back to the fire. He sat resting against the wall and, sliding the flintlock across the floor to George, said, "Clean it."

George dropped one more round of lead into the bowl of the pouring ladle, placing it close to the coals to slowly melt. He reached for the flintlock, then inched himself farther away from his partner. He caught himself beginning to hum again and immediately swallowed the tune.

Brudloe laid one wrist over the other in his lap, ankles crossed, as if preparing for a long rest, and curled one side of his mouth upwards. "Ya know, I think I know that tune. It's a sea-farin' song, yeah? Tell me, Afton, how was your crossin' over?" The open space in his gums gave the words an odd whistling sound.

"Wha'?" George asked, unsure of his meaning. He had been leaning into the hearth, gathering a taper to light a small lantern, and when the candle flared to life, he saw Brudloe's eyes on him.

Brudloe lowered his chin. "Your crossin'. Your trip across the fuckin' water." He waited briefly for an answer, his head nodding as though in congenial conversation. "I *know* how you came to be *here*, in this *shitting* house. But how did you come to be in the *fuckin'* colonies?"

"Same as you," George said, taking out the ramrod from the barrel of the gun.

"'Same as you,'" Brudloe mimicked. "No. Not the same as

me. Not the fuckin' same. What were you, in London, before you came here? Don't tell me I'm wrong. I know the city garble when I hear it."

"I manned ferries."

"Manning ferries." Brudloe's voice took on a queer flat quality. "Ferries...fairies...*fairies*..." Suddenly he laughed and George flinched, gathering the flintlock closer to his chest.

Brudloe said, "I had a partner, a fuckin' *beast* of a man. You know what happened to 'im?" He thrust out his lower jaw. "They burned 'im *alive*. The cunting rogues burned 'im alive, so don't you say 'same as you.'" Brudloe looked at him savagely for a moment more before George turned his head away, busying himself by taking from a small leather pouch the turnscrew, patches, and whisk to clean the gun.

"How old are we now, boy?" Brudloe asked. George's hold on the gun tightened; he knew very well their contact in Salem had told Brudloe how old he was supposed to be.

"Sixteen," George answered.

Brudloe shook his head slowly, his mouth curling into an ugly parody of a kiss. "Bonnie, bonnie lad, why do I doubt this to be so?" He suddenly leaned closer to George. "Tha's all right, boy. I killed my first man at fourteen. You're young for the job, but you'll play."

Brudloe abruptly stood and went for the water skin, drinking sparingly. George let out a breath, cradling the flintlock over his knees. Returning the rod to the shaft, he unscrewed the back plate, and carefully setting aside the frisson, he ran the whisk over the vent and trigger, removing the oily black powder.

Brudloe stretched out on a quilt near the fire, propping his head up on the balled-up greatcoat. He was silent for a few minutes, but when George shifted his gaze to the supine man, he saw the light of the coals reflecting dully off Brudloe's eyes.

"The cap," Brudloe said, pointing to George's head. "You're always wearin' it and it's a bloody inferno in here."

"I always wear it," George muttered.

"Take it off."

George slipped off his cap, but kept his head well down, his face in shadows. Brudloe had barely so much as looked at him for days, but now George felt the man's eyes studying the top of his head.

"I know that song you was hummin'. I heard it before. Just don't know where." There was silence for a few breaths, and Brudloe mused, "It's this place that's got me frigged. No proper streets, no proper towns. No lands' end to the west. Just trees and rocks and more trees again. It works on a man. Grinds him down to dross. Too much space. Too much light…" His voice trailed away, and when George snuck a look, Brudloe's eyes were closed. Soon he heard a slack-jawed breathing, a gentle, wet snoring sound coming from the sleeping man's mouth, the two halves of Brudloe's split lip quivering in tandem with each exhalation. George only ever felt safe when his partner slept, and even then he kept a close watch.

When he was a boy his father, or so he guessed him to be, as the man sometimes shared a cot with his mother, kept a baiting cur. The animal was small for fighting but with a large head. Wrapped tightly with muscle, all taut sinew and straining ligaments, he was banded over with the scars of endless fights in cellars and baiting pits. He was mostly silent, never barking, giving no warning of any kind before striking, and George, only five at the time, mistook the dog's quiet ways for a gentle temperament. Within moments George had had part of his lower leg torn away from the bone, the bulk of the calf muscle stripped, hanging loose like a stranded cod. It took two men to beat the dog away, and, beyond the pain, George recalled the disconnected feeling of looking at the gaping wound and remembering that moments before the attack the dog had been licking his hand. He would have bled to death if not for the ministrations of his father, who was greatly practiced, and sure-handed, in sewing up dogs for the ring. The muscle on his leg grew back whole, leaving only long scars and a lasting mistrust for quiet, self-contained dogs.

George only partially reassembled the firing mechanism, so that it would not discharge, and then he set the gun gently against the wall. The coals had begun a low pulsing, making deep shadows in the room, and Brudloe's breathing was steady and rhythmic. Careful not to rattle the handle, George picked up the lantern and stood, walking noiselessly to the window. He raised the lantern higher, pressing his face against the glass, looking for some sign of movement in the yard. His job, his true job, was only just beginning. And though he had spent days with Brudloe, cleaning his weapons, cooking his food, watching his back, he had had to wait until now for Brudloe to fall deeply asleep.

His breath fogged around the smoked windowpane, the lantern swaying gently aloft in his hand, and he caught a sylphlike reflection in the glass, like the beating of wings behind his shoulder.

The sudden impact smashed George's head against the windowpane, breaking the glass jaggedly in the casing, and Brudloe pushed his full weight onto George's back, grinding his forehead onto the emergent shards. Brudloe's other arm came around George's neck and he knew, without actually feeling the blade, that he had a knife to his throat. He could hear Brudloe's quiet breathing and felt the movement of the man's head as he scanned for intruders approaching the house.

"Who's the lantern for?" Brudloe whispered, his lips pressed against George's ear.

When George didn't answer right away, Brudloe pushed his head more forcefully into the lattice of broken glass, cutting the flesh above his eyes. George dropped the lantern, guttering the candle, the room suddenly darker than the ambient light outside. Brudloe grabbed him around the arm, flinging him hard to the ground, the back of his head striking the floor with a muffled thud. A momentary blankness of vision that was greater than the lack of lantern light made George think he had shards of glass in his eyes. He winced under the bony weight of Brudloe's knees over his outflung arms, and when his vision cleared from the fall, he could see, through a wash of blood from his forehead, Brudloe's face over his own. He felt the cold press of a knife sliding into one nostril, and a pressure, just great enough to stretch the skin, made him want to lie very still.

Brudloe's face came closer. "Who were you signalin'?"

George began to shake his head no and the pressure from the knife increased. Brudloe's hand, in the gentlest of motions, flicked downwards, and a hot spray of blood flowed into his nose flooding backwards, down into his throat. He opened his mouth, gasping in pain, and the knife's flat surface slipped in between his lips, over his tongue. Brudloe reached up with his other hand, and tousled his hair in an almost friendly way. "You crossed over on the Dutchman's ship with me, ain't that right, *Georgie?*" he said. "It came to me while I was sleepin'. I remembered yer song after all. You was supposed to be washed overboard, along with Baker. Whatever happened to Baker, do you suppose?"

The blade turned sideways creasing the middle of his tongue and the taste of salted copper sprang into George's mouth. Brudloe leaned lower still, his eyes vaguely interested in the small trench he had carved in George's mouth. He said, "Manning ferries, was it? You was an eel boy, weren't ya, Georgie? A mud-divin', coal-eatin' little bastard. I'm damned if I know how ye got off that ship, or how you ended up in Salem, but I'm bettin' it was the Dutchman, Koogin. I learned a few things from Baker about how to pull secrets from a man. He could skin a man's ballsack off with a pair of pliers the way I'd peel a boiled plum." He pressed his lips again to Georgie's ear. "He always said that the best way to get a man to talk is t' be patient. But I don't have the time."

Brudloe quickly put the knife between his teeth and hauled Georgie onto his stomach, punching him in the kidneys when he kicked out with his legs. Brudloe grabbed a handful of his hair and pulled his head backwards until Georgie thought his back would break.

"Now, then, who is coming?" Brudloe gave another brutal yank backwards when he saw Georgie's hand reaching out for the hearth, towards the pouring ladle filled with the melted lead.

Georgie, the skin stretched tightly over his throat, gagged on the blood coursing down his gullet; "D-d-d-d—" was all he could manage.

Brudloe's jutting chin rested over one of Georgie's straining shoulders, and he asked, softly, distinctly, "Who…is…coming?"

"D-d-d-d—" Georgie squeezed out. There was no air left in

his lungs to speak, and he could feel his awareness begin to fragment and break away, like a reflection of himself in water, fractured by a dropping stone. He thought he had wanted to say "Death," but he was already forgetting. A slip of wind brushed his thighs, and he wondered if his back had indeed broken, the sensation of cold a prologue to misaligned limbs.

An explosive blow from behind knocked his head forward onto the floorboards, cutting a gash in his chin, and he lay dazed for the fullness of seconds before he realized there was no more agonizing pressure against his back. He heard the grunting and scuffling of bodies, but he lay moaning, his back useless in spasm.

Gurgling, animal sounds came from behind him, somewhere closer to the door, and soon he heard the thudding sound of a falling weight. He turned his head slowly, letting himself fall onto his back, and saw the darkened shape of a tall man framed by the doorway, signaling outwards towards the yard with a swinging lantern, newly lit. The breeze he had felt on his backside, he suddenly realized, had been the door opening silently. Georgie saw Brudloe lying on the floor, an oozing curtain darker than shadows spreading beneath him.

The tall man turned and quickly walked to Georgie, kneeling over him, strong teeth yellow in the lantern light. "Three nights now, boy. I thought the man would never sleep."

Georgie could hear the creak of a wagon pulling close to the house, and he staggered to his feet, stepping over the body of Brudloe and through the door. The wagon had pulled to a stop, the driver holding a torch aloft to better see.

"Blessed Christ," the man said to Georgie. Climbing from the wagon he handed the boy a cloth for his face and briefly examined the cuts. Pulling an ax and a canvas sack from under the driving board, he jerked a thumb over his shoulder for Georgie to climb into the wagon, and the man walked into the house.

Georgie crawled onto the wagon bed and lay on his quivering back, panting, his knees drawn up towards his chest. He let his matted eyes track the constellations in the sky, grateful he still had sight, and thought about the Rat on the Dutchman's ship, the mute cabin boy who had rescued him from Brudloe and the others, who had fed and comforted him, pointing out to him with a sure and steady finger the constellations of the Bear, the Hunter, St. George's Dragon. The Rat had cried voiceless, inconsolable tears when Georgie left the ship at Boston, but Captain Koogin understood that the young landsman would never make a good seaman.

He could feel his tongue beginning to swell, the pain in his mouth now greater than his other wounds. He parted his lips to better breathe, spitting out blood from the back of his throat, and wondered if he himself would ever be able to speak again.

It was Koogin who had taken him overland from Boston to the home of a man named General Gookin. The captain had told Georgie by way of introduction, "This, boy, is my brother." He regarded Georgie's surprised face and then, in the sandy soil at their feet, etched the name "Koogin." Rubbing out the *k* and the *g* with his fingers, he transposed the letters, turning Koogin into Gookin. Standing, he erased the name with the sole of his shoe and said solemnly in parting, "I am no more a Dutchman than you are, lad. And I am not a pirate, though some would have me so. My ship serves the general, my brother, and you could do no better than apprenticing yourself to him."

It was the general who had enlisted Georgie and Robert Russell, along with a network of spies, to the scheme of ridding the colonies of the assassins come to kill the man who had dared to take the head of a king, or so Georgie had been told.

Georgie Afton, named for the eight Georges before him, a fourteen-year-old eel boy from London sold into slavery to murderers, was one of the only remaining colony men alive who knew the face of Brudloe, and one of the few who had the mettle to put himself in harm's way for the general's sake. He had been changed greatly in the few months since being abducted from England, but he believed it was only Brudloe's fixed obsession with killing the Welshman that had bought him time before being discovered. He had often thought on this moment: Brudloe's blood running freely in the dirt.

Georgie heard the thunking sounds of an ax chopping against a soft target, and Robert Russell and the wagon driver soon walked out with the ax and the sack, now filled. They climbed onto the driving seat, and a dry rushing sound, followed by a growing light within the house, caught Georgie's attention. The three of them watched the flames growing in strength, consuming the dry, untended wood with startling speed.

The wagon driver clucked at the reins, and Robert, tipping his head towards his companion on the driving board, said, "Georgie, greet your close neighbor, Goodman Daniel Taylor."

Daniel winked at him and said, "Welcome to the brotherhood."

Gingerly, Georgie propped himself up on his elbows, watching the growing conflagration, gray smoke pouring from the windows and door. The house was small and it would not last long, but its very compactness serviced the flames into a yellow-white wall of wavering phosphorescing light, and he could feel the pulsing heat even at a distance.

A dark shape emerged from the blankness of the yard like a partial eclipse, floating in front of the burning house, and resolved itself into the shape of a man. Shaken, Georgie saw that the man's height was greater than the topmost frame of the door, and he palmed his eyes, brushing away the clotted blood at his lashes, thinking his perspective was muddled by distance and injury. The man turned his back to the flames, and the punishing heat, and stood watching the departing wagon.

Georgie raised himself onto his knees, and uttered thickly, "Sweet Jesu."

Robert turned to look and quickly signaled for Daniel to halt the wagon. He reached for the sack, the bottom dripping with bloody matter, and climbed from the wagon, loping at a fast clip back towards the house. Georgie could clearly see Robert's form, distorted by waves of heat and smoke, coming to stand in front of the giant, and he watched as he pulled from the sack Brudloe's grimacing, seeping head. Robert held the head aloft like an offering, and the two men regarded for a moment the remnant with its backlit features, open-mouthed and fixed, and the giant then turned and disappeared into the woods.

Georgie gazed over his shoulder, staring at Daniel with the slack-jawed, trembling look of the battlefield injured, his eyes questioning.

Daniel gently wrapped his greatcoat around the boy's shivering frame and held his shoulders with a fatherly steadying grip. Gesturing to Robert, standing alone in front of the already diminishing fire, he said, "He's paying a debt, boy."

CHAPTER 22

Transcript of General Court Session, Town of Billerica
23rd day of the 10th month, 1673
Presided by: General Daniel Gookin, Magistrate of Concord,
Carlisle, Bedford, Wilmington, and Billerica

Formerly in Dispute, Now Resolved: 3 Acres land, promontory
lying southerly to Treble Cove on the Concord River, bounded by
Billerica Great Common Field to the North, Concord River to the
West, Fox Brook Road to the East, and Main Street to the South,
sufficiently bounded by Marked Trees and Pillars of Stone.

By Jonathan Danforth, Surveyor

It is jointly agreed between Daniel Taylor, of Billerica, and
Asa Rogers, late of Salem, that the aforementioned Daniel Taylor
shall make sale of designated land, becoming Seller, giving assurances that the three acres shall be granted to aforementioned Asa
Rogers, becoming Buyer, with full rights of ownership, and that
such Seller does hereby, fully, clearly, and absolutely give up his

whole interest, right, and title to land; and that subsequent to affixing his signature and transference of settled price, Asa Rogers can make sale of and dispose of land as he sees fit for his person, his assigns, and estate.

Asa Rogers, as Buyer, hereby agrees to make said purchase for Four Pounds Sterling upon execution of this Document.

> Witness my hand the day and year above
> Written, together with Buyer and Seller
> Gen. D. Gookin
> Daniel Taylor
> Asa Rogers
> Copied by Town Clerk: Tho. Adams

Post Script to Mr. James Davids, New Haven, Connecticut:

Dear friend James,

Forgive these hasty scratchings as I have much withal to concern me: meetings of the governor and General Council and, more important I believe to the immediate welfare of these wilderness settlements, the visitation of Indian villages. There has been of late much unease regarding relations between the colonists and the natives, and I have endeavored to begin a work which I hope to publish for the benefit of peace: "The Doings and Sufferings of the Christian Indian."

More to the point of this missive, I have sent the above copy of a court transcript for your enlightenment as it concerns the carter Daniel Taylor, also your agent in the surrounds of Boston. Goodman Taylor solicited me to help settle a land dispute between Asa Rogers and a hired man, one Thomas Morgan, a rumored regicide.

It will please you to know that Morgan is popularly believed to have been executed by bounty men, his head struck from his body (the head of which I, being responsible in part for His Majesty's Will and Charters in the colonies, have myself witnessed). This disjointed head, I must add, is most decidedly small for such a reputedly large man, the forehead cross-hatched with a multitude of scars. The skull is to be conveyed back to England on the ship The Swallow *with a captain of our very close acquaintance, Captain Koogin, for the satisfaction of the Crown. On the shipping barrel will be writ, no doubt by some wayward scoundrel: "Here lies the head of Thomas Morgan, regicide; to which state every head of state must someday find." His Majesty will want to know, through endless correspondences, I am certain, how we, the colonists, hold in regard the Royal Court to make such rustic jokes and bite our thumbs at Consequence and Ceremony.*

Once Thomas Morgan had proven to be officially dead, and therefore unable to make a claim upon the Taylor land—a cunning well-ordered spot on the Concord—Asa Rogers stepped forward most vigorously to claim it for his mill (bringing poignantly to mind that "the mills of the gods grind slow, but exceeding fine"). Rogers paid in full, and hurriedly, for his plot of land. He, upon some reflection, has taken my word as a magistrate that Thomas Morgan is gone from this earth. The more so after describing to him, in most painstaking detail, the attendant hackings, burnings, and dismemberments by Indians that may take place upon a settler without the protection of the militia, under my command.

To more felicitous duties. I had, upon completion of the sale of land, the satisfaction of officiating in the marriage of one Thomas Carrier of Billerica to a Martha Allen, late of Andover, and cousin to the wife of Goodman Taylor. As they stood, still and solemn before me, making their vows—he as exceptionally tall a man as I have ever seen, and she wearing a fine green-gray cloak — they brought to my mind stone carvings I had seen in a great abbey in London. There, resting in a shadowed, forgotten nave, were likenesses of some long-absent king and queen, both alike in dignity, their brows crimped in imponderable thoughts. And though their eyes were closed, their heads inclined together, speaking to the onlooker, "We have endured."

Goodman Taylor was witness to the ceremony and discreetly presented the bride afterwards a fine down quilt, such as is rarely seen in the colonies. In a peculiar aside, I overheard him say quietly to her that there was, within, an accounting book, a red one, if such extravagances can be believed.

"Keep it well, cousin," he told her, "until such time as it can be brought forward to illuminate a world more equal to its subject."

The couple being poor, and they being of remarkable fortitude for work, I have offered them, along with Carrier's man, John Levistone, a good plot of land from my own holdings, in return for some period of labor and a gold coin given to Goodwife Carrier by her father.

Thomas Carrier accompanied me to Boston to deliver Morgan's head, kept from corruption in a salt barrel, to the ship at Boston Harbor. Along with us came my new aide, George Afton, who is an able lad (formerly an eel boy in London, such is the greatness of opportunities in the colonies for inventive men). Along with Morgan's head was found a scroll wrapped around a small wooden stake. After gaining my permission to open the scroll, Georgie began to read aloud to us the words inscribed by the hand of the great Lord Protector of England, whose orders of battles, instructions to Parliament, and writs of execution I have seen with my own eyes. This scroll will be sent to England along with Morgan's remains.

The words are from Revelation, the meaning, and signature, of which may serve to confound and torment His Majesty everlastingly:

"You are worthy to take the scroll and to open its seals... and with your blood you purchased men for God from every tribe and language and people and nation. You have made them to be a kingdom.
Oliver Cromwell"

In God's trust, I remain,
Gen. Daniel Gookin

ONCE THE HEAD, as it came to be known, had been presented to Charles Stuart in his private chambers, accompanied only by an examining audience of the Earl of Arlington, the Duke of Buckingham, and Sir Joseph Williamson, nothing was ever again right for the sovereign.

The viewing of the barrel's contents had begun before it had even left the dock. Advance news spread across the city that the remains of the executioner that took the head of the first Charles had landed aboard the ship *The Swallow*, and carriages of nobles, titled ladies, and serving orderlies mingled with curious, rude 'prentices and common people, who all gawked, for a fee, inside the barrel. After all, the dock courier reasoned, its lid had not been secured, there being no royal seal, and the captain of the escorting guard was amenable to retaining an accommodation fee for himself. Very quickly, the joke had been had; the shrunken, tarred head with its ridiculous topknot and the scribbling on the barrel itself, alluding to the inevitable fate of kings, brought first knowing smiles and then waterfalls of derisive laughter. Tiernan

Blood, cloaked and hooded within the crowd, drew near for a peek and, recognizing the cross-hatching scars, laughed the loudest.

An old poem by a court wit was resurrected and circulated:

After a search so painful and so long,
That all his life he has been in the wrong;
Huddled in the dirt the reasoning engine lies,
Who was so proud, so witty and so wise.

Artists made sketches of the relic to be engraved onto pamphlets, which were circulated within hours to a wider populace whose dissatisfaction grew daily, pinched as they were by the taxes for the third Dutch war and the outrageous expenses of keeping the king's whores and bastards fed and housed. The secret, dishonorable pacts by the second Charles Stuart with the Catholic French, the betrayal of a morally upright Protestant Dutch king, and the lack of legitimate successors to the throne had all brought disenchantment to the English people for their bonny wayward boy-king who was now an aging reprobate: a cynic and a secret heretic to the Anglican Church.

Charles replaced the lid on the barrel, his lips curled into the public show of insouciance. Throwing the accompanying scroll of parchment, along with the little wooden stake, into the fire grate, he gestured for Arlington to dispose of the barrel. The king would now visit his mistress Louise de Keroualle and their infant son. As he left, the dozens of timepieces in his chamber struck to twelve, the sound of their gongings and tinklings following the king's footsteps, along with the clattering of the royal spaniels, roused to partner his stride. Arlington bowed as the king departed and then directed Williamson, who in turn directed Chiffinch, to remove the offending object. Buckingham had left the chamber even before the parchment had finished burning.

Chiffinch, Keeper of the Privy Closet, gestured for a guard, who in response clambered down the stairs, calling to a passing chamber orderly. The orderly opened the outward privy stairs door and called to a porter to come right quick. The porter and his mate retrieved the barrel, bumping it down the stairs, and boarded it onto a wherry, where it was directed to be thrown into the Thames farther downstream. The wherryman rowed with the current towards the docklands, discharging his cargo into the dark waters there.

After days and weeks, the rotting wood of the barrel expanded and broke apart, expelling the head like a birth into the tidal wash. By measures the skull, its prominences of brow and jawbone catching in the tumultuous mud, came to rest on the shores near Wapping, where it lay until at length it came to be found by a boy scouring the shores for eels.

From Martha Carrier's Diary: Andover, Massachusetts, Thursday, January 28th, 1692

My dearest and most beloved daughter Sarah,

If ever you are to read this, you will surely wonder at the tenderness of these opening words, as we have, so many times, been set at odds with each other. It has been said that when the daughter draws her nature from the mother, rather than from the father, there will be disharmony between them. And certainly discord has been in the house in which we have lived since the time you took your first steps. But you must know that as I have many times harshly tended to my children, scolded them, beaten and brayed at them, so, too, have I always loved them.

You would say a painful thing is this my love after you have felt the tender ministering of your aunt Mary. Sending you away to my sister's house as I did was a hard thing, and yet I hoped to save you from the pox that threatened to take the life of your brothers, and which killed my own mother. But taking you back home again, away from a gentler house, was perhaps the cruelest thing that ever I could have done, for next to my sister's sweet and exemplary nature, I must have seemed unyielding beyond bearing.

But you must believe that I know the workings of the world, and I would tell you that I did you a greater service in hardening you to the uncertainties of life, as well as strengthening you to its certainties of Age, Loss, Illness, and Death.

Some have said it is a sin to feel a greater measure of affinity for one child over another, but I have always seen in you the best, and most forward, parts of myself. I cannot say in truth that you are wholly the mirrored image of me, for where I am importune in my emotions, you are studied and cautious, like your father. Where I am quick to berate, you are more tempered in finding fault. You are brave and loyal and steadfast.

It may be that you and I will never come to a place of greater felicity, or even understanding. Perhaps it will be that the best we can hope for is a more charitable patience between us. It has been many years since I made entry to this diary, and if you have found these end pages, you will now know the history of the ones you called Mother and Father, he who has been to me, and above all else, Friend; and perhaps it may be that, in reading these words, you will come to understand, and forgive.

I have wondered countless times over the years since I began this work why I continued to keep it, dangerous as it is. Many times I have held the book over a fire, meaning to drop it into the flames. But it is a true accounting book, and the best kind; an accounting of your family, and your past. Perhaps it is only pride which keeps me from destroying these pages, an action which would keep us safer from those who would gain in status and wealth in its ransom. But, dear

Sarah, once the storyteller is gone, so, too, is the story, unless it is committed to the written word, and I would have you know the whole of us; knowing, too, the sacrifices we have made.

And now I have come to the final pages. These will be my last observances in the red book.

There is of late a brooding, unsettled timbre to the air, stirred about by gossip and the unkind thoughts of others, and throughout the goodness of these days, I feel a shadow that may one day harden and congeal itself to the hateful acts of others. It is a danger that I daily bring closer to myself by being what I am. I can no more deny the nature of myself than a lump of coal can unprove its hardness, or an egg its smoothness. And these things give up their best gifts to the world upon their demise. The coal is burned by fire and brings warmth. The egg is broken and feeds a hungry mouth. It may be that the greatest gift I will ever give you will come only after I am gone, my body broken on the wheel of time and circumstances, and you will come to understand the full measure of my love.

I hear you in the next room, struggling to wake as you lie next to Hannah, overtired from tending well into the night your sister's terrible burns. So like a little child to pull a scalding pot upon her head, not knowing for what she reaches but desiring above all else to have the very thing that is beyond her grasp. Someday it will be that you will have your own children to tend, though I now fear I will never see them.

You are even now rising from your bed, stretching out your arms, pushing away sleep.

Tell your children your mother was a woman who, with all her multitude of shortcomings, was more ferocious than kind, more contentious than agreeable, more irate than placid; but who cherished her family above all else. And when you are asked, tell them you are Martha Carrier's daughter; that you had a mother who cared for you beyond reason, beyond tepid courtesies, beyond the brief, struggling hollow that is this life. That you are, and ever will be, loved.

Final Testament

Tall against the sky it stands, silent witness
To man's frail grasp of God's unending Grace.
Beneath its branches, shades and shadows creep,
Strangers to the light they now outpace.

Blame not the oak; as I it could not speak.
Truth shared our shackles, mute.
In thrall to fear, rough hands and hearts did seek
To pluck the truth from this tree's blighted fruit.

Through boughs of glittering green I saw the dying leaves,
Drought-blasted, poised for flight.
God's seasons soon will strip these branches nude;
And then, oh then, spring-born buds will seek the light.

— AUDREY CARRIER HICKMAN

THE TRAITOR'S WIFE is a work of fiction. However, many of the novel's chief characters are based on actual people. Thomas Carrier, also referred to in early documents as Thomas Morgan the Welshman, does appear in the town records of Andover and Billerica, Massachusetts, during the second half of the 1600s. What is certain about him is that he was married to Martha Allen Carrier, who was hanged as a witch in Salem in 1692; had children with her; and died in Colchester, Connecticut, aged 109 in 1735. What is less certain, and most likely unsupportable, is that he fought in the English Civil War and was one of the executioners of King Charles I of England. These stories are based on family legends and local Massachusetts lore. Some historical sources give the name of Richard Brandon, the Hangman of London, as the actual executioner, although it was widely believed that he refused absolutely to cut off the head of an anointed king.

In the novel, Thomas and Martha marry in the fall of 1673; in reality, they were married by a Captain Daniel Gookin (not yet made a general) in May of 1674, Martha most likely pregnant with their first child, Richard. Captain Gookin, already well established as a landowner in the colonies, had accompanied Cromwell's confederates and fellow regicides Edward Whalley and William Goffe on the *Prudent Mary* from Gravesend to Boston in 1660.

John Dixwell, living under the assumed name James Davids in Connecticut, was one of the regicides, a judge who signed the warrant of execution for King Charles I, living "in plain sight" in the colonies.

The spy rings of Henry Bennet, Earl of Arlington, and Sir Joseph Williamson were very real—ruthless and extremely effective in gathering foreign and domestic intelligences during the Restoration period. Thomas Blood (renamed Tiernan Blood in the novel) was a historical figure who successfully penetrated the defenses of the Tower of London, stealing the Crown jewels. He was arrested, and after demanding, and getting, a private audience with King Charles II, he was pardoned. He went on to be a successful spy until his death in 1680.

ACKNOWLEDGMENTS

MANY THANKS TO my wonderful agent, Julie Barer, for her constant encouragement, keen editorial eye, and joyful enthusiasm. To Reagan Arthur, a writer's dream of an editor, I offer my profound gratitude for her expert guidance and sensitivity in shaping this book to its final form. My deep appreciation also to the following people at Little, Brown and Company: David Young, Michael Pietsch, Heather Fain, Luisa Frontino, Terry Adams, Sabrina Ravipinto, and Andrea Walker for all their continuing support. For the second time, I was so very fortunate to work with the sharp-eyed and exacting Pamela Marshall during copyedits.

To my family—my mom, Audrey, Josh, and Mitchell, the Hickmans, Morrisons, Orlowskys, and Muethings—I send all my love. My heartfelt appreciation also goes to my extended family and dear friends who have been cheerleaders, advisors, and sources of comfort. Finally, to Lowell and Sandy, *Merci pour tout.*

KATHLEEN KENT'S first novel, *The Heretic's Daughter,* was based on true family history. Kathleen has worked in commodity trading and for the US Department of Defense in Russia. She now lives in Dallas with her family. *The Traitor's Wife* is her second novel.